Australian Cheryl Adam was deported from Kenya in the 1960s and arrived as an unwanted guest in Sweden. She later moved to South Africa where she lived for thirteen years and had five children before returning to Australia. After her husband's stroke, she took up study, completing a Masters in Fine Arts at Monash University before taking up writing. At the age of 74, her first novel *Lillian's Eden* was published. *Out of Eden* is her second book and she is currently writing the final volume of the Eden trilogy.

Other books by Cheryl Adam

Lillian's Eden

OUT OF EDEN

Cheryl Adam

SPINIFEX

First published by Spinifex Press, 2021

Spinifex Press Pty Ltd
PO Box 5270, North Geelong, VIC 3215, Australia
PO Box 105, Mission Beach, QLD 4852, Australia

women@spinifexpress.com.au
www.spinifexpress.com.au

Edited by Pauline Hopkins and Renate Klein
Cover design by Deb Snibson, MAPG
Typesetting by Helen Christie, Blue Wren Books
Typeset in Berling
Printed and bound by CPI Group (UK) Ltd, Croydon, CR0 4YY

A catalogue record for this
book is available from the
National Library of Australia

ISBN: 9781925950267 (paperback)
ISBN: 9781925950274 (ebook)

*With thanks and gratitude for their support,
this book is dedicated to Heather and Bill, Peggy and Niklas,
John and Molly, Lotta and Erik, and Bengt.*

1

Arrival

The suitcase was heavy; it held the last three years of Maureen's life. She moved it to the other hand and lost her footing in the light flurry of snow that coated the footpath and made a grab for the lamppost to stop herself from tumbling onto the busy street. A tram rattled past and a car slewed sidewards, sending a stream of water over her, adding to her misery.

When Maureen reached the block of flats in Kungsgatan it was four o'clock in the afternoon and the day was fading. Two drunks leaning against the wall of the adjoining newspaper shop leered at her and said something in Swedish. Behind them was a poster with the latest headlines on the Vietnam War. They should join up, she thought, shoving open the heavy wooden door to the block of flats. The door banged closed behind her and she dropped her suitcase onto the floor and stood motionless, her breath making small clouds in the cold air.

For a moment she enjoyed the solitary space, closed off from the noise of the street and the frantic scramble of her day. Then she stamped the sludge off her boots, blew warm air into her frozen hands and picked up her suitcase again. The staircase steps were wide, man steps apart, and it was three flights up to her friend.

By the time she reached the landing on the third floor her hands were stinging from blisters. Dumping her suitcase on the top step, she straightened and stretched, ironing out the cricks in her back. A single light bulb hanging from the ceiling lit the dingy space between the doors of the two flats on the landing. The feeling of desperation that had dogged Maureen's day began to lift as she stood in front of Sarah's door. A sympathetic ear was what she needed, as well as a bed. Although where she would sleep in the bedsit Sarah shared with her husband and two-year-old was a concern. It was just one big room.

Yet in her present predicament, under the kitchen table would do. A nice hot bath would be welcome too, but Maureen knew that wouldn't happen. Bathrooms were scarce in older Swedish flats. They only had a toilet with a washbasin, and there were no communal bathrooms. Swedes went to the spa baths once a week. She'd have to settle for a strip wash. In fact, she'd settle for anything. Maureen lifted her hand and knocked.

Minutes passed and the door didn't open. Although it was late, maybe Sarah had gone shopping? Maureen rapped again only louder and leant her head against the door listening for life inside. A man arrived at the top of the stairs, a rucksack over his shoulder. His cold blue eyes gazed at her from a fist-ruined face. He smelled of motors and wore grease-smeared overalls over a thick polar neck jumper. An accusing finger pointed at Maureen's suitcase and he growled something in Swedish.

Maureen shrugged apologetically. "Do you speak English?"

He scowled. "You move."

A waft of alcohol hit Maureen. "Sorry." She pulled the case to the side, even though he could have easily stepped around it. He went to the door opposite and unlocked it, then jerked his head towards the door Maureen had been banging on.

"They not home."

"Do you know where Sarah is?"

"Where you from?" He looked her up and down.

Maureen noted he didn't speak English with the usual Swedish lilt. There were a lot of Yugoslav immigrants in Gothenburg, perhaps he was Yugoslavian? Anyway, he wasn't very nice. "I'm Maureen, Sarah's friend. She's expecting me. I'm just a bit early."

He snorted. "She gone visit husband in Scotland."

Maureen's shoulders slumped. Sarah's husband worked on oil rigs. Sarah had been her only hope. It was her fault they hadn't been in contact all summer because she had accompanied Nils and his crew to the yacht races in Denmark and Germany. Desperate, she gave the man her most appealing smile.

"She must have forgotten to leave me a key unless she left it with you?" He shook his head and disappeared into his flat, shutting the door.

Flopping onto her suitcase Maureen put her face in her hands. Where could she go? It was already darkening outside. Her stomach rumbled. The only thing she had eaten today was a pastry someone had left behind on a plate in the café where she'd had coffee this morning. Hopelessness gnawed at her. How could she have been so stupid? It served her right for running off with a man she hardly knew.

Maureen shrivelled against Sarah's door, tucked up her legs and pulled her thin coat around herself. She would have been wiser wearing slacks and not a mini skirt. It was the beginning of winter and freezing. What were her options? Go to the police? They might deport her as an undesirable. She didn't have a work permit. The job she'd had until this morning had been cash in

3

hand. She didn't even know how long she could stay in Sweden, as it was Nils who had vouched for her when they entered the country. He will come for me, she thought, trying to push away the day's events.

A clanging noise interrupted her thoughts. Turning, Maureen noticed the wooden steps in an alcove at the back of the landing. Short black boots, legs in thick brown stockings and a bucket came into view.

The owner of the feet emerged. She looked to be in her sixties. The brown three quarter length duffel coat she was wearing swallowed her thin frame. Her dark hair was streaked with grey and pinned off her angular face. On seeing Maureen, the woman hesitated.

"Hej," Maureen said, hoping to engage her in a conversation. Maybe she knew the caretaker and could help her get into Sarah's flat? The woman responded with a quick nod, then holding the bucket high so as not to spill its contents, she walked around Maureen's suitcase and disappeared down the stairs leaving behind the whiff of something pungent. Maureen wrinkled her nose. The woman seemed shy, furtive almost. She would talk to her when she came back.

Curious as to where the woman had come from, Maureen waited until she heard her footsteps fade and a door bang downstairs before she went over to the alcove to check the steps. They weren't like the staircase; they were made from rough wood and more like a ladder. The steps led up to a small doorway. It was the roof access. What had the woman been doing up there? She was about to take a peek when she heard the flush of the ground floor toilet and decided to leave her investigation until later. It wouldn't be good to get caught snooping around when she wanted help. Maureen returned to her suitcase and sat down, it was warmer than sitting on ceramic tiles. Propping herself up against Sarah's door she listened for the woman's return. It was hard keeping her eyes open. She fought the urge to sleep and then her head fell forward.

The exit door to the block of flats banged, pulling Maureen out of her doze and into the cold reality of her situation. Her neck was stiff and her leg had gone to sleep. How much time had passed since she'd dozed off? She stood up and stamped her feet to get the circulation going. It was stupid to stay here; she should find somewhere warm like the railway station. But finding the station meant wandering around the streets of Gothenburg lugging a suitcase in the dark. The idea didn't appeal. Either she had been asleep when the woman with the bucket had returned or she didn't live here and had only come to collect something. Hunger pangs gripped her. A reminder that she had someone else to think about. What should she do?

The sound of feet on stairs, something being dragged, grunts and heavy breathing penetrated her thoughts. Leaping to her feet she opened her handbag, pretending to search for a door key when the woman from the roof reappeared. Walking backwards she pulled a sack onto the landing, then dropped next to it out of breath and gasped something in Swedish.

"I beg your pardon," Maureen said, "but I don't speak Swedish."

"Getting too old for this." The woman replied in perfect English.

"It looks heavy. Those stairs are steep. I'd be out of breath pulling that." A perfect opportunity had presented itself. Maureen could help the old lady and find out if someone had a key to Sarah's. Her stomach rumbled. Maybe she would be offered a cup of tea? "Let me carry it up the steps for you." Without waiting for a reply, Maureen bent down and picked up the sack. It was heavy, crunching against her.

"It's coal, you'll get filthy," the woman said.

Bugger! Maureen dropped the bag on the step and looked down the front of her fawn coat to the imprint of coal dust.

It was her warmest coat. Her only coat. She held out her blackened palms and screwed up her face. "Looks like it's too late now." She grabbed the sack like she'd seen shearers drag sheep and backed up the steps. The roof door was low, not much taller than her. A six-foot man would have to duck his head. She rested the bag of coal against the door and returned to the woman.

The woman looked from Maureen to her suitcase. Shivering in the chill air, Maureen explained her situation.

"I wanted to surprise my friend." Should she admit she's Australian? Last week, students from the University of Gothenburg had burnt the Australian and American flags in a Vietnam protest. "I've come from Australia to see her but she's away on holiday. That's what the man who lives there told me." She nodded towards his door. "I don't know where else to go. I've run out of money and have to wait until the bank opens in the morning." It was half a truth because there wasn't any money waiting in the bank. "I was going to stay here for the night." There was a catch in her voice. She indicated the landing and shivered. The woman frowned and stood in silence as though considering something.

"I suppose I can assist you tonight, but it's only a temporary solution. You will have to leave first thing in the morning."

Maureen's relief was enormous. Anything would be better than becoming a frozen corpse in the slums of a foreign country. If Nils knew what was happening, he would be furious with his parents for leaving her on the street. Without a key to his flat she couldn't receive his prearranged phone call. If he called his parents she doubted they would tell him what they'd done in case it messed up his chances of winning the yacht race. She'd have to survive until he came back and this odd lady was offering her accommodation. It was the first offer of help she'd had from a Swede and she was grateful from her head to her toes. "Thank you, that is so kind of you. My name's Maureen, by the way." She held out her hand.

"Netta." The woman looked at Maureen's proffered hand but didn't take it. "You can wash your hands in the downstairs lavatory. I don't have water. Bring the bucket up with you, it's at the bottom of the stairs." She spoke English with a posh accent. She turned and started walking up the steps to her door.

Maureen's eyes widened. "Righto." No water? How did this woman live? It would be rude to question her after being offered refuge for the night. Eager to please she headed downstairs.

The reek of boiled kidneys assailed Maureen's nostrils as she opened the lavatory door and felt for the light switch. In the feeble glow, she saw the scribbles and scratched messages of desperate people on the walls and the toilet seat that leant against a wall. A smidgen of toilet paper was left on a roll on the floor. To her surprise in the murk and stench, the hand basin was clean and the lavatory bowl free of splatters. Also the floor looked clean, but Maureen dry-retched anyway. The stink from the ancient pipes was overpowering. Perching over the bowl she peed then pulled the chain. Afterwards she washed her hands using her handkerchief as a towel. The next time she would come prepared! She collected the bucket and headed up the stairs.

The door to the roof had been left ajar. "Hello," Maureen called out as she dragged her suitcase inside and dumped the bucket. Her heart skipped a beat as she gazed around, open-mouthed. She had expected to enter a small flat in the roof, but certainly not this!

It was a loft, as big as the barn on her father's farm. A carpet and a stained mattress lay on the floorboards. Surely not the woman's bed? Around the surrounding walls were small cubicles with chained doors, storerooms for the building's occupants. Oddments of furniture, piled chairs, dressing tables, coffee tables, wardrobes and numerous other items were strung across the loft. The loft smelled of pinewood and dust. The dust got up Maureen's nose and she sneezed. With a sinking heart she wondered if she wouldn't be better off spending the night on the landing. This place was freezing.

There were skylights in the roof. Some were missing pieces of glass and others were cracked. Snowflakes drifted through the breaks and melted in the air. Pigeons perched along the rafters cooed while jockeying for position as they tucked in for the night. Peering into the gloom, Maureen looked for signs of life while she argued with herself whether to wait for the woman or be sensible and head for the railway station. A lantern emerged in a gap between two wardrobes. Maureen had delayed too long. She couldn't leave, it might hurt the woman's feelings.

An arm beckoned. "Through here," Netta said, impatient, already regretting letting someone into her space. There were reasons for living in secret. But the landing wasn't a safe place for a young woman to sleep. The door to the street was never locked and drunks often found their way into the building. They used the downstairs lavatory and sometimes slept on the landings. She held the lamp high as Maureen dragged her suitcase across the wooden floor.

"Lift your suitcase – we don't want the whole building knowing we're up here," her hostess snapped.

"Sorry," Maureen whispered, lifting her case off the floor. Netta eyed the case.

"You won't get that through this narrow space. Take what you need for the night and put your suitcase behind that cupboard." She indicated a cupboard further along from the wardrobes she was squashed between. Maureen did as she was instructed, removing a pair of pyjamas and thick socks, thinking this Netta woman must be a bit paranoid. *Who else would come up here at night?*

As if reading her thoughts, Netta said, "I did have a vagrant come up here last winter. Also the tenants keep their skis in the store rooms." She pointed to the chained doors on either side of the loft. "Bring the bucket and follow me and try not to make any noise."

It was a tight fit between the wardrobes. A tangle of piled chairs on top of a table stopped their progress. Netta grunted as she dropped to her knees and struggled under the table pushing the lantern ahead of her. "Mind your head and turn left," she said. Amazed, Maureen followed. She started thinking about mummified bodies and escapees from asylums. Who would find her if the woman was an axe murderer?

Netta pulled herself upright with a grunt and set the light on a box. A collection of curtains and sheets draped over stacked furniture created a circle of cloth walls. The floor space in the middle was covered by a large carpet. Two settees and an armchair edged the carpet. In the middle was a coffee table, on its top sat a violin case. A tall bookcase stacked with books stood on one side of the makeshift room and on the other an iron stove chuffed smoke up an asbestos pipe that poked through a broken skylight. There was a saucepan on the stove and an orange glow from the coal embers that exuded warmth and cheerfulness in the strange surroundings. The room had a familiar feel; it reminded Maureen of her Aunt Maggie's place in Eden.

2

First Night

Maureen stood like a kid on a sleepover hugging her pyjamas and socks watching Netta pull bedding from a cupboard and stack it neatly at the end of one of the couches. She wondered if the bedding belonged to the other tenants?

Netta patted the couch. "You should be warm enough here."

She picked up the bucket and lamp and went over to the bookcase and stood behind it. "Follow me." She pegged up one of the drapes that hung over the furniture and stepped through.

Maureen followed her into the shadows. There was nothing behind the makeshift room but a few feet of empty space. Netta walked neck bent as far as she could get before the sloping roof met the ceiling and put the bucket down. She picked up a small square of timber that rested against a beam and placed it on top of the bucket.

"This is where you pee in case you need to go. And make sure you cover it after you use it. Only urine, anything else you will have to go to the lavatory downstairs at the entrance." She stood back and stared at Maureen. "Understand?"

Maureen nodded dumbly. It wasn't that much different to the piddle-pot she'd used at home as a kid.

They went back to the room and Maureen sat on her couch, sinking into the big cushions. It was comfortable. A damn sight better than the stone tiled landing and better than the back seat of her car. She still felt sad about the car. It was the first car she had ever owned, an Austin Somerset, with a sunroof and a back seat big enough to sleep on. She'd bought the car in the Channel Islands with the hundred pounds Aunt Maggie had left her. The money had been released on her 21st birthday and the car was a present to herself.

One of the chefs she had worked with in Jersey knew she wanted to visit Sarah, who at the time had been living in Norway. He had secured waitressing jobs in a ski lodge in Lillehammer for her and her workmate, Jane. With a month up their sleeves before starting work, she and Jane had driven to Vienna to stay with friends. Then they had driven to Munich.

The car broke down in Munich. The petrol gauge hadn't worked from the time she had bought it. "One owner, old lady, nothing wrong with it," the salesman had said. She knew now not to trust car salesmen but the world had been new to her then. She was a country kid from Australia and too trusting. The car ran out of petrol. Fortunately, she had a jerrycan and wasn't far from a petrol station. The petrol attendant filled the jerrycan. She asked him why the fuel was a blue colour. He didn't speak English and just nodded and smiled, so she thought maybe petrol was a different colour in Germany. The next garage she rattled into, the mechanic had said, "Motor kaputt!" It wasn't just the kerosene fuel; Maureen hadn't known the car had an oil leak when she'd bought it. It was probably spare parts by now.

She sighed, wondering what she would have done with the money if she hadn't bought the car. Where would she be now? She wouldn't have hitchhiked or needed a gun. She had told Nils about that episode because it had been headlines in the newspapers. *Hitchhikers abandon man in snow.*

Netta took eggs and bread from a cabinet missing its door and put the eggs in a saucepan. "Boiled eggs and toast," she said, humming as she poked the coals to get the embers sparking. When it was glowing enough she put bread on a long fork and held it in front of the fire.

Watching her made Maureen think of her mother, in the time before they had owned a toaster. She relaxed for the first time that day. "Have you been living here a long time, Netta?"

"A while."

"You wouldn't have a cup of water by any chance?" Maureen was parched.

"There's coffee in the thermos if you would like to pour yourself some." Netta pointed to the thermos on the floor by the stove. "I made it when you were downstairs, it will be nice and hot. There's water in a jug on the box next to the cabinet."

Maureen's face shone. "Coffee would be lovely. I haven't had a hot drink since this morning."

"Cups are on the top shelf, milk and a box of sugar cubes underneath. There are tongs next to the sugar cubes, use them."

Maureen leapt off the couch, humbled by the generosity of her odd benefactor. "I'm so grateful to you," she said. She downed a cup of water and refilled the cup with coffee. It smelt wonderful. Using the tongs, she picked up two sugar cubes and plopped them in the cup, then took a teaspoon from a neat tray of cutlery where all the spoons and forks faced the same way and stirred her coffee. The cup warmed her hands as she lifted it to her mouth, the aroma teasing her senses.

"I'll pay you back when my boyfriend returns from Greece. He's sailing in yacht races there." She hadn't gone with him because of her job. So much for that, she thought. Closing her eyes, Maureen sipped the long awaited hot beverage. She carried her cup back to the couch and curled her feet up.

A frown creased Netta's forehead. She straightened up from toasting the bread and transported it on the end of the fork to a plate on the sideboard, then removed a pack of butter from the kitchen cabinet. It was refrigerator cold. Netta dug into its hard surface with a knife, removing five blobs of butter. These were arranged on the pieces of toast, with one in each corner of the bread and one in the middle. She watched the blobs soften before spreading it evenly over the toast. Her lips pursed, thoughtfully. "Boyfriend? I thought you had just arrived from Australia to visit your friend?"

Maureen blinked. "Well, not just arrived. From Australia that is. I have been travelling in other countries. This is just the first time I would have met up with Sarah since I've been in Sweden. Sarah is Australian. We are from the same town." Maureen's eyes widened as she looked at Netta, who seemed to be watching her intently. "Sarah married a Norwegian boy and moved to Norway. That's why I went to Norway. Her husband works in shipping and moves around a lot."

"Your boyfriend is Norwegian?"

"Swedish. We met in Lillehammer at the ski lodge where I was working." She smiled, remembering the way Nils' deep blue eyes had followed her around the dining room. "He's very handsome, blonde, and has really nice teeth." She hugged her cup of coffee to her chest. The first thing he had said to her was that she looked like Claudia Cardinale, the film star. She didn't feel like a film star now, perched on a couch in a loft, beholden to the generosity of a squatter. She combed her fingers through her thick dark hair, recently cut into a bob that was the latest look here, conscious of her crumpled appearance.

Netta opened a sideboard and removed two trays, putting a plate on each. She drained the water from the pot of boiled eggs into a bowl and put the eggs into two egg cups. "How long were you in Norway?" she asked.

Maureen's brown eyes became glued to the food. "About six months."

"So, you and your boyfriend worked together?"

Maureen wriggled on the couch. "He was a guest at the lodge."

"You didn't know him long then?"

Maureen drew a deep breath. It seemed to be a problem for everyone who knew them. No self-respecting girl would move in with a boy and not be married, let alone one she hardly knew. That was brought home to her when she first met Nils' parents. The questions his mother had fired at Nils. *What do you know about her family? Why isn't she at university? Why is her skin so dark? Why was she travelling around the world on her own?* Nice Swedish girls didn't do that.

She'd said her father was a farmer. And that her skin was suntanned, because she was used to the Australian sun and she had just come back from a summer of sailing in Denmark with Nils. That she was a country girl and universities were only in the cities too far for her to travel. She didn't say that none of her family had been to university. That she would have loved to have gone, but her parents believed university was a waste for girls because they got married and had children. They would have spent their money on her brother Johnny, except Johnny never wanted to go to university. Maureen's adventurous spirit had been nurtured by her mother's stories about growing up in England and her father's stories of when he travelled the world

14

in the navy. She had wanted to meet her relatives in England. It had taken her three years to save up for a one-way ticket. Lots of Australian girls travelled on their own.

The tray Netta handed Maureen had two eggs, one in an eggcup and the other on a plate with toast cut into fingers. It crossed Maureen's mind that the food could have come from a dustbin. But a teaspoon and knife lay on top of a perfectly ironed white linen serviette. Maureen noticed Netta's clean hands, her trimmed fingernails, the white cuff of her blouse. There was nothing about Netta that conjured up an image of a vagrant. Maureen took the neatly arranged tray.

"Thank you." She dived at the egg, smashing the top with the teaspoon, peeling the bits of shell off with one hand, while pushing toast into her mouth with the other. Her gut gurgled with delight, giving her heart. The woman watched Maureen devour the food, saying nothing, waiting. Maureen knew she had to satisfy Netta's curiosity. She owed her.

"It was the end of the ski season and I was going to return to England, so Nils suggested I visit Sweden instead and get a job in Gothenburg. He said I could stay with him." Maureen saw the tweak of Netta's eyebrows and lifted her chin. "So, I thought, why not?" There was no commitment but Maureen was totally smitten. And at the time she had thought if it didn't work out, she could always hop on the ferry to England. She had relatives there. Maureen hung her head under Netta's stare. How naïve and impulsive she'd been.

"I'm sorry you have to share your food with me. I reckon I'm in a bit of a mess at the moment."

Netta didn't reply. She fetched her tray and settled on the couch opposite Maureen. Picking up a knife, she sliced the top off her egg, checked the centre with a spoon and scooped a small portion into her mouth. She nibbled a finger of toast and dabbed her lips with the napkin. Her fastidiousness put Maureen's mind to rest about the dustbin. Netta ate her food in silence.

Maureen had finished her toast and was already into her second egg when she realised Netta seemed to be waiting for her to speak. Filling the silence Maureen obliged. "I guess it's weird really, but I didn't think about Norway and Sweden being different countries at the time. I mean the language sounds similar." It had seemed to be like travelling from one state to another in Australia. Seeing the look of disbelief on Netta's face, Maureen blushed. She hadn't learned anything about Scandinavia in school other than they were all Vikings. Dutch wore clogs, Swiss yodelled, Germans started the war.

"Nils went guarantor for me. I didn't have a visa to work but I did have a job until this morning." A heaviness settled in her chest. "I was an au pair, paid like a babysitter, I didn't need a visa." The sob sounded like a hiccup. Maureen covered it with a cough and dug a hole in the bottom of her eggshell. How stupid she must sound.

Netta's eyes narrowed. "What happened to the job?"

"Nils' mother didn't approve of me. She telephoned my employer and told her I had a bad character. I was fired. They changed the locks on Nils' flat too. He doesn't know that yet because he's away sailing in Greece."

"Good heavens," Netta said.

Maureen looked at her plate. "I'm not a bad person. I didn't know Nils' family was rich when I met him. I wouldn't have cared anyway."

The only time she'd gone out with someone she hadn't been interested in was with a friend of The Rolling Stones, who took her to one of their parties. Maureen covered a yawn. She was exhausted. She didn't want to explain herself any further. She stood up and looked around for a place to put her tray.

16

"Leave your dishes in the bowl on the sideboard," Netta said. "I'll pour some water over them later. I don't like to use too much water as I have to empty it in the pee bucket, which makes it heavy to carry downstairs. Why don't you get into your pyjamas while I pay the bucket a visit?" Netta put her plate in the bowl and went behind the curtain. A radio blared somewhere in the building, and voices argued beneath them. Netta's pee was camouflaged by the sounds of the tenants, home from a day's work and settling in for the night.

Maureen shivered out of her clothes and dived into her pyjamas and socks. They were the only pieces of clothing she had kept from the parcel of clothes her mother had sent when she'd written to her saying she was freezing in Norway. She remembered how embarrassed and angry she'd been unpacking her long-awaited winter clothes, all the way from Australia. The clothes she had requested, her brand-new woollen suit with its braided edges and mini skirt that had taken two months on layby to pay off, hadn't been in the parcel. Nor was her red mohair jumper and new jeans. Instead, there was an old mustard-coloured mohair cardigan, missing a button, a pleated skirt that was too large, a pair of green woollen trousers with baggy knees and an elastic waist that looked like they'd been worn in the garden. And Maureen recognised as her mother's a couple of long sleeved singlets with stains under the arms, pyjamas and three pairs of knitted socks. The letter from her mother had said she'd given Maureen's clothes to her young boarder, thinking Maureen would live in Africa with her uncle's family – which was where she'd gone after leaving Australia and stayed for a year before travelling to Europe – and not need winter clothing. Maureen couldn't believe it. The Norwegian girls whom she worked with had all gathered in her bedroom to watch her open her parcel. No one had said a word as Maureen held up each item of clothing.

She put on the pyjamas, missing her mother, wondering if Netta had pen, paper and an envelope.

'Your turn," Netta said, holding the lamp out. "I'll put some coal on the fire and light a candle."

Maureen took the lamp and ducked under the drape, walking as quietly as she could to the bucket. She removed the wood covering and sat on the bucket, wincing as the hard metal edge stuck into her bum. She crouched above it, hands against the roof to steady herself and peed loud and full like a horse, hoping Netta wouldn't hear her above the creaks and sounds of the old gothic building. When she'd finished, she put the lid on the bucket.

The circle of comfort Netta had created held Maureen as she pulled back the drape. Soft light, playful shadows, a glowing fire and couches covered in blankets in that bleak roof filled Maureen with sadness for Netta. She had tried to create a home.

Feeling like an invader, she tiptoed to her couch-bed. Netta was in her pyjamas with a doona across her shoulders tuning her violin. Maureen waited until Netta put her violin in its case. "I don't suppose you have paper and an envelope so I can write a letter to my mother?"

Netta leant over the back of her couch and lifted an old sheet that served as one of the walls. Behind it was a tin trunk. She rummaged through the trunk withdrawing a brown leather writing case. "You'll find what you need in here," she said, handing it to Maureen. The leather case had the letters DHI engraved in gold next to the brass lock.

"Thank you. Is it yours?" The question had popped out and she instantly regretted it when she saw Netta's mouth compress. "I'm sorry, I didn't mean …"

"It is mine." Netta went back to her couch. "We'll have to put the lamp and candle out soon, don't want downstairs seeing lights through any cracks in their ceilings."

Maureen nodded. She made her bed and climbed in. The rugs were warm from being near the stove. Lying on her back she propped the leather case against her knees and took out a writing pad and a biro. How would she start her letter? How much would she tell her mother? Not that her mother would bother answering; she hadn't had a letter from her since she'd arrived in Sweden. For all her family cared she could be dead. Her pen burrowed a full stop at the top of the page where she usually put her address. What address could she give?

"Damn!" She slapped the case. Netta's head jerked up. "Sorry, I don't know what address to put? I can't use Sarah's, as the postman will slip her letters through the door and I won't be able to get inside to get them."

Netta's brow furrowed. "Leave the address off until you're ready to post it and ask at the post office what you can do. Why don't you use your boyfriend's address? He'll probably be back before you get an answer?"

"He's actually my fiancé. And his mail goes to his parents' house. Something to do with their income tax if his flat is empty."

"You're not wearing a ring?" The single gold band that indicated engagement was in Maureen's bag. When they married, she would wear two gold rings which was the Swedish custom.

"We had to keep it a secret from his parents." But she didn't have to keep it a secret from her parents. It might be a good place to start her letter. Being engaged would make her more respectable and her family wouldn't condemn her so harshly for running off with Nils. Maybe they would write to her again?

3

A Job in Sweden

The pigeons went off like an alarm clock creating pande-
monium in the rafters. Maureen shot up from her troubled
sleep and gazed around, bewildered. A fly-by pigeon splattered
its early breakfast on her rug and left through a skylight in the
roof. Her stomach seesawed. Hand to her mouth she raced for
the bucket. There was no muffling the sound of her vomit.
She tried coughing and hoped it was enough to fool Netta.
Feeling normal again she had a pee and went back to her couch.
Netta was up adding coals to the feeble glow of the few embers
that had lasted the night. She put a pot of water to boil for their
morning coffee.

Covering her mouth with her hand Maureen faked a cough.
"I hope I haven't picked up a bug."

"Toast?" Netta asked.

"Yes, please." It was strange that she always felt hungry after a vomit in the morning. Once it was out she could eat a side of bacon. She looked around for something useful to do to show her gratitude. The place was neat, Netta's blankets already folded and stacked on the end of her couch. "Can I make the toast for you?" Maureen said.

Without replying, Netta sliced the bread into thick chunks and handed them to her along with the toasting fork. Sticking the prongs into the bread she crouched in front of the fire. Another wave of nausea struck her. She dropped the fork and ran for the bucket. When she came back, she was shaky and pale. "Sorry, it doesn't usually happen twice. Please, I'll do that." She put her hand out for the fork.

"No need, it's done." Netta removed the toast from the fork and put it on a plate. She gave Maureen an enquiring look. "Are you pregnant?"

Maureen looked at the floor and nodded.

"I was pregnant once, lasted two months and then I aborted," Netta said.

Maureen's hand went to her stomach. "Were you married?"

Netta looked past Maureen, butter knife suspended, then shook her head to remove a thought and went back to preparing breakfast. "I was at the time. Not that marriage is important," she said. Maureen's back straightened. "Does your boyfriend know?"

"Yes." Maureen hesitated. "He was trying to get me to have an abortion but it's illegal in Sweden. Swedish girls go to Poland. I need a visa for Poland, which would take three months. Too late by then."

"Do you want an abortion?"

Maureen thought for a moment. Nils hadn't asked her that. "No, I want to keep it and marry Nils."

"Well, you should tell him. He has to take some responsibility. You are engaged." What man would leave his pregnant fiancée on the street? Once upon a time, Netta had been married to someone she'd believed in. He was dead now. She looked into the rafters, most of the pigeons had gone. "The newspaper shop should be open in an hour," Netta said.

The bell tinkled as Maureen pushed open the door to the shop. The owner cut the string from around a bundle of newspapers and looked up. Maureen pointed to the telephone on his counter, mimed picking it up and putting it to her ear. "Could I use your phone?" She held out one krone. He took it.

"You may use. I speak English." His chest grew.

"Tuk, I only know a little Svenska," Maureen apologised. She went to the phone, dialed the operator and asked for Lizette, the girlfriend of one of Nils' crew members. They had become friends. After a few exchanges between the telephone operator and the number, Maureen was put through to the housekeeper. The family was on holiday.

The telephone missed the cradle as she replaced it, her eyes too misty to see properly. "Sorry," she mumbled to the shopkeeper. "Thank you for letting me use the phone." Would Netta let her stay longer? Did Netta have enough food for her? Nils wouldn't be back from Greece for another five days.

She felt despondent as she made her way back through the passage of furniture and under the table to Netta's hideaway. *It will all turn out alright* she told herself. She hauled herself up and dusted her knees then caught sight of Netta. Her mouth dropped open.

Netta chuckled. She was wearing glasses with white rims and a blonde wig that curled around the edges of a black fur hat. Her green wool dress, belted at the waist, ended just above black leather boots. The look was that of a stylish hippy and nothing like the Netta Maureen had left half an hour ago.

Netta pulled on gloves and a black overcoat, then gathered up a bulging carpet bag and her violin. "Did you speak to your friend?"

"She's away on holiday."

"A lot of Swedes travel in autumn and winter."

Maureen twisted her hands. "Would you mind letting me stay longer?" She felt like a beggar standing in front of Netta. The look on Netta's face wasn't encouraging. "I won't get in your way and I'll pay you back when Nils comes for me." She noticed the bucket of pee on the floor next to the coffee table. "I can empty the bucket for you?" She picked it up.

Netta looked at the bucket and nodded. It would save her an extra trip up the stairs.

"If any tenants see you, just say you're assisting the janitor. There isn't a janitor but they don't know that. You can stay one more night and then we'll see." She looked thoughtful. It wouldn't be wise for Maureen to stay in the roof on her own during the day. There was always a chance one of the tenants would access their storeroom and a desperate Maureen might give Netta's presence away. "Can you sing?"

"What? Can I sing? Not really. Why?" Maureen said.

Netta shrugged. "Just a thought." She picked up her violin and bag. "Get your coat on, you're coming with me." Maureen didn't argue.

Light snow danced towards the ground melting on contact. The glazed sun held no warmth in spite of the blue sky. Maureen clung to Netta's carpetbag and occasionally the rail as she negotiated the crisp puddles on the pavement. Netta strode ahead carrying her violin case. They came to the recessed entrance of a large clothing shop. The mannequins in the window wore red Santa Claus hats or a ring of candles on their heads. It wasn't long until Christmas. Netta set down her violin and motioned to Maureen for her bag. Out of the bag came a folded metal stand, a music book and a small rubber mat. The stand was set up and a book placed on top, then Netta took her violin from the case, leaving the case open. She plinked a few notes tuning the violin. Then smiled at the shoppers passing her and began to play.

The chills up Maureen's neck weren't from the cold. The music was haunting. People stopped to listen, money was thrown in the violin case. Netta could have been giving a recital in a concert hall. After an hour they went inside the shop to warm up and use the ladies' rest room. The contrast from the cold outside to the shop's warm interior made Maureen's cheeks burn. "You play beautifully," Maureen said, enjoying the hot water running over her hands. A toilet flushed behind her.

"How do you know how well I played?"

"I lived with my aunt and uncle in Melbourne. My uncle was in the orchestra and I often went to recitals." Taking a comb from her bag she did her hair and applied some lipstick.

"Come, we have another call to make," Netta said, pulling at the blonde tendrils of her wig so they could be seen under her fur hat. Maureen had nothing else to do, so she was happy to follow Netta. It was interesting to see how she spent her time.

They went down an alley and into the back of a restaurant. The kitchen was a clatter of pans and raised voices. When Netta walked through the kitchen, the chef and his two staff stopped what they were doing and greeted her politely. Netta led Maureen into the dining room. The floor was covered in a deep blue carpet. Gold curtains draped the windows, Lautrec paintings hung on the walls. The tables were round with white tablecloths and fanned napkins. The chairs were cushioned in paisley. A piano rested on a raised dais to the side of the room. It was a glamorous setting that spoke of expensive food. A short man, in a striped waistcoat that strained around his ample middle, and wearing a yellow cravat with a diamante brooch, moved around the room flicking bits of imaginary fluff off tables and straightening cutlery. He looked over as they came in.

"Henrietta," he swept a bow and came towards her. "You are early today, my dear." He looked around her at Maureen. "Who is this you have with you?"

"Bernard, meet Maureen." Bernard kissed the air both sides of Maureen's cheeks.

"A flower," he said, holding her out and appraising her from top to toe. Maureen giggled, liking him instantly. "What do you play?" he said.

"Pardon? I …"

"She's with me today, locked out of her apartment. But there is something she could do for you. Weren't you short of a dishwasher?"

"Too pretty for a dishwasher. I could use another waitress?" Bernard's smile was wide and cheerful.

"She doesn't speak Swedish."

"I'm Australian," Maureen said, taking charge of her situation. "And I am a good dishwasher. I've worked in hotels."

"Consider yourself employed," said Bernard. He turned to Netta, "Are you playing for us at lunchtime or have you just come for lunch?"

"Playing," said Netta. "And we will have an early lunch before your guests arrive."

"Magnifique, I will join you." He left for the kitchen. Maureen followed Netta to the ladies' room.

"Netta, thank you for getting me the job, but I don't have a work visa?"

"We will pay you cash," she said. She shook her head, "I mean Bernard will, of course." Netta stripped off her dress and was lathering a face washer she'd taken from her carpetbag. She washed her armpits, then wetting and soaping the cloth again, she disappeared into a lavatory cubicle. Maureen hesitated, then pulled off her jumper and soaked her handkerchief under the tap and scrubbed her armpits. When Netta came out, Maureen wet and soaped her own handkerchief and went into the lavatory to wash her nether regions. She dried herself on toilet paper. *When in Rome*, she thought. Netta was ready and waiting when Maureen had finished.

The three of them sat at a table close to the kitchen. One of the kitchenhands came out with a platter of chicken and an array of vegetables. Maureen loaded her plate.

"Eating for two," Netta said.

"You don't say?" Bernard responded without much interest. His lips twitched. "When are you leaving your convent?"

"That is my business," Netta said, flicking her eyes towards Maureen and frowning at Bernard.

"Where are you staying, ma petite?"

"Netta was kind enough to put me up last night," Maureen said.

Bernard's head went back and he stared at her in shock. "Non! With the pigeons? That is horrible." He looked at Netta.

"It was cozy and I'm grateful that I had somewhere to stay. In Australia we have cockatoos instead of pigeons. They make a lot more noise."

Bernard stared at Maureen, his lips a small circle. He brushed some crumbs off his waistcoat. This girl was desperate.

"Can you help in the kitchen today? See how we do things?" he said.

Maureen clapped her hands. "Yes, I can definitely work today. Thank you so much." She couldn't believe her luck.

"Come. You will meet the chef." They entered the kitchen and Bernard waved the chef over. "Bengt, this is Maureen from Australia, she will be helping with the dishes."

The chef wiped his hands on his apron and shook Maureen's hand, frowning. He spoke to her in Swedish and she shook her head. He threw his hands in the air and said something to Bernard. Bernard's smile disappeared. There was a quick exchange of words, a flurry of hands. The chef glared, staring at the floor. Bernard flipped his hand in the air and took Maureen over to the sink. "This is where it is done." He pointed to the draining boards and showed her where the scourers and washing-up soap was kept. "You will do what Bengt asks you. He looked across at the chef and gave a little toss of his head. "Make him happy. He would like his niece for the kitchen job but she's in school for more time. We cannot wait so long."

The job gave Maureen new hope. She would do her best to win the chef over. Rolling up the sleeves of her jumper, she pulled on the rubber gloves hanging over the tap and put the plug in the sink.

"I'll start on the pots first in case the chef needs them." Picking up a pad of steel wool she got stuck into a saucepan. Bernard nodded his approval.

"You will do," he said.

Netta came into the kitchen and stood next to Bernard. Maureen looked at them through the steam from the sink and it struck her what an unlikely twosome her rescuers were. She remembered her mother's words, *never judge a book by its cover*, and smiled.

4

Eden – Letter Home

Lillian heard the postman's whistle and put down the trowel she'd been using to dig around her roses. She wiped her hands on her apron and went around to the postbox at the front gate. There were a few palings missing off the fence. Perhaps that was a job Eric could do, she thought, opening the box and retrieving the letter. The letter had an express airmail sticker. Turning it over she saw it was from Maureen, care of a post office box number in Gothenburg, Sweden. The new address made Lillian feel a trifle anxious.

Taking the letter into the kitchen, Lillian hoped there would be some answers to the questions she'd asked in her previous letters. It was odd that Maureen didn't mention her Swedish boyfriend. Was he kind to her? Did he have a sense of humour? What was his family like? She would have thought Maureen would have been excited to tell her about him, but other than his name and that he was a student she'd said nothing. Nor had she commented on any of the town gossip Lillian spiced her letters with, not even when she had written about the death of one of Maureen's school friends in a car accident. It was as though she hadn't received any of her letters.

Lillian sat at the kitchen table and tore the envelope open. After reading it twice, she put the letter aside. Something wasn't quite right. Maureen was skimming over things, which wasn't her style. Her letters were always in-depth, describing the country, the people she met, the food she ate, the weather. This one left Lillian with a lot of questions, although she did mention her boyfriend was away sailing in Greece. But why did she want to move in with Sarah? Was there a problem with the boyfriend? It was lucky the woman who lived in Sarah's block of flats offered her somewhere to stay until Sarah came back but moving in with someone she had never met was a bit foolhardy. There were a lot of things that didn't add up. Like asking for money because she'd lost her job. Maureen had never asked for money before. She had always been a good money manager. Unlike me, thought Lillian. She gazed out of the kitchen window to the Pacific Ocean. It seemed cold and distant, like the miles between her and her daughter, filling her with foreboding.

Maureen's father would have to help her with money, as most of hers had been spent on trips to Melbourne to see her mother, and on Splinter's wedding. The idea of asking Eric for money fired up Lillian's reflux. She went to the fridge and found a bottle of Rennie's Quick Ease on the top, popped one in her mouth and chewed it. Approaching Eric would need a plan. She remembered his reaction to Maureen's previous letter, informing them she had moved to Sweden to live with a boy she had only just met.

It had been at one of their Sunday family get-togethers after the divorce. Lillian had saved the letter to read when they were

29

all together. Eric was gobsmacked, his chair hitting the floor as he'd leapt up, roaring. "Bubs has shamed this family. I forbid any of you to write to her until I say so. Do you hear me?" To keep the peace, they had all agreed. Later, Lillian reminded Eric that their own relationship had started with a holiday romance when his ship docked in Portsmouth, in England. When the ship returned a few months later they had married. The time they actually spent together before the wedding totalled five weeks. Most of their courtship had been through correspondence. Admittedly the Second World War was about to break out and it was uncertain times, but … Lillian's only hope was that her daughter's choice would turn out better than hers had.

Ignoring Eric's demand to cut contact with Maureen, Lillian had written immediately. She had said how disappointed they all were, but she would support her. She had finished off by saying, "Just don't end up living on the other side of the world."

Pushing back her chair, she got up and put the letter on top of the fridge. Ingrid had asked her to afternoon tea. There was something important Ingrid wanted to tell her. The grey sky suggested she should wear her mackintosh and the news had said a southerly was building. An umbrella wouldn't work in a gale, so she put on a scarf.

Lillian bent into the wind as she passed the Eden Whale Museum. It had just had a new coat of paint and a busload of tourists was outside. Tom the Killer Whale had become a big attraction. Lillian pulled her mackintosh tighter and followed the track through the ti tree down to the wharf. The wharf leaned into the bay, white caps slapping at its pylons. On both sides, trawlers banged and pulled at their moorings like tethered dogs. Lillian could see the boat her son worked on. Johnny was probably up at the Fisherman's Club with some of his mates.

By the time she reached Ingrid's gate, she was panting. The lookout hill had taken its toll. Before she could knock, Ingrid had the door open and was pulling her inside and sitting her in the lounge. Two glasses of sherry were poured.

"This you vill need," Ingrid said, handing a glass to Lillian. She wasn't usually so dramatic.

"Thank you. Now what's all the cloak and dagger about?" Lillian said, taking a sip. The grinding of the Hills hoist outside the lounge window caught her attention. The wind had turned the sheets into sails turning the Hills hoist into a merry-go-round. It reminded Lillian of her washing. It would wrap around the clothesline in this wind and take her ages to untangle. The next appliance she would save for was going to be a Hills hoist.

"I can't stay long, Ingrid. I have to get the washing in before it rains."

"Ja. I vill tell you news but first we have the strudel." She cut two wedges of her famous strudel. It was worth the two-mile walk, Lillian thought, as she took her first bite.

Ingrid settled herself opposite Lillian. "It is Eric," she said. Lillian's lips pursed. Eric could go to hell. She didn't want to be bothered with him anymore. Maureen's news had unsettled her enough, but she waited to hear what her ex-husband had been up to.

Listening to the story, Lillian was glad it was Ingrid she was hearing it from. Better a friend than someone wanting to see her squirm with embarrassment. Not that she wasn't doing that now. Eric's doings stank worse than the cannery.

"Surely not?" Lillian downed her sherry and held her glass out for a refill. Ingrid topped up their glasses.

"Ja, tis true. Eric says in Fisherman's Club he had heart problem and needed housekeeper. This woman leave her husband, Quick Parker, because she says he's stupid," she tapped the side of her head. "Quick gets farm in money trouble. That is okay but Quick says she is sharing a bed with Eric. His kids told him. Mein Gott! The woman is twenty-five and has three children?"

31

Lillian frowned. "I know her. Kathy Parker, a big hefty girl with dark curly hair. She worked as a nurse in Bega Hospital. I think she was a class above Splinter at school. I can't believe he's having an affair with someone the same age as his own daughter. What's he thinking for Pete's sake?" It was incredible that he had the nerve to say Maureen had shamed the family. It was the pot calling the kettle black. Lillian gave a thin smile. "If Aunt Maggie was still alive, she'd prune his dick with her secateurs."

Ingrid laughed. She had listened to many of Lillian's stories about Eric's feisty old aunt. "It is good you got a divorce."

"It doesn't seem like ten years ago. I manage to survive on my boarders, and he has his farm. I don't mind doing his washing on weekends, but I won't do it if he has someone living with him. It's not myself I care about, Ingrid." Lillian had weathered too many of Eric's treasons during their marriage to bother about what he did. She had no feelings for him anymore. "I care about the kids. How could he humiliate Splinter and Johnny? Shacking up with someone they went to school with? It's a small town. The kids will never live this down." She needed to warn them. Not Maureen, she was too far away for it to affect her. Lucky her, Lillian thought.

The window rattled as the southerly picked up. Lillian put her empty sherry glass on the coffee table and got to her feet. "Thank you for having the courage to tell me Ingrid, you're a good friend. I'm not looking forward to telling the kids, but better they know so they can fob off the gossip." She pulled on her mackintosh and picked up her handbag. "Your turn to visit me next." They hugged goodbye.

Walking down the wharf hill after leaving Ingrid's, Lillian went over how she would tell Splinter and Johnny about their father's doings. She could picture her children's shocked faces. Better to get it over and done with and leave Johnny a message at the club on her way home. She would phone Splinter, invite them to tea tomorrow night while Johnny's boat was in.

"You must be kidding, Mum?" Johnny lowered his fork full of steak and kidney pie. He had lost his virginity to Kathy; how could she root his father?

Splinter gagged. "No! I went to school with her. She's got three kids. She was a tart at school. He's an old man."

Lillian shrugged. "You know your father. He was always that way. I believe Kathy's husband has gotten into debt with their farm and is going to lose it."

"So, Dad's an easy way out for her? Take advantage of an old goat? She's probably sucking him dry."

Johnny coughed.

"Well, that may be, but there's nothing we can do about it. The problem is how to deal with the gossip when it gets around town." In the past Lillian had hidden indoors, sending her children up the street to do the shopping as though she were the guilty person. Her lips pruned.

Splinter let out a moan. "I'm a schoolteacher. The kids will hear it from their parents. I'll have to ask for a transfer to Bega or somewhere."

"No, you won't. It's not your fault. You just look them in the eye and say nothing. It's none of their business." Lillian had gained courage under the tuition of Aunt Maggie. No more hiding her head.

It wouldn't be that easy for Johnny though, all his mates knew he'd rogered Kathy. They would be merciless. Johnny chewed his pie in silence. His father had to pay.

"While I've got you both here, I want to share another problem." Lillian went to the fridge, retrieved Maureen's letter and handed it to Splinter. "This came today. It's from Maureen. I want you to read it and tell me what you think." Lillian watched Splinter's face for a reaction." Splinter frowned, then turned the single page over to see if there was anything written on the back.

"Short letter for Bubs," she said. "Is she in some sort of trouble?" She handed Johnny the letter.

"I don't know, and I haven't got any money to send her this month, too many bills due. I was wondering how we could approach your father?"

"Well, don't look at me," Splinter snapped. " I wouldn't go near him with a barge pole. Bubs shouldn't have spent all her money having a good time." She was usually kind to her young sister, but Bubs wasn't here to share the humiliation of their father.

Lillian looked at Johnny and raised her eyebrows. He had a soft spot for his little sister.

Johnny scowled at his plate. Bubs had moved to Melbourne to live with their aunt and uncle when she was fifteen and then gone overseas. He hadn't seen her in seven years. He was more concerned about getting back at his father for shagging Kathy. "I could pinch that new Buick he bought. Flog it in Sydney?"

"Don't be ridiculous, you'd end up in gaol. Anyway, it would take planning and Maureen needs the money now." Lillian couldn't help smirking at the thought of Eric's face if he discovered his prize possession missing. "What else can you think of?"

They ate their food in silence. Then Johnny banged the table with his fist, making the crockery and his mother jump. "I've got it! My mate's a bookie in Melbourne. I'll tell Dad he's given me a tip on a race. That it's a sure thing and I'm going to Melbourne to place a bet. I'll say my mate won't take less than a hundred dollars bet. I'll pay him a tenner to back me up in case Dad phones him." Of course, Johnny would pay himself twenty dollars for all the effort he'd have to go to. "It will serve the old buzzard right." Johnny gave his mother a narrow-eyed look and grinned.

Lillian knew that look. He'd conned her a few times. Well, if anyone could con Eric, his son could. "Righto, ball's in your court. Don't waste time, it's urgent."

Johnny was dressed in his good clothes to support the story he was about to tell his father. He went over it in his head as he drove to the farm.

Kathy opened the door as he stepped onto the verandah. Johnny gave her a hard look. "Where's the old man?" He noticed she had the grace to blush. She was no oil painting, wearing his father's dressing gown. He'd knocked her off when he was seventeen, a lot of his mates had. None of their fathers though. His jaw clenched and his green eyes flashed.

Kathy patted her hair and let the dressing gown fall open revealing a satin petticoat with lace trim that stretched across her large bosom and accentuated the rolls around her gut. Johnny was a handsome fellow. "He's dagging the sheep in the back paddock," she said.

Johnny's nose wrinkled; it wasn't a job he was going to help with. He didn't thank her. He turned and walked away.

"Your father's not well," she called out. "I'm only here as his nurse."

"Yeah, right!" He yelled back.

"Good to see you, mate," Eric said, a sheep between his legs and a pair of shears in his hand. "Could you hold her head for me? She's been fly struck so need to cut her close. She might get a nick or two."

"I'm wearing my good pants, Dad. Leaving for Melbourne

tonight. Going to the races." Johnny grabbed the sheep's head anyway. He had never stood up to his father.

"Races, eh? Got a tip?"

"Matter of fact, I have." It was going to be easy.

Three days later, Lillian slipped the fifty-dollar postal note into an envelope along with her letter and lists of questions and sent it express post to the new address Maureen had given.

5

A Bad Cold

Maureen had spent two nights with Netta and nothing had been said about her moving out. The rugs remained folded on the end of Maureen's couch. She did the bucket duty and went to work.

The kitchen was readying for its lunchtime guests and Maureen waited at her post, rubber gloves on. Netta entered the kitchen through the back door, dressed in glasses, hat and wig. She waved to the staff, nodded at Bernard and went into his office off the kitchen. Bernard poured two coffees and hurried after her, closing the door behind him. How kind of him, Maureen thought, making time for a woman who lived in a roof. When Netta came out of the office she went into the dining room and settled herself at the piano. Maureen wondered how many instruments she played and if she ever played the violin in the restaurant.

The dining room soon filled with guests. Maureen's arms were soaped to the elbows and her back sore from bending over the stacks of dishes in the sink. To keep her mind off her discomfort, she tried to understand some of the Swedish flying around the kitchen, picking up occasional words, mostly swear words. Swear words were the first thing she'd learned. Nils' yacht crew had been dedicated teachers. She wondered what he was doing now? The Scandinavian yachtsmen competing in the races in Greece were all staying at the palace because King Constantine was married to a Danish princess. She imagined Nils sitting at a banquet table toasting the king, while here she was, washing dishes and sleeping with pigeons in the roof! She laughed at the strangeness of it. It wasn't much different for Netta though, sitting in a swanky restaurant playing Tom Jones' latest hit, *What's New Pussycat?*

She hadn't pushed Netta to reveal anything about herself; instead she put her in the category of her eccentric Aunt Maggie who she had lived next door to as a child. Maureen could accept anyone. She had met all types of people after leaving Eden and moving in with her musician aunt and uncle in Melbourne. She hummed *What's New Pussycat?* as she washed the dishes. It was Nils' and her song. It had been playing when he proposed to her on the dance floor in the Copenhagen yacht club. His name for her was Pussycat. She felt a flutter in her stomach. "I know you're there," she whispered, giving her tummy a pat. She wondered if it was a boy or a girl? Nils' parents would change their minds about her once they knew they were going to be grandparents. She thought about her own grandmothers. Her maternal grandmother had been kind but her paternal grandmother had been horrible to her mother Lillian and to Maureen and her sisters. It was possible Nils' mother might not react the way Maureen hoped.

After the guests had gone, tables cleared and dishes done, the staff had their lunch. Netta and Maureen were joined by Bernard. Maureen sat quietly while Netta and Bernard conversed in French with a lot of frowns and gestures. Netta put her hand up, stopping Bernard's monologue and stood up.

"Excuse me, it's time I went home." She turned to Maureen. "You can come back with me; Bernard only needs you for breakfast and lunch shifts." Netta picked up her carpetbag and went to the lady's room. Bernard drummed his fingers on the table.

"That is a stubborn woman." He smiled at Maureen. "How do you manage in that bird poo poo, place?" Maureen was surprised Bernard knew how Netta lived.

"Fine." She felt a surge of loyalty for Netta. "Netta has made me very comfortable, thank you." She wouldn't have to stay there much longer. "When my fiancée gets back from Greece, I'll stay with him." They would get married at a registry office with his crew and Sarah's family in attendance. She would also ask Netta and Bernard to her wedding. Once they were married there was nothing his parents could do about it.

"It is my worry Henrietta is getting too old for such discomfort. Does she seem well to you?" Bernard gazed at Maureen, concern in his eyes. "It is ridiculous. Non?"

"Where else can Netta go? She doesn't have any money except what she earns from busking." She hadn't seen Bernard pay her for playing. She was probably doing it for the meals she ate. "How long has she lived there?"

Bernard scratched his head. "Eight years, I'm thinking." The spoon in Maureen's coffee went still. He shrugged. "It is her choosing."

Why would anyone want to live in a roof without water, electricity, a toilet and in the freezing cold? Some people didn't have a choice. Bernard didn't know what he was talking about.

But eight years? Maureen felt sorry for Netta. She had shown her kindness and was obviously an educated lady. "Does she play the piano here every day?" Maureen asked.

Bernard nodded. "She brings customers. She is a mystery to them. Once she was professional musician."

"Gosh! Was that before she was married? Did her husband die? Have you known her a long time?"

Bernard checked his manicured fingernails and picked at the light pink polish. He loved to gossip but there were boundaries where Netta was concerned. "You must ask her these questions, my little pigeon. Now I have work to do." He took some notes from his wallet. "This is for your work. I will pay you each day."

Bernard handed Maureen the standard wage for a kitchen hand. "You can eat here for free, no boyfriend or friends though." He beckoned to the waitress to clear their table. "Au revoir, until tomorrow." He turned to go as Netta came out of the lady's room. The white-rimmed glasses were gone, her hat and wig too, and she had changed her dress for a skirt.

Bernard raised his hand to farewell Netta and lowered his voice to Maureen. "Sometimes customers wait for her outside. She doesn't want them following her home, so she disguises," he shook his head.

On the way back to Netta's, Maureen carried the violin. They passed a bakery. The sweet scent of baking bread tugged at Maureen. She stopped. "I'll buy a loaf of bread for tonight," she said, wanting to pay her way, however small. She bought a loaf of *limpa* bread, a rye bread with honey and aniseed. It wasn't Maureen's favourite, preferring white bread without any sweeteners, but *limpa* bread was expensive and she wanted to give Netta something special.

Maureen had found it hard adjusting to Scandinavian food: raw fish for breakfast, blood pudding and *lutefisk*. The *lutefisk* was the worst. Her gut roiled at the thought of the rotten-smelling fish Swedes ate at Easter and Christmas. Nils had encouraged her to eat it and she had tried for his sake, but most of it ended up in a serviette hidden in her lap.

Netta sliced some cheese and cut the *limpa* bread while Maureen boiled two eggs. They sat on their couches and ate in the glow of the fire and four candles.

"When is your baby due?"

"I'm not sure. I think I'm three and a half months pregnant."

"Didn't the doctor give you a date?"

"I haven't seen one yet."

Netta sat back. "Really?"

"I can't afford to go. Nils is taking me when he gets back from Greece." She saw Netta's lips purse.

"He should have taken you at the beginning. You can go to the hospital for free in Sweden. I can't understand why this Nils boy hasn't mentioned that. A miscarriage can be dangerous. So can an abortion. Which it's obviously too late for."

Maureen stiffened. It wasn't up to Netta to give an opinion. She hadn't done so well with her life. Maureen felt the need to defend Nils.

"He said he had to secure an abortion first because once I was registered as pregnant, I would be checked up on." The words tapped at her. There was something not quite right.

The grim look on Netta's face took hold. Maureen chewed a fingernail. Nils had been more concerned about getting her an abortion than her health. He'd said he would make enquiries in Greece. She tried to quell the prongs of anxiety that threatened the wriggle in her womb. She shut down her negative thoughts. Nils loved her. He would look after her. If not, she would manage. Hadn't she left home and moved to Melbourne at fifteen and left Australia on a one-way ticket when she was nineteen? She wasn't going to talk about it with Netta anymore.

"I'm going to get ready for bed. I'm feeling a bit tired."

Maureen rinsed her dishes and put on her pyjamas. She had a job to go to tomorrow. Everything would work out.

The temperature dropped overnight. Snow covered the skylight in the roof. The pigeons remained in the rafters, bodies fluffed, and heads tucked under their wings.

A wave of morning sickness brought Maureen to her feet. Wrapped in a rug, she rushed for the bucket and heaved. The acrid smell of her vomit clung to the chill air. She wiped her mouth, had a pee and went back to the couch. In the light of a candle, Maureen checked her wristwatch. Six o'clock. Early to bed, early to rise, time to get dressed for work. She leapt from her pyjamas into her clothes, anticipating the warmth of the restaurant kitchen. Two more nights in the cold dark loft and Nils would be back. She smiled on the inside.

Netta stayed curled on the couch. "I won't busk today. I'll see you at lunchtime." Her voice was hoarse. A hacking cough brought her to her elbows.

"You don't sound too good. Why don't you stay in bed all day? I can bring you back some lunch? Maybe a hot toddy? My aunt Maggie always drank hot toddies when she had a cough. She used to warm up brandy, lemon and honey and down it with two asprins.

I can ask Bernard to mix it then you can heat it up?"

Netta gave a small smile. Bernard had taken care of her before, when she'd had a fall. On that occasion he'd brought her food. Her circumstances had horrified him, and he had tried to get her to move out of the roof. Even threatened to call in the social workers. It was a threat without substance. Bernard wouldn't have wanted to expose Netta's situation and open a can of worms.

"I will stay home, thank you. The bucket will need emptying before you go." Maureen couldn't help a grimace, but it was her vomit and pee as well as Netta's. She felt a rush of guilt that Netta had had to empty her vomit.

"Of course, I'll do that now."

There was toast and coffee waiting for Maureen when she got back from bucket duty. Netta sipped her coffee tucked up on the couch.

"How did you meet Bernard?" Maureen asked as she ate her toast. Her question was greeted with silence and for a moment she thought Netta wasn't going to answer and wished she hadn't asked.

"I knew him when he opened his restaurant. I was invited to play the violin at the opening."

"Bernard said you played in an orchestra?"

"London Philharmonic."

Maureen stared at Netta in disbelief. If it was true, but how could such a talented woman end up in this place? She looked around the makeshift room and back to the huddled form swathed in blankets. "I don't understand why you're living here when you can still play so well? You should be living in a nice warm house and playing in a orchestra."

"I have all I need. You should be off to work." There was nothing more to be said.

Maureen collected their cups and put them in the dish on the sideboard and added more coal to the fire. "I'll see you about three o'clock then."

"The pigeons haven't left their perch so it must be snowing outside. You had better take my umbrella."

Streetlights, headlights of cars and the glow from shop windows made crystals out of snow gathered on ledges. Maureen was glad of the fur-lined boots and beanie she had bought in Norway. A car slowed next to her. A leering face leaned over and rolled the window down, motioning her over with his hand. "I don't speak Swedish," she yelled, glancing at him. He patted the seat. Maureen stared straight ahead and walked faster. The car kept pace with her. She was reminded of the lift she and her travelling companion, Jane, had accepted when they were hitchhiking to Norway eighteen months ago which turned into a kidnapping. They were lucky to escape unscathed.

Now Maureen was more cautious. Rather than show her pursuer where she was going, she walked past the restaurant and when the car was a few feet ahead, unable to turn around in the traffic, she doubled back at a run, ducking down the alleyway beside the restaurant. She burst through the back door of the kitchen out of breath slamming the door behind her. The chef's head whipped towards her.

"Helvita!" he said.

"Sorry, I was being followed," she gulped. The chef received her apologetic smile with a grunt and went back to stirring his saucepans.

While Maureen washed the dishes, she kept an eye on Bernard's office door, waiting for an opportunity to speak to him. He had had meetings all morning. Finally, he emerged as the first of the lunch guests appeared, rushing to greet and seat them. He came back into the kitchen and Maureen seized her chance.

"Netta can't come in today, Bernard, she has a bad cold," she called out. Should she mention the lunch? The chef couldn't object if she offered to pay.

"I said I would take Netta some lunch. I can pay for it?"

"Non!" Bernard turned to the chef, draping an arm around him. "Bengt, you will fill the thermos flask with le bouillon de poulet." The chef nodded and Bernard kissed his ear. Maureen was suddenly aware that the relationship between Bernard and the chef was an intimate one. Living with her dancer aunt and musician uncle in Melbourne had opened her mind to many types of relationships. "Maureen, if Henrietta needs the doctor, you must bring her here in a taxi. I will pay. I must speak sense with her. She cannot stay in the cold roof anymore. If she dies, my business go boom!" He clapped his hands.

Maureen suppressed a smile at Bernard's dramatics. "It's just a bad cold, Bernard. The soup will make her feel much better, though. You are very kind."

"Kind? My little pigeon, you know nothing." An hour later, at Bernard's insistence, she left the restaurant armed with the thermos flask and a paper bag with eggs, cheese, milk and lingonberries.

Pushing the roof door open Maureen peered into the dark. There wasn't even the faintest glow coming from Netta's hidey-hole. It looked bleak and unfriendly. She switched on the torch Bernard had given her, after she'd mentioned how they had to creep around the roof with candles.

"Mon dieu," he'd said, tugging his manicured hair.

She scrabbled her way through the furniture and arrived in Netta's space. She shone the torch on the bundled form on the couch. A hand went up to shield the light. Maureen aimed the torch at the stove. The fire was out. "How are you feeling, Netta?"

"Not the best," she wheezed. She sounded dreadful.

"I have some nice chicken soup for you." She put the thermos on the table, found a cup and poured Netta some soup. Netta struggled into a sitting position.

"Very thoughtful, thank you." After a few sips she held the cup out to Maureen. "My throat's too sore. I'll save some for later."

"No, you will finish it." Maureen and her sister, Splinter, had nursed her mother's migraines, mixing Bex powders, wetting flannels to put on her head as far back as she could remember. She would nurse Netta.

"I can't tell Bernard a lie if he asks how much you ate. He said

I was to take you to him in a taxi if you aren't well. What if Nils arrives tomorrow? I can't go off and leave you sick in bed." She expected him any day. She would leave a note on Sarah's door telling him to come and fetch her from the restaurant.

Netta grunted, had another mouthful of soup and sagged back on the couch, too sick to argue.

Maureen twisted up newspapers, added coals and lit a match. The newspapers fired up and caught the coal. Embers licked into flames. Maureen shut the grate and put the kettle on the stove to make coffee. She sat back on her heels wondering what she should do about Netta tomorrow. If she hadn't improved by the morning, she would call a taxi. But how would she get Netta to go if she refused? And what would happen to Netta if Bernard alerted the social workers? Netta lived here because she didn't want to be found. Perhaps Maureen should find out why she was hiding so she could decide what to do?

6

Waiting for Collection

The day began with the rustle of pigeons; there were more coming into the roof as the weather grew colder. Maureen sat up ready to run for the bucket to vomit. But the usual hot feeling at the back of her throat and the queasy feeling in her gut weren't there. Was she over her morning sickness? She'd heard it only lasted a few months. She dressed in a state of excitement; Nils might be back today, if not, then definitely tomorrow. She could scarcely believe everything that had happened since he'd been away. She stoked the fire, putting the kettle on to boil, then went over to Netta who had coughed all night keeping them both awake. The hot toddy hadn't helped, even with the double dose of brandy.

"How are you feeling, Netta?" Maureen whispered, not wanting to wake her if she was sleeping.

Netta poked her head out of the blankets, face flushed and eyes glassy. "Not so good," she croaked.

"Bernard said I was to take you to the restaurant, and he would call a doctor if you weren't well today." She looked too sick for Maureen to leave on her own in the freezing roof. "I'll go to the newspaper shop and call a taxi. Bernard said he would pay for it."

Netta shook her head. She didn't want a doctor. She sat up and swung her legs out of bed. The floor tipped and Maureen became two people. Netta fell back on the couch. "Alright, it's probably better you call a taxi." She closed her eyes to stop the roof from moving. Her throat throbbed.

Maureen felt a rise of panic. Netta looked really sick. "I think we should go down to the telephone together so we will be ready when the taxi comes. Would you like me to help you get dressed?" Netta gave a small nod and held up twig thin arms. Maureen guided them into her jumper. Legs not much thicker, slipped into the elastic waisted woollen pants Maureen held open. And long bony feet went into her socks and boots.

When she had finished helping Netta dress, Netta's hot dry hand squeezed hers. "Grab my arm and I'll help you up." She propped Netta against the arm of the couch while she reached for her hat, wig and glasses. "Do you want these?"

"No, but I will need my bag to show the doctor my identity." She pointed behind the couch. Maureen picked up the bag and handed it to her. Shadows danced around them as the fire grew in the grate.

"Wait a bit, I'd hate to set fire to the place." Maureen knew about fire, she was Australian. She removed the kettle from the stove, spread the coals in the grate, and shut the grate door. "We'll have our coffee and toast at Bernard's." It was taking advantage of Bernard's kindness, but he had asked her to look after Netta.

In the shop, while they waited for the taxi, Maureen tried

Nils' phone. There was still no answer. The taxi arrived and between Maureen and the newsagent they managed to get Netta in the vehicle. The traffic was light, and it didn't take long to reach the restaurant. Maureen asked the driver to wait while she got Bernard to come out and help her assist Netta inside. On seeing Netta, Bernard threw his hands in the air.

"Mon dieu! She needs the hospital. You will take her in the taxi, Maureen. I will phone and say you are coming."

"Is that alright, Netta?" Maureen wasn't sure if Bernard was overreacting. Netta managed a nod.

At the hospital, an attendant brought a wheelchair out to the taxi and collected Netta. He left her in a queue inside. Maureen waited beside her to ensure she would be admitted. It was the first time Maureen had been inside a hospital since a school bully had broken her leg when she was five years old.

A young doctor saw Maureen, gave her an appraising look and, ignoring the queue, came over. He addressed her in Swedish, but before she could reply, Netta gasped a few words in Swedish and thrust her bag in Maureen's hand. The doctor put his stethoscope in his ears and listened to Netta's chest, smiling up at Maureen. He moved the stethoscope backwards and forwards then pulled up Netta's jumper and listened to her back. His face tightened, head cocked, the flirty smile gone. He removed the stethoscope and hung it around his neck. "I will need to examine your motter in the examination room. You must attend paperwork at the desk." He pointed to the reception desk where another queue waited. "When the paper filling is finished, you can wait for your motter in the waiting room." Maureen was about to say Netta wasn't her mother, but he was already pushing Netta towards an examination room.

"Please, identity." The nurse held out her hand. Maureen pulled a man's wallet from Netta's bag and went through the contents. She found an identification card with the name

Deborah Henrietta Irwin, born 8th February 1903, Kent, England. So Netta was English. And she was sixty-three years old. Maureen handed the card to the receptionist who wrote the number of the card on a form. She looked up.

"Address?" The receptionist's eyebrows went up while Maureen dithered. What address could she give? She didn't know the street number of their building nor could she use any of the other flat's addresses in the building. She wrote down the restaurant's address. Bernard would cover her if they telephoned to check.

"Sign, please." The receptionist pointed to where the signature was required. Maureen signed not knowing what the document said.

In the waiting room she flipped through magazines looking at pictures of elegant models standing outside plush apartments wearing Dior. Why was she looking at these when she could hardly afford a tube of toothpaste?

She watched visitors peep around doors then enter rooms with forced jocularity and wondered whom they were visiting. To keep herself occupied, she made up stories about them. The squeal of a baby caught her attention, its mother was playing hide-and-seek, covering and uncovering her face to the child's squeals of delight. A tickle in her womb confirmed that she too would be doing that one day.

Half an hour later the doctor returned. "Your Motter has pneumonia. She is very sick. She will stay in hospital some days. You will come back tomorrow please."

It was too far to walk back to the restaurant so Maureen asked the receptionist to call a taxi, sure that Bernard would be willing to pay. The sun was out and the sky blue and clear. Buildings with domed roofs shone like scoured pots, cleansed by the previous day's fall of snow. Rugged up people filled the streets eager to grab the few hours of daylight and sun, their breaths ghosting in the cold air as they chatted to their companions. Maureen gazed at the passing scene and wondered how things were going back home in Australia. If her mother had answered her letter, she should get a reply soon, that's if it hadn't gone sea mail, which would take five weeks. The taxi drew up outside the restaurant.

"Please wait and I will get the fare," she said. The driver followed her into the restaurant.

On seeing Maureen, Bernard rushed over. "How is Henrietta?"

"I'm sorry I took so long at the hospital, Bernard. She is very sick. It's pneumonia."

"Mon Dieu!"

"I had to take a taxi back and I haven't got any money." She pointed to the driver hovering behind her. "Would you mind paying for it? It can come out of my salary."

"Of course, I will pay. Nothing from you." He went to the till, removed some money and handed it to the driver. Maureen went into the kitchen and put her apron on.

"What is the report?" Bernard asked, trotting after her.

"They said she'll be in hospital for a few days."

"Good!" Bernard said. "She is not going back to the pigeon roof. I will find a place for her. You can do her packing, Maureen."

Maureen stared at Bernard. "I wouldn't know what to pack. There's lots of furniture and food and kitchen things." She had no idea what belonged to Netta.

"Start with clothes and books. The furniture I will see her about. You can pack in empty kitchen boxes. You can ride back with me and the boxes." Maureen was struck by Bernard's kindness towards a homeless woman.

"You do so much for her, Bernard. She is lucky to have you as her friend."

"She was my business partner's wife. He died. Now she is my partner."

"God!" Maureen's hand went to mouth. It was impossible. Netta owned half of this grand restaurant? "I don't understand?"

"She can tell you when she chooses." Bernard put his hand up to stop any questions. He'd already said too much. "You must pack for her. She will not go back there."

"I have to leave a message for Nils in case he comes to pick me up."

"You can leave at reception; I will tell them."

Five empty boxes were loaded into Bernard's Saab with one resting on Maureen's knee. They parked in front of the building and Bernard helped her carry the boxes to the roof.

Maureen shone the torch while Bernard stacked the boxes inside the roof entrance.

"Would you like me to make you some coffee?" She knew it was a ridiculous offer.

"Non, chérie. I do not dine in bird cages." He pulled a face and Maureen laughed.

The roof felt different without Netta, more like the empty attic it was. The dark shadows and emptiness made her jumpy. She tried to take comfort in the filtered sounds of the tenants beneath her to hedge off the loneliness she felt.

How had Netta lived here all those years? With no visitors? No radio or television set? If she had died up here no one would have known. What if I died up here? Maureen closed her thoughts down. Nothing like that would ever happen to her, she was being silly. It was time to occupy herself.

She began checking drawers and cupboards, not feeling quite right about going through Netta's things. What if Netta refused Bernard's demands and came back to the roof? Maureen emptied one drawer that she had seen Netta rifle through. It was full of papers and documents with a pile of photographs held together with a rubber band. She removed the band and looked through the photographs. In one, a woman who looked like Netta was playing a violin. Another photograph showed the same woman with a man. Both were wearing smart suits, hers had a corsage pinned to the lapel and he wore a carnation. The couple were the same height. He was well-groomed with a dimpled smile. The type women went for. Maureen looked at the back of the photo. It read: *Phillip and me on our wedding day*. There was another photo of an older Phillip with his arm around a smaller, younger woman. She was clutching his hand, leaning into him and looking up at his face. On the back of the photo Netta had written: *Bigamist!* What did she mean? She stared at the photo. The girl was wearing a wedding ring. Was Netta's husband a bigamist? She sorted through more photos. Most were of Netta with members of an orchestra or band.

There were English newspaper clippings featuring her as a soloist violinist. Another newspaper clipping, in Swedish, had a picture of her next to a policeman and an ambulance with a body on a stretcher. Maureen recognised Bernard's restaurant in the background. She identified the Swedish word for dead. Maureen scanned the article trying to make sense of it. She put the papers and photos back. Netta wouldn't want her to see this.

Tiles rattled on the roof and the pigeons started up a noisy conversation in the rafters. A coffee was what she needed to warm herself up and help her think. Pulling a rug around herself she loaded the fire with more coal, stoking it into flames.

She filled the kettle from the water container, noting the water level was low. It could wait until the morning when she emptied the bucket. Thinking about tomorrow lifted her spirits. No more sleeping in a freezing roof. She would be snuggled up with Nils.

Through the night Maureen listened to every creek and groan, her mind too busy with Nils to sleep. She decided she wouldn't show Nils where she had been living. It was possible he might not like her washing dishes in a restaurant. His parents were snobby. But she needed to work – she didn't want to live off him and end up like her mother, so dependent on her father that she'd had to beg for everything. It wasn't going to be like that for her. After all it was the '60s – although in reality things hadn't changed that much for women. Many lost their jobs when they married. And unmarried girls who had babies were called 'sluts'! In Australia some were put in asylums. It was fortunate she had Nils because she could never return to Eden with all the wagging tongues.

The first thing Maureen did when she woke up was write Nils a note instructing him to pick her up from the restaurant after she visited Netta in the hospital. She pinned the note to Sarah's door, knowing he would look for her at Sarah's place. Then she tidied up and packed her suitcase. She wasn't looking forward to lumping her suitcase all the way to the restaurant, but if she left it by Sarah's door it might get stolen.

The day couldn't pass fast enough. Maureen hummed *What's New Pussycat?* as she washed the mountain of dishes and pots. The staff yelled and swore in Swedish. Maureen yelled a few swear words back, too excited to care. Even the chef's brusque manner didn't faze her. At the end of her shift, she knocked on Bernard's office door.

"Can I phone for a taxi to go to the hospital, Bernard? I will pay for the taxi this time." She owed Bernard enough and a taxi would have her back in time for Nils to pick her up. He shrugged, called a taxi, then phoned the hospital for Netta's room number, which he wrote down and handed to her.

"Tell Henrietta I will visit soon. She must get well." He kissed Maureen on both cheeks and waved her out of the office.

54

It didn't take long to find Netta's room. But it was hard to see Netta through the oxygen tent. Maureen pressed her face close to the tent and saw Netta smile. She reached through a flap and held her hand.

"You don't have to talk, Netta. Just squeeze my hand to answer questions." She felt Netta squeeze her hand. "Bernard is worried about you returning to the roof. He thinks you will get sick again and he wants me to pack up some of your things." Maureen bit her lip. "I haven't done any packing because I don't know what belongs to you." Netta moved her head from side to side and pulled her hand out of Maureen's. "Alright, Netta I will wait until you're better." Netta's hand pressed hers. "I won't be staying in the roof anymore. Nils is collecting me this afternoon, but I will come and visit you. Of course, I'll see you in the restaurant anyway, when you play." Another hand squeeze. A nurse came in and spoke in Swedish, which Maureen understood was time for her to leave. She let go of Netta's hand and picked up her handbag. "I'll visit in two days." It would give her time to spend with Nils.

The evening guests were already arriving and still Nils hadn't come to the restaurant to pick her up. Hugging her coat around her, Maureen paced. Had someone taken her note off Sarah's door? She had phoned his flat but there was no answer. He would have to go to his parent's place to collect the key. She pictured the argument they would have when he found out she had been locked out of his flat. Poor Nils. She was about to give Bernard a message for him when she heard a voice behind her.

"Hello, Pussycat." She whirled around and there he was, six-foot one inch of him, tanned, blue eyes shining. He hugged her close and she let the tears come.

55

7

Staircase

The relief of being in Nils' arms was enormous. Everything collapsed inside Maureen. It was like being released after weeks of confinement. She slumped against Nils and his arms tightened around her.

"Hej Pussycat, I'm here. All will be good." He lifted her chin and smiled. "I'm taking you home." Tears left a smudge of mascara on the back of Maureen's hand as she wiped them away.

"I thought you didn't get my note," she said, leaning back and looking up into his face. "Your parents changed the locks and I couldn't get into your flat. They had me fired from my job. I tried to phone you." Her eyes searched his face. He looked away, then deep into her eyes.

"I love you, Pussycat."

"Did you get the keys from your parents?" She saw the creep of annoyance cross his features.

"I have keys. I will talk at home." He took her hand to leave when Maureen stopped. "Wait. My suitcase. It's in Bernard's office." She tugged Nils' hand, pulling him towards the office, too afraid to let him go. She knocked on Bernard's door.

"Entre." Bernard saw Nils and patted his hair in place. "I meet the Nils?" Bernard stood up smiling and held a poised hand across his desk. Nils stretched his arm and briefly touched Bernard's fingers then put his hand in his pocket. He didn't smile.

"I've come for my suitcase, Bernard."

"Please, ma chérie." He pointed to the case behind the door. "You will be back tomorrow?"

Maureen picked up her suitcase. "Of course, I will."

"That is good. And no more pigeons." Bernard winked at Maureen.

She beamed up at Nils. "I work here, in the kitchen. Bernard's been very kind and given me a job." She laughed at Nils' look of surprise. "I'll tell you about it when we get home." She waved goodbye to Bernard. He twiddled his fingers back at her. Nils gave a stiff nod, took Maureen's suitcase from her and steered her through the door towards his Volvo sports car parked in the side street. It was the same car *The Saint* drove, in the television series they loved to watch. Nils opened the door for Maureen, put her suitcase in the boot and climbed in next to her. They hummed out into the traffic. All the way to his flat he gave Maureen an excited account of his trip.

"The palace was beautiful. We had waiters and maids looking after all our needs. The first night we dined with King Constantine and Princess Anne-Marie, and we drank a lot of aquavit." Nils laughed. "I think he made us all drunk so we could not race well the next day. But Viking men you cannot beat on water. Sorenson beat him. I came third because Olaf made a wrong tack and we went too wide of the buoy."

Maureen listened, but her mind was elsewhere. He hadn't asked about the baby.

Nils carried her suitcase as they entered the foyer of the elegant old apartment block where he lived. A sweep of marble stairs curved upwards. Maureen tilted her head and looked up the well of spiral stairs. It would be nice if she could walk in a door without a climb, she thought. The flat was on the second floor.

"You walk ahead of me. I like to look at your legs," Nils said. Conscious of him behind her she accentuated the swing of her hips. When they reached his door he grabbed her and kissed her. "Jag alskar dig." He said, breathing heavily.

"I love you too," she whispered. They bundled through the door and made love on his soft black leather couch. Afterwards he mixed them a vodka and tonic and they sat cuddled together. Maureen put the drink to her lips and grimaced after the first sip. It made her nauseous. She put the drink on the coffee table. "Sorry. I haven't been able to drink alcohol since I fell pregnant. It makes me feel sick."

Nils put his elbows on his knees and swirled the vodka in his glass. "I speak to friends in Greece about your baby. It is too late for an abortion." That news made Maureen sigh with relief. "A job has been offered to me by a sail maker in Italy. I can sell for them. We can live in Italy. What do you think?"

It was a message from heaven. Maureen threw her arms around Nils. "Yes! God! Yes! I was so worried about what we were going to do."

"I will take care of you," he said. And for the first time since she'd fallen pregnant, he put his hand on her belly. "Both of you."

While Maureen unpacked her suitcase, she thought about living in Italy. She could speak some Italian, having learned it from Carmela, a girl she worked with in Australia. She would ask Nils to borrow an Italian phrasebook from the university library so she could brush up. She fetched a bundle of clothes hangers from his walk-in wardrobe and put them on the bed. Nils came over and picked the hangers up.

"Do not hang up your clothes, Pussycat. It is better you leave them in the suitcase and keep them where no one sees." He smiled. "My parents don't know you are living here. It is good we keep it like that." Maureen looked at him, confused. He stared at the floor. "They own this flat, Pussycat, and have keys. It is possible they will visit me. You will not have to hide for long." He squeezed her hand. "They do not know about the baby yet. We will give them time."

He didn't want to face his parents with news of a pregnancy after their last encounter.

Furious that his locks had been changed, he had stormed into his parents' apartment shouting that they were treating him like a child and had no right to interfere in his life. His mother had screamed at him. Never had he experienced such fury from her before. When everyone had calmed down enough to have a discussion, he had begged his parents to accept Maureen, even cried, but his mother remained unmoved.

"Your father and I are not paying for you to live with girls. Especially not a foreign girl you've picked up on a holiday. If you want to do that, then get a job and find your own place. That girl just wants a nice life in Sweden. Next thing you know she will try and get pregnant and force you to marry her. You are only twenty-four and still have to finish university. Find a nice Swedish girl with money and good heritage. Australians come from poor backgrounds. They are Irish and criminals. Your father has investigated them."

"We are not paying for her to live in our flat," his father had added. "You stay with her and I will sell your yacht." That had been the worst blow. Nils didn't tell Maureen any of this.

"What happens if they visit and find me here?" Maureen

looked around the apartment. There was the entrance hall, a walk-in cupboard and, at the end of the hall, a toilet with wash basin. Nils' office sat in the centre of the flat and was the largest room. It opened onto a small balcony that overlooked a tree-lined street. On either side of the office were two small rooms. One was Nils' bedroom, with a single bed and set of drawers. The other served as the lounge room. The flat had a good-sized kitchen. The only place she could hide from unexpected visitors was the walk-in-wardrobe, but she was claustrophobic.

She didn't want to face his parents on her own. She was afraid. They had already cost her a job and put her on the street. They didn't care what happened to her. Nils hadn't mentioned her job loss, obviously embarrassed by their actions. She wasn't going to tell him she had been sleeping in a roof. "When are you going to tell them I'm pregnant and that we are getting married?"

"I must finish the year at university and work everything out with the job in Italy. One more month, Pussycat."

In one month, she would be four and a half months pregnant. It wasn't too long to wait. Sarah would be back from Scotland and they could plan the wedding. Tomorrow she would visit the post office and see if her mother had sent any money. "We can wait one month," she said pushing her stomach towards him. "Soon you will have to buy a bigger bed."

Nils was asleep when Maureen rolled out of bed in the morning. She wasn't looking forward to going to work. She would rather spend the day with him. He hadn't put up an argument about her working in the restaurant, although he mentioned there had been a big story some years ago that involved the restaurant owners. He didn't remember the details, but said he would look up old newspapers on the fiche when he went to the library to do some study. Maureen hadn't told him about Netta. She would ask her permission first.

She pulled on long socks and trousers, blouse and jumper, a

fur-lined beanie with ear flaps that Nils had given her, and a coat and gloves. She kissed Nils' forehead and waited a moment to see if he would wake up, but he was dead to the world. Outside it was pitch dark. The air was like an ice block. Maureen's torch lit the way to the tram stop. A fifteen minute ride and ten minute walk to work.

The day dragged. At the end of her shift she decided to give the hospital a miss and go home via the post office. She felt guilty but she was longing to get back to Nils. Fingers crossed, if her mother had answered straight away there should be a letter for her. It hurt her that none of her family had answered any of her letters since she'd been in Sweden. This time she had made her request urgent, writing in capitals, PLEASE REPLY.

The postal clerk turned to the alphabet boxes on the wall when he saw Maureen and flicked through the envelopes, withdrawing a letter with blue and red stripes around the edges. Express mail was stamped on the top. He put it on the desk.

Maureen squealed and grabbed the envelope. The clerk laughed as she ripped it open. Eureka! A fifty-dollar postal note. "Thank you, Mum." She held the note up for the clerk to see and kissed it. He gave her a pleased nod. She put the note back in the envelope. The letter would be read in the tram on her way back to Nils' flat. Tonight, she would write and tell her mother everything that had happened to her. That she was pregnant, and she and Nils were getting married.

"Look," Maureen said, waving the postal note at Nils. "I have enough to pay for my ticket to Italy when we go."

"That is good, Pussycat. You must bank it so it doesn't go away." He dangled the chain around his neck that held the gold disc with her name engraved.

"That wasn't a waste of money, it's your engagement present," she said. His parents would have seen a ring on his finger. "We could put the money in your bank account for safe keeping until

61

I open an account. You may have to go guarantor for me. That's what we do in Australia." Nils lifted a nonchalant shoulder and put the postal note in his wallet.

A blissful few days passed with Maureen rushing home from the restaurant to cook for Nils. Bernard had been giving her cooking tips, and spaghetti bolognese and pasta with meatballs were very tasty. Nils was only eating at his parent's place twice a week now, instead of most nights, which he had done before Maureen moved in with him. His excuse to his parents was that his friend had just moved into a flat and they were taking it in turns to cook and eat at each other's places. When asked about the friend, Nils had said he was a Danish student studying in Gothenburg.

They were cuddling on the couch listening to music when a key turned in the lock and they heard his parents' voices. They looked at each other in panic. Nils jumped up from the couch and rushed to the entrance to give her time to hide. Voices snarled in Swedish. Maureen recognised one word, *Flicka*. It's what his mother called her. It meant Girl. Her heartbeat quickened. She looked around for somewhere to hide, but they were already in the lounge before she could get off the couch.

The mother was a big woman, blonde, with a broad face. Arctic eyes glowered at Maureen. The father, a mouse of a man, stood next to her. A smudge of dark hair ringed his bald crown. She felt her throat clog. All her instincts urged her to jump up and run. She looked to Nils for guidance, but he stood to the side, avoiding her eye. Stumbling over a Swedish greeting, Maureen forced a smile. Neither was returned. The mother snapped at Nils and he sat on the couch next to Maureen, leaving a space between them.

There was an exchange of Swedish too fast for Maureen to follow. She looked from one to the other, not understanding, yet knew from the finger pointing she was the subject of their anger.

The father could speak English, but Nils had to interpret for his mother. He hung his head.

"I'm sorry, Pussycat. They know you are pregnant. One of my crew told his mother and she told my parents. My mother wants to know whose child it is?" Nils waited for her to answer.

She stared at him. Why had he asked her? Why hadn't he jumped off the couch and ordered them to leave? They had been together nearly a year, were in love, there was no one else. He knew she wasn't a bad girl. The fact she had to answer suffocated her.

"Yours of course." She could only manage a whisper. She opened her palms and tried to smile at his mother, wanting her to know she was a honourable girl. Wanting to be accepted. The mother tossed her head and snapped at Nils.

"My mother said you are laughing at her."

Maureen was shocked. She looked at his mother's glacial face. "No, I smiled at her because I want her to like me." Nothing she did would melt this woman.

Nils exhaled a big sigh and slipped sidewards on the couch, away from her, his eyes closing in a swoon.

The parents rushed to their Viking son. His mother held his face between her hands and the father clasped Nils' shoulders and gently shook him. Nils sat up and looked around in a daze.

The father turned on Maureen. "You see what you have done? He is too worried."

Nils slid a look towards her. The faint had been staged to win their sympathy. It hadn't aroused any in Maureen. It made her angry. He should be on his feet telling his parents to mind their own business. And that they were getting married and his parents could go to hell.

His father leant over her. "You are after our money. You are a farm girl. Nice girls don't travel around the world on their own."

Maureen shook her head, too choked up to speak. Why

wasn't Nils sticking up for her? She put her hand on his knee, but he didn't touch it. There was so much confusion inside her. A defendant on trial. Where was her champion?

Nils stood up. "We shall go," he said. "I will meet you outside."

Heart pounding, Maureen picked up her handbag. She didn't look at his parents as she passed them. She felt the flay of their eyes on her back, triumphant. She stumbled through the door and onto the landing to wait for Nils. The mother was shouting inside. How could they be so mean to her?

A moment later the door flew open and a torrent of fury charged out of the flat, shrieking in Swedish. Nils' mother hurled herself on Maureen. Her nails dug into Maureen's scalp, hands coiled around her hair, snapping her head back. Tears burst from Maureen's eyes as she cried out in pain.

The weight of his mother's body propelled her towards the bannister. The railing pressed into her back and Nils' mother bent her over it. The fist in her hair wrenched her head to one side and through a blur of tears Maureen could see the stone floor, a long way down. Maureen clung to the bannister, heart pounding in her throat as Nils' mother bent her backwards.

"Hora!" the demented woman shrieked. Her spittle covered Maureen's face.

"Nils!" Maureen screamed. He ran out of his flat and wrenched his mother off her. Maureen collapsed to her knees, her legs shaking so hard she had to use the bannister to pull herself up off the floor. Nils struggled with his mother. She pulled her arm free and slapped him across the face.

"Run to the car," Nils yelled. Maureen's flying feet echoed down the stairwell.

In a state of shock, they didn't speak until Nils pulled up outside Sarah's block of flats. He got out of the car and removed her suitcase from the boot. She hadn't even realised he had brought it with them. She climbed out of the sports car sensing a distance between them that filled her with despondency.

"My mother," he said, swallowing. "I was engaged before you and she chased that girl away. A doctor said perhaps my mother had pressure on the brain."

Maureen touched the scratches on his face, and he turned away walking ahead of her up the stairs. If only she had known this, perhaps things could have been different. She followed at the heels of his expensive shoes, noticing for the first time that he wore the inside of his heels down. The building had never seemed so dingy.

On reaching Sarah's landing Nils set her suitcase down. "I would rather not talk to Sarah or anyone," he said. "I will leave you here and come by the restaurant tomorrow." He bent down and kissed her. Eyes averted. "I am sorry, Pussycat."

She could have told him Sarah was away but didn't want to stress him any further. Her body was a boulder. All she had the energy for was to lie on her couch in the roof. Maureen pulled his head down and kissed his lips. "I'll be fine, you go and sort things out. We'll see each other tomorrow."

He didn't linger. The street door closed before she crumpled over her suitcase and cried her heart out. For half an hour she huddled outside Sarah's door in the freezing gloom before she could bring herself to climb up to the roof. Inside Netta's refuge, the rugs were still folded on the end of her couch as though expectant of Maureen's return. She sat on the couch going over the traumatic events that had just taken place, hardly believing what had happened and why, and worried what Nils was going to do. A throbbing ache started behind her eyes. Thoughts of her mother's migraines came to mind. She wasn't going to end up with those. She needed something to block the attack from her mind. There was a writing pad and a pen in the drawer. She would write and thank her mother for the money. Tell her how happy she was that she had started writing to her again and how much she missed her.

When the letter was finished Maureen wrote a separate note to her father in the hope he had forgiven her, wishing him success with the farm and sending him love. She slipped the note in with her mother's then curled up on the couch and imagined she was home in Eden, where her family loved her and life was calm.

8

Eden – A Bottle of Pills

Eric walked into Lillian's kitchen and dropped his bag of washing on the floor as if he owned the place. She sucked air between her teeth and eyed the bag. What did he take her for? A door mat?

Lillian noticed that he looked a bit pale around the gills. There were bags under his eyes and stubble on his chin. Probably worn out from shagging a young woman. Folding her arms, Lillian gave him a dead eye. "Surely you don't expect me to do your washing while you have a live-in-maid, or whatever you call your schoolgirl?"

Eric looked sheepish. "It's just a few things, Lil. There's only a tub and wash board at the farm."

Lillian's face darkened. Eric stepped from one foot to the other, unsure of himself. A silence fell between them. Lillian's hands went to her hips and she glared at Eric. His feisty Aunt

Maggie had taught her well. She was glad of the years she had spent looking after her.

"A tub was good enough for me. It's all I had for years. How many times did I ask you to buy me a washing machine? I had to win a crossword puzzle in *The Women's Weekly* to get this one." She saw his eyes go that snake grey, but she wasn't scared of him anymore. She strung him out like he used to do her. "You can pay me and I'll send the money to Bubs. She's in a pickle in Sweden and needs money while she looks for a job." Lillian removed an envelope from the top of the fridge and took out a page, which she handed to Eric. "Here, she sent you a note with mine."

Eric stared at the page, snatched it from Lillian and thrust it in his pocket. "I told you not to contact her until she stops living with that boy. It's a disgrace."

Lillian's face hardened. "Well now, is it any worse than what you are doing? Living with your children's school mate, Kathy Parker and her three kids?" The cheek of him. "The gossips are having a field day. Did it occur to you that Splinter is a schoolteacher? Think how ashamed she must feel with the whole town knowing." Eric's eyes shifted around the kitchen. She saw a flush of red above his collar. It was a small victory.

"I've not been well and she's there as my housekeeper." He fished in his pocket and pulled out a five-dollar note. It was all he had. He wasn't sure why that was. He couldn't remember his bank account number to make a withdrawal. He would have to ask Kathy. Lillian relieved Eric of the fiver.

"I'll owe you three dollars. I don't have any change until I get the rent next week." She put the note in her apron pocket. It was the most expensive washing in Australia and would keep her in food for two weeks. Normally Eric would have argued but he seemed in a daze.

"Had any luck with the horses lately?" She turned to her new stainless steel sink to hide her smirk and gave its immaculate shine a wipe with a tea towel.

"I haven't been placing any bets," Eric lied. His brow crinkled. "What's Johnny been up to? He told me he was going to Melbourne last Tuesday to see a mate, but I could have sworn I saw him up the street when I came to town to buy some sheep dip."

Lillian went still. "Maybe you made a mistake?" The washing suddenly caught her attention and she busied herself rummaging through Eric's clothes. He needed distracting. "I'll have to do two washes. I can't put your white shirts in with these overalls. I'll do the whites first. Come back in an hour."

Eric looked taken aback, he had expected a spot of lunch, at the least a cup of tea. "Where am I supposed to go?"

"Don't ask me. I have to get lunch ready for my boarder and it wouldn't look good if you're hanging around when she comes home. We don't want anyone talking about us, do we? I can't afford to lose the rent if my tenant thinks she's living in a house of ill repute." Her tenant was a bone of contention between them. The house had belonged to his aunt and in his mind should still be his regardless of their divorce. The rent, in his mind, should be shared. Lillian waited for some cutting remark, which didn't come. Instead he shrugged and went outside, looked around the garden and started walking towards the shed.

"Gate's the other way," Lillian called out. He stopped, gazed around confused, then made for the gate. Lillian's body relaxed. He still put her on edge.

She watched him leave from the kitchen window. He seemed a little unsteady on his feet. She felt a nudge of concern. Perhaps he really was sick and hiring Kathy to nurse him? Even so, according to Kathy's husband they were sleeping together, and the gossips believed it. Let his nursemaid take care of him. She put the white shirts in the washing machine and switched it on.

After ten years the machine still looked like new. And now that she wasn't washing by hand her dermatitis had gone.

Taking her annoyance out on her boarder's lunch, Lillian slapped a piece of lard in the frying pan on the electric stove. The stove and other new appliances had been bought with the bonds Lillian had found in Eric's late Aunt Maggie's tea caddy. The kitchen, once her purgatory, had become her favourite place in the house. Two sausages followed the lard. Lillian stabbed them with a fork so they wouldn't explode and added a mash of leftover vegetables for bubble and squeak.

The boarder lifted her nose as she entered the kitchen and sniffed the air. "Something smells nice." She was wearing what had once been Maureen's good jeans, now three years old and a bit worse for wear. Lillian wished she hadn't given her the left behind clothes. She could still remember the furious letter she had received from Norway. Perhaps that's why Maureen had never responded to any of her news when she wrote? Still it was a long time to keep the animosity going. It wasn't like Maureen to dwell on things, too busy flitting around the world to bother about what was going on at home.

Lillian broke an egg in the pan. The boarder helped herself to a glass of water from the basin tap. No more running out to the tank stand thanks to Aunt Maggie. The boarder leant against the sink and gave Lillian a 'by the way' look.

"I passed Eric going up the road. He looked like he'd had a few?" Her eyes shone expectantly.

Lillian frowned. It was none of her boarder's business and she knew Eric hadn't been drinking. He never drank before lunchtime. It was his rule. He wasn't a big drinker anyway. When he went to the Fisherman's Club it was usually to keep up with what was going on in town. "He's not been well." Lillian flipped the egg onto its other side and watched the edges darken.

"I hear he has a housekeeper taking care of him?" The boarder kept her eyes on Lillian.

"We are divorced. Whatever he does is his business." When would people get the message that Eric was nothing to do with her? She needed to stop doing his washing and letting him waltz in whenever he felt like it. Lillian put the egg, sausages and bubble and squeak on a plate and put it in front of her boarder. "I've got to hang out some washing, so I'll leave you to it." Bloody nosey parker, she thought, as she closed the kitchen door behind her.

The washing machine completed its final spin. Lillian removed the shirts putting them in her clothes basket. She picked up the wash bag and shook out Eric's overalls. A bottle of pills rolled onto the floor. She picked up the bottle and read the label. Valium. Bega Hospital issue. There was no patient's name on the label. Lillian put them on the shelf next to the washing powder to give back to Eric.

When Eric returned an hour later a basket full of wet washing was waiting for him. He stared at it. "It's not dry?"

"You said you'd hang it out at the farm?"

"Did I?" He squinted for the memory, shook his head and picked up the basket. "Righto."

"Are you feeling alright, Eric?" She regretted her moment of concern when he gave her his curled lip look.

"Why wouldn't I be?" he snapped.

Her mouth thinned. "You're looking old today."

That did it. He turned his back and stomped out of the laundry, lifting his thumb as he went. His signal for up yours. After he'd gone, she remembered the pills. It might be a while before she saw him again. He'd have to go to the doctor for another script if he didn't remember where he had left them, which in the dazed state she had seen him in was quite likely.

Maybe Splinter could drop them off at the doctor on her way to work? A whistle blew outside. It was the postie.

The letter was marked airmail and care of Post Office, Gothenburg. Excited, Lillian went inside, made a cup of tea and settled herself at the kitchen table. She slid a knife along the flap, withdrew two pages written on both sides and started to read. Thank God Maureen had received the money and promised not to tell her father. At some point she would write and tell her how they had swindled him. Her daughter's gratitude was warming, and she was pleased that she'd been able to do something for her.

Then the word pregnant jumped off the page and the breath went out of Lillian. She lowered the letter to think over the news. Falling pregnant was always a risk when you lived together.

Hadn't she written and warned Bubs about that when she first went to live with Nils? It surprised Lillian that Bubs hadn't been able to get an abortion in Sweden. Wasn't it lauded as the land of free love? There seemed something a bit strange about a country being open to encouraging sex before marriage yet imprisoning doctors if they were caught giving abortions. Thank goodness Bubs hadn't tried to find an unqualified person to give her a back-street abortion as so many went wrong. Lillian realised how fortunate she had been to find a doctor when she needed one. Thanks to Ingrid all those years ago. Lillian still carried the guilt.

Reading the next page rocked her with shock. It was unimaginable that Nils' mother would physically attack her daughter. The poor kid. If she could afford to go over there and bring Maureen home, she would. Who were these people? It was understandable his parents were angry. No parent wanted their child pressured into marriage because of a pregnancy. But to try and kill her? Something clutched at Lillian's heart as she remembered her own mean mother-in-law and the way she had been treated when she was so homesick for England. Lillian paced around the kitchen, eaten with anxiety, thoughts racing. She needed to calm her nerves. Go for a walk, clear her mind.

She went out to the back porch and removed her shell-collecting bag from its hook. The bag was made from a potato sack she had cut in half, threaded with elastic and added handles. Lillian put the bag over her shoulder and left the house.

The sapphire sea rolled in, leaving a meringue edge on the clean yellow sand, filling her footprints. The only ones on the beach. High tide didn't offer up many shells, so she sat on the beach curling her toes in the warm sand, loving its coarseness. It didn't stick to everything like the fine white sand further up the coast. After half an hour she gave up the hunt for shells and made her way through the ancient stand of banksia trees that edged the dirt road to the lake. The tidal lake was full. Birds shrieked, some twittered and others floated on its surface. Eden's garden of delight.

Her thoughts took flight. Maureen and Nils' mother would never overcome the attempt on her life. Who would Nils be true to in the long term? His mother or Maureen? A pelican glided by and landed with hardly a ripple on the lake. If only life was that easy, she thought with a sigh.

On the way home Lillian walked through the graveyard, stopping to read some of the old headstones. Death by drowning, sadly missed. She looked at the tiny cot graves of children and said a prayer for the child she had lost and the one who was living so far away, desperate and in a freezing country.

9

Missing Nils

It was crushingly cold in the roof. Pigeons cooed to let Maureen
know it was time to light a fire and leave them some crumbs.
She went to her suitcase, unpacking the thick pyjamas she had
previously worn in the roof – the slinky black nightdress was
only for Nils – and a change of clothes for tomorrow. How long
she would have to live up here again she didn't know or want
to think about. The fact was, she could never live in Nils' flat
again. The thought of facing his mother gave her the terrors.
The woman wanted to kill her. Nils would have to find another
place they could share. Tomorrow she would speak with Bernard.
Perhaps he had a friend who might rent them a cheap flat where
they could be independent of his parents?

Maureen made a fire in the stove, then lit the lamp. The kettle
sloshed when she picked it up. Good! There was no need to
traipse downstairs for water and enough in the kettle to fill the

hot water bottle. She wondered how Netta was going to react when she told her she had returned to the roof? Guilt stabbed at her. She hadn't gone back to the hospital to see Netta when she had said she would. The glow from the fire created a play of shadows on the mismatch of fabric that was draped over the furniture walls. The kettle whistled and Maureen whipped it off the stove before it signalled her presence to the other tenants. She made a pot of tea and filled the water bottle with the rest of the hot water. Next came an opening of a tin of sardines and a packet of plain biscuits. "I hope you like fish," she said to the baby in her stomach.

After she'd eaten and the pigeons had cleaned up her crumbs, she curled around the water bottle on the couch, pulled the blankets up to her nose and waited for the worst day of her life to disappear.

The pigeon alarm went off and Maureen struggled awake. A darkness that she'd never felt before crouched inside her. She forced herself out of bed, stoked up the night's remaining embers and emptied the water from her water bottle back into the kettle to make coffee. Coffee grains would kill the rubber taste, she thought. In the cabinet was half a loaf of bread covered in mould. After trimming off the mould, she managed to salvage enough for a slice of toast. The coffee tasted of rubber and the toast crackled between her teeth. A pigeon waited by her feet to peck the crumbs that fell from her toast. Netta would have chased it away but it was company, so Maureen let it be. She packed a face cloth, soap and towel in a paper bag, dressed and left for work.

When she entered the kitchen, she didn't smile and greet everyone like she normally did, going straight to the sink instead. Minutes later she was waking up in the chef's arms as he carried her to a chair. The overhead lights were spinning. She turned her head and vomited on the floor.

"So sorry," she whispered wiping at her mouth and trying to sit up in his arms. He sat her on the chair and knelt beside her.

"You rest. I have medicine." He left, returning with a bottle of smelling salts and waved them under her nose. The sharp aroma snapped her to full alert. He held up a mug of hot liquid and forced her to sip. It tasted of brandy and something she couldn't identify.

Bernard spoke to him in Swedish and the chef looked at her, concerned. "You must sit until you feel better," he said. Maureen looked around her. The kitchen hands had stopped work and were staring at her. She flushed with embarrassment. The last thing she wanted was to be a burden on them and risk losing her job. Not now, when things were so messed up. She stood up, fighting the giddiness.

"Thank you. I will be fine." Bernard clucked his tongue but didn't protest when she went over to the sink and donned her rubber gloves.

There were too many guests, and everyone was needed. Dishes came and went like on a conveyor belt and the time passed quickly. At the end of her shift Maureen sat by the reception desk to wait for Nils.

Two hours had passed since her shift had finished and there was still no sign of him. Maureen called his flat from Bernard's office, but the phone rang out. Perhaps he was waiting for her at Sarah's? She had intended to ask him to take her to the hospital where she was going to introduce Netta as the building's manager. It was important she let Netta know she was staying in the roof again. Maureen tossed up what she should do. Get a taxi to the hospital, stay put or go to Sarah's building? Two hours was long enough to wait for anyone. The restaurant was busy, and she didn't want to bother Bernard. Nor did she want to waste money on a taxi. Light snow fell as she walked back to her building.

Before she reached Sarah's landing, Maureen called out. "Nils?" There was no answer. Somewhere deep down, she knew he wouldn't be waiting for her, yet she still rushed up the stairs. The man from the flat opposite Sarah was standing in his doorway.

"Have you seen anyone waiting here?" Her voice had a pleading edge. His eyes crept over her and he shook his head.

"My friend was coming to meet me here, thinking I was living with Sarah. Which of course I'm not. I have a room down the street until Sarah comes back from Scotland." It sounded lame and she wished she hadn't yelled up the stairs and brought him out of his flat. He lounged in the doorway with a leer on his face. "Well, if you hear a man knock on my friend's door would you tell him I'm at the restaurant? He'll know what I mean." She gave his suspicious face a smile and retreated downstairs. He mustn't see her climbing into the roof.

Maureen tried the paper shop next door to phone Nils, but it was closed. Her only other option was to go and see Nils at his flat, but what if his parents were there?

She sat on the stairs near the entrance waiting for Sarah's neighbour to go back inside his flat. Her frozen backside told her she had waited long enough. Creeping up the stairs, Maureen stopped to listen before reaching Sarah's landing. The coast seemed clear. She continued to creep up the steps and into the roof.

In the morning she emptied the bucket before the tenants were up, hiding it behind the stairs until she returned from work. The waitress who had been teaching her Swedish tried to engage her in conversation, but Maureen just gave a wan smile. She didn't feel like joking around.

She repeated her actions from the previous day, phoning Nils until the phone rang out and waiting. It was dark by the time she left the restaurant.

The next day she stood by the sink staring at the water, despondent, afraid and angry. If something was wrong, surely Nils would tell a friend to contact her? How could he abandon her without a word? A hand rested on her arm. She jumped.

"What is the matter, chérie? You do not smile. Come into my office. We must talk." He led her into his office and sat her down.

"I haven't heard from Nils." She cried into Bernard's handkerchief and told him what had happened. It was a relief to be telling someone. Bernard picked at his nail polish while she spoke. "Something could have happened to him. His mother did try to kill me."

"Ahh, love makes a lot of killing," Bernard said. "Why do I not phone his mamma and ask where he is? I make up a story that I am his friend looking for him?"

It was a great idea. Nils' parents wouldn't suspect Bernard. She turned grateful eyes towards him. "That's so good of you, Bernard."

"We will find the number."

"His father is Sune Classon, he lectures at the university." Maureen hung over Bernard's shoulder as he went through a list of names.

His finger went up in the air. "I have 'im." He picked up the phone and dialled a number. Maureen drew a deep breath as Bernard introduced himself.

"Fru Classon? Mitt namn is Bernard Leclair, jag skulle villja prata med Nils?" He waited for Nils to come to the phone. "Nils? Pardon, Herr Classon." Bernard went quiet, he blinked rapidly, lips prim. He rattled off in Swedish, voice rising. Maureen watched Bernard's face; it didn't bode well.

"What's he saying? Are you speaking to Nils, Bernard?"

Bernard shook his head and covered the mouthpiece. "'Tis Nils' merde bastard father." He took his hand off the mouthpiece and snapped into the phone, listened, then banged the phone back on the cradle. He sat back, bristling with indignation. "He tells me Nils is called into military service; he cannot be contacted for the first month. I tell him I am your friend and he have a responsibility. He tells me Nils is not responsible for your baby. It is not his. Then, merde bastard father, says he remembers a man died in my restaurant."

Bernard pressed his fingers to his forehead. "It was in the newspaper, years ago. They say my food could 'ave been contaminated. It was proved not true, Henrietta was there. But merde father says he is a lawyer." His eyes were reproachful, "You said he is university lecturer, chérie? You did not say he lectures in law. He said he will make bad publicity for me if I help you. He is not a good man."

Maureen tried to take in what Bernard was saying, but all she could think about was that Nils had joined up to do his military service. Why, when he had once told her university students were exempt until they had finished their degree? What had happened to their plans to go to Italy? Nils must have made the decision to leave her. She felt an icicle pierce her heart.

Bernard wrung his hands. "It might be better you do not work in my restaurant for now. It is for Henrietta's sake." He looked at her imploringly.

Why bring Netta into it? God! He had just told her she had lost her job! Maureen put her hand to her throat. "No! Please Bernard. I need money for food, for things. What am I going to do?" A chasm opened in Maureen. She put her hand on her stomach. Nils had her money and she couldn't contact him.

"You can come for food every day. I am sorry, chérie." Maureen hunched forward her arms around her body. Food was important but what about other things like soap, tram fares? She cursed Nils' parents. The last thing she wanted to do was write to her mother and explain her predicament, ask for more money.

10

Eden – Intensive Care

The Country Women's Association were having a meeting to raise money for the Eden Town Hall. Lillian sat, pen poised, taking the minutes. A hand went up seconding the motion to hold a craft stall in the main street. Lillian noted the name. It was now Ingrid Kasbauer's turn to give a summary of the finances which, since Ingrid had held the job of treasurer, had improved. Lillian saw the look of pride on her friend's face as she gave her report. It had taken the resignation of the chairwoman before Ingrid had been allowed to join the CWA. The chair had lost her husband in the Second World War and Ingrid had been on the wrong side of the war. Her acceptance was due to Lillian's rallying efforts behind the scenes.

Lillian's second success, Judy Thompson, once excluded because of holding séances that most of the women attended in secret, looked around the group of chatting women. She was about to tap her glass to call the meeting to attention when there was a knock on the door and a man's head appeared. All eyes turned towards their male intruder. Judy Thompson waved him in.

The intruder was the young constable, Trevor Price-Jones alias PJ, because his mother didn't know if his father was Jim Price or Brian Jones. He removed his police cap and brown hair fell into his eyes. Licking his fingers, he patted it to the side. He had rosy cheeks and looked about twelve years old. Scanning the women around the long table, the constable's eyes rested on Lillian.

"Please excuse the interruption, ladies, but I have an urgent message for Lillian McKinley." He turned the hat in his hand. Lillian's heart flipped, her first thought being something might have happened to Maureen. She gripped her pen. All eyes swung towards her.

"I'm sorry to have to inform you, Mrs. McKinley, but your husband has been taken to hospital with a stroke."

The instant concern she felt was quelled. "I am divorced. I don't have a husband. Are you referring to my ex-husband?" He wasn't her responsibility, but he was the father of her children. Concern for her children filled her. They loved him. The constable shuffled.

"I didn't know who else to inform."

Lillian fought the question she knew all the women in the room were hanging out for and then threw caution to the wind. "Did you inform his housekeeper?"

Around the table, lips moistened.

The intruder cleared his throat, eyes occupied with the ceiling. "There's a bit of a problem there," he said, cheeks reddening.

Lillian's gut tightened. What in blazes was going on? She pushed her chair back. "Perhaps we should have this conversation in private?"

Disappointment clogged the air as Lillian left the room. Silence followed and ears leant towards the door. Judy Thompson tapped her glass. Lillian had been the one to invite her to join the CWA and had spoken up on her behalf. Now she was the chairlady.

"Attention, ladies. Our business for today has been concluded and we should adjourn for a cup of tea and Ingrid Kasbauer's delicious strudel." The strudel was not to be missed. Lillian could be put on hold. They would all find out what was going on soon enough. The table emptied towards the kitchen.

"What's going on, Constable?" Lillian asked.

'I'm afraid to report that Eric was found unconscious at his farm by Boomer Kelly." Boomer Kelly's real name was Patrick, but his voice had been reduced to a whisper after his pet kangaroo had clobbered him in the throat when he was training it to box. "I'm afraid we haven't been able to contact Kathy, his … er, housekeeper."

Lillian's hand went to her heart. "God, how awful!" She needed to let Splinter and Johnny know. "I'll have to go to the hospital."

"Can I give you a lift?" He liked Lillian; she had babysat him on a few occasions. Hopefully, she didn't have a good memory.

"Yes, please, Constable. Before we go though, would you mind if I phoned my daughter to let her know?"

"Happy to oblige, Mrs McKinley."

"You can drop the 'Mrs', Constable, I'm divorced, call me Lillian." She enjoyed her divorcee status even though divorcees were still considered disreputable.

"And you can still call me PJ, unless of course we're in the company of felons, that is."

"Right, well, I think we had better make a move. I'll get my bag." Lillian went back to the meeting room and collected her bag. She looked towards the kitchen and caught Ingrid's eye and crooked her finger for her to come over. Ingrid sidled out of the kitchen.

"What, is it?" she said, taking Lillian's hand.

"I need a favour. Can you find Johnny and tell him Eric's had a stroke? He could be in the Fisherman's Club or down at the wharf. I'll phone Splinter and go to the hospital."

"I vil see to it. You go." They pecked each other's cheek. Lillian left with the CWA ladies waving her off, unsure whether they should offer commiserations to a divorcee or not.

The police car pulled up next to the telephone box for Lillian to call her daughter. The telephonist plugged her through to the school's bursar. "It's an emergency, I need to speak to my daughter, Mrs Louise Gilles."

Lillian fidgeted while she waited. She didn't want to upset Splinter at work; she'd break it to her gently. Splinter answered, panting down the phone. The bursar had charged into her class and told her she had to come immediately as there was an emergency call. No use beating around the bush now.

"Your Dad's had a stroke, love, he's in Bega hospital." Lillian pulled the phone away from her ear and winced. Splinter's shriek was followed by a barrage of questions.

"I don't know how he is. I'm on my way to the hospital now. Constable PJ is giving me a lift." Lillian looked perplexed. Splinter was babbling something about Kathy being responsible for Eric's stroke because of the pills. The doctor had told her they were dangerous, could addle the brain and were usually given to people with nervous disorders. Splinter sounded in a state of shock. "Calm down, love. I'm sure Kathy didn't try to kill him. We'll talk when you get to the hospital." She sent a kiss down the line and hung up.

"Poor girl's in a steam-up, thinks her father took some pills that gave him a stroke."

Constable PJ's eyebrows shot up. "I'll have a chat with her later," he said.

It was obvious to Lillian that Splinter was in a panic and not thinking straight. She couldn't deal with it now. Not with a siren going and hurtling around corners. She clung to the armrest and closed her eyes.

Intensive care was a buzz of machines, flashing lights and alarms. Nurses came and went, writing reports and pressing buttons. Eric lay on the hospital bed with tubes in his arms and down his throat. A monitor tracked his heart rate. Lillian looked at the unconscious Eric. This was not the man she knew. Robbed of his bravado and strength he was no longer the formidable person who had once controlled her with a look. She sat by his bed and waited for Splinter.

On seeing her father, Splinter's hand went to her mouth. "Mum, is he going to die?" Her father's scandalous behaviour with a girl she'd gone to school with was now on the back burner.

"The doctor said they won't know how badly he's affected until he's conscious and they don't know how long that will be. He could end up in a wheelchair or with brain damage. Her eyes fixed on Eric's hospital gown. "Your dad will need pyjamas, dressing gown, slippers and a comb and toothbrush." An image of Kathy popped into her mind. "I don't fancy going to the farm to get them."

"I can do that, Mum. Geoff's in Sydney collecting a consignment for the shop. He won't be back until the day after tomorrow." Splinter had done well for herself; she'd married the local draper's son whose father had retired and left him to manage the shop. They had a two-year old daughter, Olivia. The business had flourished due to Splinter's clever suggestions.

Lillian was proud of her eldest daughter. Unlike Maureen, she had never given her a moment's worry.

"That would be a great help, love." A nurse came over with a tray of tea. Lillian and Splinter helped themselves, smiling their appreciation. "Perhaps we could take it in turns to visit?"

"Righto. I'll have to tell the school I'm taking the afternoon off tomorrow. I'll pick his things up from the farm before I go to the hospital."

"That's fine. I'll catch the mail bus in the morning and come back at lunch time. That way he will have someone with him all day." Lillian sighed. "I suppose I should write and let Maureen know in case anything happens." Splinter gave an anguished moan. Lillian squeezed her hand. "It is something we have to think about, love." If Eric died, Maureen wouldn't be able to get home for the funeral. It was important to tell her that her Dad had forgiven her so she wouldn't have any guilt.

Standing side by side, Lillian and Splinter gazed at Eric's grey sunken face and the tube in his throat. His chest rose and fell with the help of the oxygen pump.

Johnny materialised beside them. "He's not looking good," he said, eyes filling with tears. He had been worried his father was going to have a go at him over the hundred dollars, but the man in the bed couldn't raise a finger, let alone speak.

"Mum and I are going to take it in turns to visit Dad. Do you want to be in on that?" Splinter said.

Johnny's hands went into his pockets. "We might be going fishing again so I can't make promises. Better count me out." He hated hospitals. The smell, machines, all of it made him feel faint.

"I have to get Dad's pyjamas from the farm tomorrow if you want to come with me. I'd like the support."

"Nope, that's girl stuff and I'm not going near that whore."

Splinter's brown eyes darkened. "Well, I'm … going to give her a piece of my mind."

The next morning Splinter pulled up outside Eric's shack. Biddy rushed towards her, tail wagging. "Hello girl. Where's the tart?" Grim-faced, Splinter walked up the rickety front steps. The front door was shut. She rapped on the door and stood arms folded, waiting. A child came around the side of the cottage.

"Where's your mum?" Splinter said, hard eyed.

"She said I was to see who it was," the child replied.

"Take me to her." Splinter walked towards the child who turned and ran. She followed him at a trot.

Kathy was sitting on the back verandah having a smoke. She saw Splinter and frowned. "What are you doing here?"

"In case you didn't know, my father's in hospital in intensive care." Splinter looked at Kathy, stiff-faced.

Kathy put her hand on her heart and widened her eyes. "When did that happen? I was in Bega yesterday. I thought he didn't come home last night because he was helping Boomer fix his truck."

Splinter lifted a disdainful eyebrow.

"No, Mum," a small helpful voice said. "Poppy Eric was home. Remember? He went wonky and said he had a headache and you made him a bed on the verandah."

Kathy's head whipped towards her son. "Shut your bloody mouth and get out of here, big ears. I'll deal with you later."

A look of fear crossed the five-year-old's face. He turned and ran, the dog behind him. Splinter felt sorry for him. Kathy's children had often arrived at school covered in bruises.

"I've come for Dad's clothes, but I also have a message for you." Splinter pulled the bottle of pills she had shown the doctor from her pocket and held them up. I think these belong to you, or at least the Bega Hospital where you stole them from. I've shown them to the doctor who has informed the hospital pharmacy. These could have killed my father, but I bet you know that. Now I suggest you pack your things and get off my father's

86

farm before I take them to the police." Splinter put the bottle back in her pocket. "You can start packing now."

Kathy jumped to her feet. "Look here, I was trying to help him. He wasn't sleeping. He was only meant to take a couple and then I was going to return them. I didn't know he'd been dosing himself every day."

"Well, you can tell that to the police if he dies. The doctor might tell them anyway." Splinter crossed the verandah and entered the two-bedroomed cottage. The place was a rubbish tip. Toys, clothes and dirty dishes crowded the sideboard and table. She went into the main bedroom averting her eyes from the unmade double bed and grabbed the dressing gown hanging on a nail behind the door. She pulled open the dressing table drawer and took out a pair of pyjamas. Kathy hovered behind her. "You'd better start packing."

Kathy stormed out to the verandah, put her fingers to her lips and whistled. The kids came running.

"What, Mum?"

"Go to your room and pack your stuff. We're leaving."

"Leaving? But we're building a cubby?"

"Get your bloody stuff. The bitch is kicking us out." Kathy turned on Splinter. "Fancy kicking bloody kids out of their home."

"It's your doing, not mine." Splinter pushed her father's things into a beach bag she'd brought with her. "I'll get the police constable to check you've gone this afternoon."

"Bitch!" snarled Kathy.

"Killer!" Splinter replied, looping the beach bag over her shoulder and striding off.

The next day there was still no change in Eric; he lay comatose in intensive care. Lillian sat by his bed with a book, occasionally reading him a line that appealed to her. She looked up as Splinter walked in, smug faced.

"How is he?"

"No change. Why are you looking so pleased with yourself?"

"I've just kicked Kathy out; told her I had taken the pills to the doctor and knew they were stolen. Told her I was sending PJ around to make sure she'd gone," Splinter grinned. Lillian looked at her daughter with admiration and then a thought came to her.

"But what will happen to your father if he recovers and needs to be looked after?" The possibility was numbing.

"She was trying to kill him, Mum! Johnny can run the farm and look after him."

"No he can't," Johnny said, entering the room and approaching his father's bedside. "I've got plans." When the fishing season was over, he was heading west. He wanted to work his way around Australia. "You'll have to have Dad," he said to Splinter.

"No bloody fear. He's not coming to live with me to boss us around." They looked at their mother.

"I'd rather live in a tent than have him back," Lillian said. The only sound in the room was the whoosh of Eric's ventilator. "I'll leave you kids to it. I have a bus to catch." Lillian exited the hospital at a fast pace.

Eric's recovery played on her mind all night. She wondered what would happen if he was permanently incapacitated. She didn't want the responsibility of it. Over the past ten years, free from Eric's control, Lillian realised how badly he had treated her during their marriage. Remembered the beatings. She couldn't face his domination again. But it wouldn't be fair to land Splinter and Johnny with their father either. Her shoulders bowed with the weight of it all.

The lounge room clock chimed seven in the morning. There was plenty of time for a morning walk before going to the hospital. Lillian switched the jug on and made a pot of tea in her new thermos. A birthday gift from Splinter to take on her walks. Two Sao biscuits and cheese, wrapped in a serviette, went in her shell-collecting bag with the thermos. The writing pad and biro pen were added as an afterthought. The lake would be a good place to write to Maureen. Lillian checked her watch against the kitchen clock and left.

Black swans floated between two sunrises. Orange and pink streaks painted the sky and water. A whip bird called from the blossoming ti-tree behind Lillian and a blue-headed wren flitted past. Lillian let out a sigh embracing the solitude. If there was such a thing as reincarnation, she wanted to come back as a bird. She wondered why the lake was called Lake Curalo and not Bird Haven? A kookaburra laughed nearby. Lillian hoped it was a good omen. She put the writing pad on her knee and started her letter to Bubs. It was hard telling her about her father's stroke and just as hard advising her to have the baby adopted. The finished letter went into her shell bag and she lay on the grass listening to the birds and the sound of the distant surf as the sun climbed in the sky.

11

An Unwanted Visitor

Nine thirty in the morning and the streetlights were still on. Maureen walked towards the tram, ears aching from the icy air. Her hair and beanie were not enough to balk the cold. She buried her hands in the pockets of her thin overcoat and boarded the tram. Voices drifted the length of the tram, low and respectful. There was an occasional laugh and breath of alcohol. She kept her eyes on the stations' names as the tram rocked on. A man stood up and offered his seat. He had noticed her bump. She needed to buy some loose clothing to hide her pregnancy. The gloves she was wearing hid her hands so no one could see she wasn't wearing a wedding ring. She smiled her thanks and sat down. Something somersaulted in her womb. The baby was becoming more assertive. Maureen slipped her hand inside her coat and stroked her stomach until she reached the hospital.

Netta had been moved from intensive care to a ward. Unsure

which way to go, Maureen tried to read the Swedish signs, annoyed at having left Bernard's note behind with the room number on it. Nurses hastened past her, white-capped with efficiency. A doctor was ambling along, reading a report. She put out her hand and stopped him, excusing her English.

"I need to find the information desk?" He pointed to the end of the hall and made a right with his hand. She thanked him, following his instructions until she came to the nurse's station. The nurse didn't speak English. Maureen wrote down Netta's name. The nurse wrote 32 and pointed to the signs on the wall.

The oxygen tent had gone and Netta was bright faced, perched up on pillows. Her face lit up on seeing Maureen.

"Hello, Netta. How are you?" She was pleased to see the improvement in Netta. She pushed the visitor's chair closer to the bed and sat on the edge.

"Much better thank you." Netta's eyes swept Maureen. "You're looking a little wan?"

Maureen's hands twisted in her lap. It was always her motto to get the worst over with first. "I'm sorry for not visiting when I said I would Netta. Nils is back and I've had a bit of a shock." She couldn't control the tremble in her voice. "I hope you don't mind, but I've had to move back to the roof." She swallowed, waiting for Netta's objections. Instead Netta gazed at her and nodded as though it was expected. "I've nowhere else to go. It's only until Sarah gets back and then I can stay with her." Maureen took a deep breath to hold back the tears that threatened while she explained what had happened.

Netta was attentive, shaking her head in disbelief at Nils' mother's attack on the stairs, setting her jaw at Nils leaving her at Sarah's without knowing his pregnant fiancée was sleeping in a roof. Her silent responses gave Maureen heart.

"I've been trying to get in touch with Nils. Bernard tried to speak to him on the telephone but didn't get past his father. Now

Bernard has fired me because the father threatened him over the food poisoning incident you were involved in years ago. He said if the matter was raised again it might put you in a bad situation."

Netta lurched forward. "Me? What about him? He wanted to save the restaurant," Netta hissed.

Maureen jerked back, alarmed at her sudden change of mood. "I don't know what you mean?"

Netta scanned the room, leant forward, her voice low. "It's a long story and I can't tell you in here. However," she stared at the counterpane on her bed, picking at the pilling, "I've been wrestling with an idea and you have just made up my mind. I don't want people nosing around in my life. I've been thinking about moving since Bernard mentioned hearing about a home for retired musicians in England. I will move there, so you can stay in the roof as long as you need. Tomorrow I'm being discharged, and I'll be back in the roof. We'll talk then. There are a few things to sort out before I return to England." Netta lay back, strong and determined.

Maureen bit her lip. It was her fault Netta was in this predicament. "I'm really sorry, Netta. You have been good to me. I don't know where I'd be if you hadn't helped me. I've caused you a lot of trouble and now you have to leave." Maureen huddled in her chair.

Netta patted her hand. The move to England wasn't the girl's fault. Netta had forgotten what it was like to live in warmth and comfort. She was enjoying the care in the hospital. "I've done my penance. It's time."

"Bernard is still feeding me by the way."

"You will have to plan ahead my girl. You can't live in a roof if you intend to keep your baby."

Shocked, Maureen looked at Netta. "Of course I'll keep my baby! When the baby is born Nils will come back to me."

Netta's eyebrows rose in disbelief. "I wouldn't bank on it, child, but it's your decision."

Maureen shook her head. Why did Netta have to be so negative about Nils when she needed to believe in him? She hated the niggle of doubt Netta always managed to stir. She took Netta's hand in both of hers. "I'll be alright."

The look Netta gave her said she was delusional. "We'll speak tomorrow," Netta said. Her eyes settled on a pregnant girl visiting the patient next to her. "Have you been to the hospital for a check-up yet?"

"No, I was waiting for Nils to take me." There had been too much going on for her to think about check-ups. It wasn't as if she was sick.

"Find out about the maternity clinic before you leave and make an appointment." The appeal in Netta's eyes couldn't be ignored. Maureen sighed.

"Righto. I'll do that now." She leant forward to kiss Netta's cheek but Netta's hand settled on her chest holding her back. They exchanged pats on the arm. "I'm calling into the restaurant to collect some food if you want me to pass a message to Bernard?"

Netta shook her head. "I'll see him tomorrow." She pointed to the door. "Maternity clinic." Maureen sighed. She'd have to attend the clinic at some time so she may as well sign up now to stop Netta nagging.

The nurse at the station handed Maureen pamphlets all written in Swedish.

"Do you have anything in English?" Maureen asked. The nurse gave her a look as though to say *another immigrant on the welfare system*.

"I will write down for you." She wrote down the dates and times on a notepad, tore the page off and handed it to Maureen.

"Sometimes waiting is a long time so good to bring book and lunch." The nurse dismissed Maureen to attend another enquirer.

"Thank you." Maureen scanned the dates and put the note in her bag. She'd wait until Sarah returned, then she would have someone to interpret for her.

The kitchen staff greeted her like a long-lost friend when she entered the restaurant. The chef sliced some beef, put it on a plate and ladled a thick brown sauce over the meat. He added julienne potatoes and string beans, then motioned her to follow him as he carried the plate to the dining room where a place had been laid for her. He even pulled her chair out.

"Thank you," Maureen said, tucking into the meal. The chef touched her head like a father and called out to the waitress. The waitress came in with cheese and bread in a brown paper bag and put it next to her plate. Although embarrassed at their charity, she enjoyed the attention. Bernard had done a good job in telling her story. While she ate, she kept one eye on the door, vetting the drift of early guests to make sure Nils' father wasn't amongst them to check up on Bernard. Before she left the restaurant, she nicked a bar of camphor from the lady's room to put in the downstairs toilet.

Everything was ready for Netta's arrival. The downstairs lavatory cleaned and smelling fresh. The pee bucket clean. The pigeon poo removed from the carpet and couches. There was a fire in the stove and water in the kettle to make coffee. Maureen plumped the pillows on Netta's couch and settled down to wait, thoughts crowding her head. The thoughts were always the same .... All the what ifs.

What would she do if Nils didn't come for her and the baby? She was convinced he would, but what if he didn't? Without money there wasn't much she could do. The darkness that crouched inside her grew. She pushed it away, determined to believe she would cope without having to give her child up. The baby would need clothes when it was born. That was something she hadn't thought about. Where would she get the money for baby clothes and nappies? She should make it something. Knit! It would help pass the time while she was holed up in the roof.

Maureen pulled aside the cloth walls to search the cupboards and drawers for knitting needles, wool and a pattern book, but there was nothing other than a few old tools. She picked up a screwdriver and thought about Sarah's door. Sarah was a great knitter; she'd have needles and wool. Perhaps she could unscrew the lock and get into the flat?

Armed with a screwdriver and lots of determination, Maureen surveyed Sarah's door. It was a heavy door with a brass lock held in place with two countersunk screws. She tried to unscrew them, but they were both smaller than the screwdriver. "Shit!" Wouldn't something work out for her?

Heavy steps on the stairs. Someone was coming. Maureen shoved the screwdriver up her sleeve and made a pretence of having just left Sarah's flat. A head appeared above the stairs. Maureen's heart faltered as she recognised Nils' father. Nils must have told him where she was staying. He stepped onto the landing, his eyes as hard as the screwdriver up her sleeve. There was no greeting. For a moment Maureen's brain froze.

The father's eyes rested on her stomach and his mouth tightened. She drew her jacket closed and hugged her arms across her stomach. He looked around the dingy landing and pursed his lips in disdain. It was what he had expected. She was an opportunist who was after his son. His hand went into a pocket inside his coat and returned with a wallet.

"You will leave Sweden," he said, tapping his wallet on his palm, cold eyes boring into her. Maureen's throat constricted.

"No. I want to see Nils first."

"He will not see you. That baby is not his."

"Jag alskar Nils."

"Love?" The father snorted. "Love passes." He opened his wallet and withdrew folded notes. "Your fare to Australia."

Maureen shook her head. She wanted this man gone. Her whole body was shaking. "Hall kafun," she swore. "For it helvete." The words didn't sound bad to her, not like English swearing. All she'd said was shut up and go to hell, but it hit the mark. He was a prestigious lawyer and university lecturer; no one swore at him especially a woman.

White-faced, he thrust his head inches from hers. "I researched you. You worked illegally in Norge. Australians don't have work agreements with Norge like England and Europe. Nils tell me he paid guarantor money to get you in Sverige. You didn't have entry to Norge stamp in your passport. The newspapers in that time say two English girl hitchhikers threaten man with a gun. They hide his car keys and leave the man in car in snow. The man was all night in the car. He nearly died from cold. Police were looking for those girls." His eyes glinted behind thick glasses. "I think one of those girls was you."

The room wobbled. Maureen knew if she told the police about the kidnapping they wouldn't believe her. She was twenty-two years old, pregnant, unmarried, in a foreign country with nowhere to live. Jane, the only one who could prove her story, was in England. The problem was they had parted after an argument when Maureen said she was going to Sweden. She didn't have Jane's address. Herr Classon bounced on the balls of his feet with glee. A movement behind him caught Maureen's eye.

"I can have you deported," he snarled, shoving his face into hers.

Maureen's fists clenched by her side. "Would Nils like you to do that? Deport his pregnant girlfriend? How would that look in the newspaper?" She saw the shift in his eyes and felt a surge of triumph.

He stepped back. "You had your chance," he said, slipping his wallet into his overcoat pocket.

"Tell Nils he has my money and I need it," Maureen said.

"Hora!" he shouted wheeling towards the stairs. He bumped into Netta who had appeared on the landing. Startled he stepped sidewards and stumbled over the top step, flinging his arm out to catch the railing to stop from falling. He muttered something to Netta and stomped down the stairs.

Netta bent down and retrieved the wallet that had fallen from his pocket. Maureen was about to call after him when Netta put her hand up. "Let him come back for it."

"I don't ever want to see him again."

"You can post it but inconvenience him. He deserves it. Horrible man." Netta opened the wallet and counted the notes. "There's enough here for your return to Australia."

"I want to have my baby in Sweden. For Nils."

Netta looked at Maureen, exasperated. "And pigs will fly," she said.

"You're not me."

A noise came from the other flat. Netta motioned with her head towards the roof steps. Once in their hidey-hole, Netta sank on her couch. She was feeling shaky after being in hospital. Maureen put the kettle on for cups of tea.

"I was checking if I could get into Sarah's flat when he turned up," she explained. "He threatened me with the police, said he knew I was the hitchhiker they were looking for. If they come, I can't say I live in a roof." She spooned tea leaves into a teapot and added the boiling water, gave the pot a stir and filled two cups. They sat on their couches, sipping tea, deep in thought. A few minutes of silence passed.

"Tell me about the hitchhiking." Netta said.

Maureen stared into her cup the way her mother did when

she was reading tea leaves. She looked up at Netta, "I'll tell you what happened if you tell me why you came to live in the roof."

A pigeon cooed in the rafters. It was a long time since Netta had talked about that night. She nodded in agreement.

"Right, well …" Maureen took a deep breath. "It happened on our way to Oslo, before I met Nils. My friend, Jane and me, we decided we wouldn't take rides if there was more than one person in the car. We'd had a difficult time with a couple of randy old hoteliers who had picked us up in Denmark.".

"Hitchhiking seems a fool hardy thing to do," Netta commented.

Maureen shrugged, "What else could we do? I lost my car." If Netta was going to judge her she wouldn't tell her the story. She hated being judged. The people who judged weren't perfect. She sipped her tea.

"Not for me to say though is it? Times have changed. Come on," Netta encouraged.

Maureen stared into her cup. "I left my broken car in Munich and my friend Jane and I had to hitchhike to Norway where we had jobs waiting at a ski resort. It was in October. Really cold. I skinned the palm of my hand putting my suitcase down because it had frozen to the metal handle. We didn't have gloves or beanies, or money to buy them." Maureen hugged herself.

"We were on the outskirts of Gothenburg. It was late afternoon. A man in a VW beetle stopped. He looked okay although we couldn't see much of his face. We were about an hour down the road when he started on Jane. She was sitting next to him and I was in the back. He pushed his hand between her legs. She yelled and tried to fight him off, but he was too strong. The car went all over the road. I thought we'd have an accident. The man told us he was taking us to his bedroom for some fun. He had turned off the highway without us knowing. Jane was kicking and fighting. Yelling for me to do something. I tried to grab his hair, but the seats were too high and the gap between them too hard for me to reach him. "We had been given a gun by a friend; it was a gas pistol. Shoots blanks and teargas. It was loaded with blanks. Harmless, I thought. I had it in my sock with my pants pulled over the top, hidden. I know how to shoot, my father taught me when I was a kid. We used to shoot bottles off our lavatory roof with his rifle.

"Jane was screaming for me to do something, so I pulled the gun out and pressed it behind the driver's ear. I shouted, 'Stop the car I have a gun!' He laughed. I held the gun up for him to see in the rear-view mirror. He stopped the car. Jane got out and grabbed our luggage. The man got out, pulled the seat forward and held the door open for me. I kept the gun trained on his face as I eased past him. Suddenly, he lunged at me. I fired. The sound was deafening. He fell forward and cracked his head on the car. At first I thought I had killed him, but then I could see he was breathing. Jane and I pushed him into the car. We were scared he would follow us when he woke up, so I dropped the car keys on the floor, just under the pedal.

"It was nearly dark. We didn't have a torch. There was thick snow everywhere. No buildings. We were in the middle of nowhere. We ran for ages, terrified. Eventually we got to a crossroad and a truck picked us up. When we reached the Norwegian border, we were both asleep. The truck driver didn't wake us up to have our passports stamped.

"Eventually the story got into the newspaper because the man had nearly frozen to death. He said we'd attacked and robbed him. I guess that was to protect himself in case we went to the police. Not having our passports stamped was a good thing though, because the police couldn't trace us."

Maureen felt the bore of Netta's eyes. They hadn't left her face since she'd begun her story. She moved away from Netta's line of vision and refilled her cup.

Netta lay back on her cushion and gazed into the rafters at a pair of pigeons tucked up together. "We are a good pair, you and me. Birds of a feather," she mused. The coal in the stove flared. Netta turned to Maureen. "Tell me? If the gun had been loaded with bullets would you have pulled the trigger?"

The question slammed into Maureen. Her immediate thought shocked her. She didn't answer. She didn't have to; Netta had read her response. The question was unfair. Maureen set her jaw. She'd just revealed her secret. Now it was Netta's turn. They had an agreement. "Would you like another cup of tea before you tell me your story, Netta?"

Netta didn't answer, her forehead creased in thought. Then her head jerked towards Maureen. "It is important for you to be seen as living in a credible abode, so Herr Classon doesn't have anything else against you. I'll speak to Bernard; he may know someone who can help you get into Sarah's flat." Netta paused. "I can see you will need to know my story in case I get dragged into being your character reference."

12

Break In

Shadows moved in the firelight. Netta grappled with her thoughts. Maureen would be the first person to hear her full story. The guilt and remorse were still with her.

"I was with the London Philharmonic orchestra. We were appearing in Gothenburg. Phillip and Bernard's restaurant had just opened, and I was asked to play the violin. The orchestra people dined there regularly. I met Phillip. We fell in love and I moved to Gothenburg to live. I still travelled with the orchestra for big events. After we had been married for twenty-three years, I learned Phillip had another wife and a child. She was much younger than me." Netta's fingers plucked at the rug covering her.

"He always travelled a lot. Said he was trying to find new business prospects. I gave him money to assist in his so-called business ventures, but looking back, I realised he was with her. It was Bernard who told me what was going on. He said Phillip objected to his relationship with the chef and he was trying to force Bernard into selling the restaurant without my knowledge so he could ditch me, take all the money and live with the other woman. I was devastated.

"I didn't tell Phillip I knew about his other wife. Instead I found out where she was living and contacted her. Told her who I was. In the beginning she didn't believe me and naturally was very upset. When I finally convinced her, we arranged to confront our husband together with a dinner at the restaurant. Bernard was in on the plan."

Netta's voice hardened. "Phillip got the surprise of his life when she arrived. Unfortunately, he died during the meal. He had an allergy to peanuts. It happened so fast." Netta looked beyond Maureen to the scene in her memory. "The chef swore he didn't use peanut oil in the cooking, but it was discovered in the salad. We tried to save him. Gave him mouth to mouth and massaged his heart. The problem was we delayed calling the ambulance because we were scared. Bernard didn't want the restaurant to get a bad name and lose custom. He wanted us to carry Phillip outside and then phone the ambulance.

"I knew there would be publicity because I was a famous musician as well as Phillip's wife. We didn't want the bigamy story to come out either. The chef was terrified he'd be under suspicion because he had a past. It all happened in a matter of minutes. I don't think the ambulance would have gotten to us in time anyway."

Netta's voice caught in her throat. "It was never discovered how the peanut oil got in the food. The story was in the press, of course, and the restaurant boomed, aided by the curious. Eventually the bigamy story came out and the police started to question us. They said I had a motive to let Phillip die, as did the other wife, also Bernard who was against selling the restaurant and had been overheard arguing with Phillip. It was me the press hounded the most because I was famous. The publicity wasn't good for the orchestra's profile, so I was asked to take leave. I started a quartet, which became successful, but all the publicity had taken its toll and I had a nervous breakdown. That's when I decided to disappear and found this roof to live in.

"Bernard discovered me busking and, of course, tried to rescue me. He told me I owned Phillip's half share of the restaurant and tried to get me to join him. But I didn't think I deserved Phillip's share because I had arranged the dinner. If I hadn't, he might still be alive."

She dabbed at her eyes with the rug. "We agreed I would play the piano at the restaurant. I wasn't known as a pianist, whereas if I'd played the violin his clientele might have recognised me. I took the added precaution of disguising myself."

She gazed past Maureen. "When I analyse my actions, I think I moved into the roof to punish myself for letting Phillip die. I loved him, you know." Netta slumped into the couch.

"Oh, Netta!" Maureen rushed over and hugged her. Netta didn't push her away. "That is so sad for you. And I'm sorry I have caused you even more problems."

"You have brought an end to my self-punishment and that is good. You can make me a coffee and then go and phone Bernard to get someone to help open Sarah's door."

Maureen made the call from the paper shop, whispering down the phone. "It needs a small screwdriver, Bernard."

"I will send the chef after his shift."

"The chef?" The door needed a locksmith.

"Oh! The things I do for Henrietta," was all Bernard said, before hanging up the phone.

Maureen returned to the roof. "Netta, he said he would send the chef. What would the chef know about breaking into a flat?"

"A lot," Netta replied.

Nothing more was explained. Maureen went up and down

the roof steps a dozen times to check if the chef had arrived. When he did turn up, he was dressed in a black overcoat, ski gear, sunglasses and a black knitted beanie. She didn't recognise him. He looked around and signalled to her.

"Which door?"

Maureen pointed to Sarah's. The chef removed his sunglasses and switched on a small torch to inspect the lock. Then he opened an attaché case and removed a bundle of keys. It was all so furtive that Maureen began to doubt Phillip's death was accidental. She pushed her misgivings aside. Netta's husband was dead and these people were taking a big risk in helping her. She owed them. After a handful of keys were tried, the lock turned, and Sarah's door opened. Maureen squealed and clapped her hands. The neighbour opened his door and stared hard at Maureen.

"Hello neighbour. My friend Sarah sent me a key and said I could stay in her flat, so I'm here now." She waggled her fingers at him and turned to the chef, putting her arms around him.

"Goodnight, Bengt, it was kind of you to help me move my things." The chef slid a look at the neighbour and gave Maureen a quick peck on the cheek.

"It is good you are living here." He averted his face as he turned to the stairs. "Goodnight."

He hurried down the stairs. Maureen gave the neighbour a cool look and closed Sarah's door. She switched the light on and leant against the door, listening for the neighbour to go back inside. The door slammed and Maureen let her breath out. A moment later there was a light tap on her door. She opened it a crack and saw the chef holding up a key.

"You cannot leave your flat without this," he whispered, giving her the key.

"Thank you and thank Bernard," she whispered, closing the door after he had disappeared down the stairs. She put the key in her pocket and turned the heater on to warm the flat. Tonight, she would sleep in Sarah's bed in case Nils' father had notified the police and they turned up early. She locked Sarah's door to report her success to Netta.

"The chef was very professional. He looked like he's done it before." There was no reaction from Netta. She wasn't giving anything away. "The neighbour thinks Sarah sent me a key and the chef was there to help me move in. I'm going to take my suitcase down to Sarah's."

"I'll come with you so we can plan what you say to the police."

Maureen carried her suitcase over to the roof door and was about to descend the steps when she heard a loud knock on the neighbour's door. She put her hand up to stop Netta. They stood in the shadows, listening. A door opened.

The gruff sound of Sarah's neighbour greeted a visitor; the door closed. Maureen relaxed. "That was close, I thought it was the police." They crept down the stairs and entered Sarah's flat.

"You'll be fine in here," Netta said, seating herself and looking around the neat, sparsely furnished flat.

Maureen didn't say, but she was elated not to have to pee in a bucket or dodge pigeon poo. They settled into discussing her police statement.

"The best thing you can do is write down what happened and read it over to make sure it sounds correct. Tell the truth but leave out what might convict you. Like hiding the car key."

"I put it on the floor. That wasn't exactly hiding it."

Netta lifted her eyebrows. "Just say you don't know what happened to it. You were too scared at the time." Netta tapped her lips with her finger. "Where is the gun?"

"Jane has it. She's in England but I haven't got her address. We lost contact after I came to Sweden. I wish I had kept in touch."

"Adam wished he hadn't bitten into the apple so don't waste time looking back. I doubt you will be visited by the police straight away. I'd better get back. I left the fire without shutting the grate." She went to the door, opened it a crack and peered through. The landing was empty; it was safe to leave.

"See you later then," Maureen said.

Netta frowned. "When later?"

"What? Oh, that's just an Aussie saying when we leave someone."

After Netta had gone Maureen felt a pang of homesickness. She imagined her mother in her sun hat on her knees weeding the garden or daydreaming at her kitchen window with a cup of tea, watching the ships pass on the horizon. Her mother had been so proud of her moving to the city for work and saving her fare to travel overseas. How far she had fallen. She made a mental note to check for mail tomorrow.

Sarah's flat seemed like a hollow log after Netta had left her alone. Maureen would have asked her to stay in the warm, but it was bad enough she had broken into the flat without Sarah arriving to find she also had a friend with her. The couch come bed was tucked into the alcove of the large bay window that overlooked the street. The window was double glass and muted the noise from the busy road. She pulled at the couch. It expanded into a bed and Maureen flopped on top. She rolled onto her back, lying spreadeagled, imagining what Sarah would think having her flat broken into. If the shoe was on the other foot, she would be glad Sarah had trusted her enough to take the liberty. A friend in need, she thought. A huge surge of tiredness covered Maureen and she dissolved into the bed, eyes closing on her worries.

The baby kicked inside her. Maureen's hand went down and stroked her stomach. She hadn't pulled the blind down when she'd fallen asleep and a sepia light filled the bed-sit. She was still in yesterday's clothes and hadn't a clue what time it was. Her stomach rumbled. Groaning she swung her legs out of bed and pushed her feet into Sarah's slippers. It was an effort to get up. The past few days had exhausted her. She went into the lavatory and looked in the mirror above the basin. Her hair was oily. The pixie cut that showed up her nice cheekbones was now all sticking out ends. Her large brown eyes were hollows with dark smudges. She looked drawn and colourless. Today, she would try and smarten up. If the police came she needed to make a good impression, not look like a suspicious desperado.

The kitchenette yielded a packet of porridge and two tins of condensed milk. She put half a cup of oats in a saucepan, covered it with water, and put it on the gas ring. Then cooked up a pot of coffee.

Tray on her knees, Maureen sat on Sarah's bed eating her breakfast, wondering how she was going to spend her day. Maybe visit the hospital and have her pregnancy checked? It was no good waiting for Sarah or Nils, and it would take her mind off her worries. She'd ask Netta if she wanted to go with her.

Maureen cleared up the breakfast things, filled the hand basin with hot water, found soap and towels in the cupboard beneath the basin, stripped off and gave herself a head to toe scrub. It was refreshing. She washed her hair in the sink and filled the porridge pot with water to rinse her hair, towelling it dry. Such luxury after the roof. The trousers she put on wouldn't do up at the waist. They had fitted her last week. She found Sarah's sewing box and a safety pin. The pin held the waist part together but left a gap beneath it. Her mohair jumper covered the gap. When she was ready to leave for Netta's she thought about the police. She didn't want them knocking on her neighbour's door. She wrote BACK SOON on a piece of paper and jammed it in the door as she left.

"Sleep well?" Netta asked as Maureen emerged from under the table. Strewn across the mat was a pile of books and photographs Netta was sorting through.

"I did," Maureen said. "I thought I'd go to the hospital for a check-up this morning and wondered if you were going to see Bernard, maybe we could get a taxi and visit the hospital on the way? I'm a bit worried about filling out forms and not having a Swedish identity card. You could say you were my aunt or something?"

Netta pulled a face. She'd had enough of hospitals and there was a lot of sorting to do. "Tell them you've mislaid your identity card along with your passport when you moved abodes." She looked thoughtful. "They won't turn a pregnant girl away if you give them the name of the father. He's a Swedish citizen, that makes your child a Swedish citizen."

Maureen perked up, she hadn't thought of that. It was one worry she could let go.

"Right, I'll leave then. Unless you want me to accompany you to Bernard's?" Fingers crossed there might be a letter from Australia for her.

"No, just phone for a taxi and tell them to pick me up at the newspaper shop in …" she opened a small travelling clock, "two hours." Using the arm of the couch Netta pulled herself up off the floor grunting with pain. "It's certainly time I left this place, my bones must have become used to the heating in the hospital. I'll look out for you at lunchtime. We'll have a welcome back lunch. I'll tell Bernard to put a bottle of champagne on ice."

13

Eden – Waking Up

Johnny walked into the Hotel Australasia and scanned the bar to see if there was anyone he knew and spotted Boomer and Quick Parker in deep conversation. They were the last two people he wanted to talk to. With a bit of luck, they hadn't seen him. He turned to go and was stopped by a whistle. Boomer's hand went up waving him over. Shit! Johnny forced a grin and headed towards them. Boomer said something to Quick who stopped talking and looked around as Johnny approached.

"G'day, Johnny Boy. Sorry to hear about yer old man, how's he doin?" Boomer said in his hoarse whisper.

"Not good," Johnny replied.

Quick Parker smirked. "Kathy's probably exhausted the poor bugger. Worn his dick out. I was glad to see the back of 'er."

"That's enough, Quick. Johnny's dad's in a coma," Boomer said.

"No wonder, mate. She's just done a runner with his accountant."

"What do you mean?" Johnny said, ears twitching.

"Don't wanna be unkind or anyfink, but she shot through yesterday. Left me with the kids. Somethin' to do with your sister visitin'."

"Your wife's a tart," Johnny said. He didn't give a bugger who Kathy had done a runner with as long as she was gone. On the other hand, if Kathy had gone there was no one looking after the dog or the cow. It was a pity Splinter hadn't thought about who would look after the farm when she'd kicked Kathy out. The boat wouldn't be going baiting until tonight, so he'd have time to drive out there and pick up the dog. He would collect his father's chequebook, grandfather's gold watch, the radio, and have a look around in case Kathy had nicked or sabotaged anything. The need for a beer suddenly left him. He didn't want to sit in a pub talking about his father.

"I've gotta go." Johnny walked off, leaving Boomer and Quick to their gossip.

Johnny could hear Biddy howling when he reached the farm gate. He skidded to a stop outside the house and rushed over to her kennel. The bitch, Kathy, had left her chained up without water or food. Johnny was nearly in tears as he let her off the chain. Biddy pawed and licked him, wobbling on her feet from the effort. He picked her up and carried her to the cottage.

The front door wasn't locked. He went inside, put Biddy down on the kitchen floor and began to hunt through the kitchen cupboards for food. He found a tin of Greenseas Tuna nicked from the Eden cannery, grabbed a can opener from a drawer and emptied the contents onto the floor next to the starving dog. He found some eggs and broke them onto the floor. Biddy devoured the lot, licking the floor when she'd finished, tail wagging with gratitude.

The dog followed him into the bedroom. It was a mess. Clothes, pulled out of cupboards, lay on the bed and floor. They were all his father's. Gritting his teeth, Johnny combed through the mess. The chequebook was lying on the dressing table. He flicked through it; there were still some cheques left. He put the chequebook in his pocket and rifled through the drawers. His grandfather's watch was at the back. He wound it up, heard the tick and put it in his pocket. The fountain pen, a gift to his father from the water polo team he had captained when he was in the navy, joined the watch. He went through the house looking for the radio and out onto the verandah. It was littered with broken toys but there was no sign of the radio. The bitch must have taken it! He considered cleaning the house and remembered the cow.

Grabbing a bucket off the tank stand, he gave it a rinse and went looking for the cow. He found her by the river, udders bigger than footballs, exploding with milk.

"Come on old girl." Johnny put a rope around Jenny's neck and tied her to the fence. She stood quietly as he milked, grateful to be relieved of the pain. Biddy lapped up the first billycan full and Johnny rinsed and filled it to the brim again, putting the lid on. He led the cow to the car, put the billycan inside for his mother, and took the cow across the river to the neighbour his father hated.

When he got back to Eden, he dropped the dog and billycan off at his mother's before heading down to the wharf to go baiting.

Seven days later, Eric woke from his coma. Lillian, Splinter and Johnny approached his bedside and he recoiled when he saw them, horror on his face, batting away Lillian's hand as she reached out to stroke his face. His voice was a croak, words unintelligible. The nurse leant over his bed and patted his arm.

"Mr McKinley, it's your family come to see you. You remember your family?" Eric squeezed into his pillow, eyes full of fear.

"Hello, Dad. It's me, Splinter." She took his hand. Eric pulled his hand away and looked from one member of his family to the other, puzzled.

"They are our kids, Eric," Lillian said. "We're not married anymore though." The doctor came over and took Lillian's arm and led her to the nurse's station.

"Eric was cognitive early this morning, so I gave him a quick test to see whether he had brain damage or not. From what I can gather he has short-term memory loss and thinks he's much younger than he is. We will need some photos of your family from when they were young and in their growing stages. Your daughter's wedding photos, things that will bring back his memory. We don't know if he is physically incapacitated yet. I will send him to our rehabilitation wing once he's stable. It can be a slow process."

Keep calm, Lillian told herself as she went back to Eric's bedside and her traumatised children.

A nurse came over and pulled the curtain around Eric's bed. "Visiting times are over," she said.

They stood next to Eric, undecided whether to kiss him goodbye or just leave. The fear in his eyes directed them to the door. No one spoke until they were in the hospital corridor.

"Do you think Dad will ever be normal again? Splinter's face streamed with tears.

Lillian gave her back a rub. "He survived, that's the main thing. We'll go home and have a family discussion." She must let Maureen know her father had recovered. Lillian sighed with the weight of it all.

They sat around the kitchen table glum faced. "We have to talk about what to do if he doesn't improve," Lillian said.

"You must take care of him, Mum. Dad can't go back to the farm," Johnny informed her.

Lillian went cold. She knew she had to take Eric in; there were no other options. Splinter lived in a caravan on a block while they saved money to build a house. She had two-year old Olivia. There was no room for her father. And as for Johnny, he was about to take off around Australia. It just wasn't fair. All her life had been spent caring for people. Bringing up her siblings, her own children, looking after her husband's two aunts and his sister, her mother. Lillian felt a pang of envy for Bubs, living on the other side of the world away from it all. Under the table, the dog lay its head on her foot. Distracted she leant down and gave her a pat. They were getting on well together.

Eric's chequebook landed on the table in front of her. She sat up and stared at it uncomprehending.

"You'll have to go to the bank, Mum and get your signature on Dad's account so you can buy a wheelchair if he needs one, or anything else he might need," Johnny said. Lillian gave him a grateful look. She hadn't considered Eric's finances.

"That's thoughtful of you, son."

"I'm going to take Dad's car. He won't be able to drive it," Johnny said.

"No, you won't. What about, Mum?" Splinter could see what Johnny was up to. "Mum will have to learn to drive if Dad can't walk. She'll need his car to take him to the hospital for check-ups."

Lillian cringed at the thought of getting behind a steering wheel. The only time she had tried was on a back road before the kids were born and she had hit a kangaroo. Eric had to slit the poor thing's throat and kill its joey to put them out of their misery. She wasn't going to have her children deciding her life when she'd not long ago reclaimed it for herself.

"Who's going to look after the farm?" She was feeling hemmed in by all the decisions that had to be made.

"If we sell the farm, Mum could buy her own car and I can still have Dad's." Johnny loved the Buick.

Splinter got up and cleared the plates off the table. She put them in the sink and stared over at Aunt Maggie's old house. Nobody had lived in it since she'd died. According to the town it was haunted. "Mum and I should go and see the bank manager tomorrow about signing Dad's cheques. Also, let's give Dad some recovery time before we go selling or taking anything," Splinter said, giving Johnny a meaningful look.

"I'll go with you," Johnny said. "I should be able to sign too; in case anything happens to Mum." He saw his mother's eyebrow raise and Splinter's lips purse. "She might get a migraine or get bulldozed into something," he said, on the defensive. "Anyway, I'm the eldest."

After her children had left, Lillian stood at the window and watched a group of fishing boats trawl for some unsuspecting snapper. She really had to make sure she kept her hands on the wheel.

14

Nils Calls By

The administration nurse at the maternity clinic checked the information sheet Maureen had filled out. "You are Miss, not Fru?" she said.

Someone tutted their disgust in the line behind Maureen. She felt the heat climb up her neck into her cheeks and lowered her head. "Yes. But I am engaged to the father." It was important to Maureen to make that known because the child of an engaged couple in Sweden was called a true love baby and had the same rights as one born within a marriage. Also, she wouldn't be looked down on. Her chin lifted and she stared at the nurse.

"It is good." She handed Maureen a card. "This you give to doctor. You may take a seat and wait. They will call."

The waiting room was half full. Maureen sat at the end of a row and observed the women. Some were knitting, others chatting and laughing. The camaraderie in the room made her feel isolated and lonely. Nils had blamed her for becoming pregnant, said she should have been on the pill. She didn't blame him for the pregnancy but why wasn't he helping her? How could he just dump her onto her friend and walk away without any explanation? He hadn't said he didn't love her.

"Mereen MLinly? Mareen Mcelinely?" A nurse looked around the room. It was her they were calling. Maureen grabbed her bag and hastened over to the nurse holding a file.

"I'm Maureen McKinley." She felt flustered, nervous. The nurse smiled, said something in Swedish and walked off. Maureen nodded, followed, even though she didn't understand what was said. The nurse opened a door to a pale green room and Maureen's heart stopped.

In the centre of the room was a monstrous reclining chair with stirrups and overhead lights. A doctor, gowned, gloved and wearing a light on his head pointed to a cotton wrap on a stool and spoke to her in English.

"Please, undress and put on the gown." Maureen shuddered. Oh, God! An image of her father with his arm inside a pregnant cow flashed before her. Without knowing how, she managed to get into the gown and onto the chair. A nurse put her feet in the stirrups and Maureen concentrated on the ceiling and answered the questions that came from a voice between her legs. At the end of the session she was a trembling mess with the knowledge she was six months pregnant, three weeks further on than she had thought. Traumatised, she left the hospital with a wad of pamphlets and a referral to a social worker.

Scarves and beanies covered the faces of people as they crunched towards her. Maureen held her coat together with gloved hands, dodging patches of slush and ice. By the time she reached the entrance to the block of flats she was exhausted.

The downstairs lavatory flushed, and a tattered man came out, his fly undone. Maureen sidestepped him and hastened up the stairs to Sarah's flat. Her cold fingers fumbled with the key. Once inside she pulled off her coat and fell onto the couch bed.

A knock on the door woke her. She looked out of the window into a fog of grey. The streetlights were on. It was late afternoon. She had missed her lunch with Netta. She got up ready with her apology. "Just a minute," she called out, combing her fingers through her hair. She cracked the door open just in case it was the police and not Netta and pulled back, hand to her mouth.

"Nils!"

The strength went out of Maureen's knees. She sagged against the door then pulled it open and leapt at him. His rough army coat made their hug uncomfortable. She pulled him inside and shut the door. He removed his coat. "I knew you would come for me." She laughed, excited. He looked different in his military uniform, slimmer, very handsome but for some reason the uniform made her feel shy.

He held her away from him and looked at her stomach then beyond her. She saw him swallow or was it a gulp? She wasn't sure.

"I missed you so much. I tried to get in touch with you but didn't know how. Bernard rang your father." Maureen snuggled into him.

For a moment he held her and then thrust her away, reaching for a chair to sit in. "We have to talk," he said, looking at the floor.

A sense of foreboding quelled Maureen's excitement. "Coffee?" Her voice sounded high. He nodded. Alarms were going off in her body as she filled the coffee pot. "Do you like the army?" It was small talk, a distraction to cover her confusion.

"I don't mind it. Very busy, not much time to think about liking." He cleared his throat. "You are well?"

"Yes. I saw the doctor today. He said I'm six months pregnant, not five like we thought." She looked at Nils to see how he had taken the news, but he didn't respond. "I was trying to think where we were six months ago," she kept her voice light. "It was on that island we visited in your boat. Smorgen, I think it was called. I remember how we had the sea to ourselves and we swam naked and lay in the sun. So beautiful. We saw a mink run into the rocks. Do you remember?" Maureen turned and smiled at Nils, the memory a softness between them.

He grinned. "You were a water nymph and I was Poseidon."

"Except you couldn't catch me in the water because I am an Australian and can swim better than a Swede," she teased. The coffee was ready. Maureen poured two cups and sat across from Nils to feast on his presence.

"Maureen?" his face reddened. Her heart missed a beat. "I have to ask first if my father left his wallet?" She'd meant to post it. It was in the roof with Netta. How could she get it without giving away the roof? No, he should know he'd left her in a bad place, with nowhere to go. That his father had treated her badly.

"I found his wallet, it's safe, but I have to go into the loft to fetch it." He looked startled. "That's where I have been living until yesterday. Sarah's away visiting her husband who is working on an oil rig in Scotland. I haven't seen her since summer. There's a couch in the roof where I've been sleeping. It's very cold up there." Her eyes were full of hurt. He lowered his head and clasped his hands between his knees. "Someone helped me break into the flat." The stricken look on Nils face filled her with satisfaction. "You must promise not to tell anyone I broke in or that I slept in the roof."

"Pussycat," he was half to his feet, reaching towards her and then shook his head and sat back down. "I am sorry." He whispered.

"What are we going to do, Nils?" She had to know.

He rubbed his forehead. "It is difficult." His Adam's apple rose and fell in his throat. "My father said he came here to help you and you swore at him."

Maureen nodded. Swearing in Swedish didn't mean much to her. She had needed to express her anger and make his father understand. Saying shut up was mild in English.

"You have made it too hard for us. My mother is sick now. My father is not speaking to me."

Stunned, Maureen stared at him. What about how hard they had made it for her? "Your father doesn't believe this is your child." Maureen's hand went to her stomach. "He offered me my fare back to Australia. Called me a whore. Threatened me. I was scared of him."

"They are my parents. They only want the best for me." His words punched into her. Didn't he think she was the best?

"You said you didn't care where I came from. I told you about myself. No, I am not rich like you. I didn't know anything about you when we met. It didn't matter to me if you were rich or poor. There's a baby now. What of the baby?"

Nils looked at her and then his eyes slid away. "I am not finished at university. I cannot be a father yet. My family insist on a blood test. It is best you adopt. Many Swedes from good families want babies. You should consider this."

"Oh, my God!" Maureen started to hyperventilate. The room was closing in on her.

Nils bumbled to his feet. She stood. "It is time I go. The wallet for my father, Maureen?"

Although her arms folded across a breaking heart, her anger held her together. "You have my money, Nils. I need it." Nils put his hand inside his serge jacket and removed his wallet. He put forty kroner on the table and said it was all he had on him.

"I will send the rest."

Somehow Maureen managed to get herself out of the flat and up the steps into the roof with Nils following behind. Beyond the stretch of bare boards and stacked furniture a faint light flickered.

"I must have left my torch on," Maureen said. "Stay here."

The pigeons were making a racket in the rafters, their coos echoing in the emptiness. Nils stood awkwardly at the edge of a pile of discarded furniture, head hung. Maureen disappeared between the cupboards and crawled out from under the table into Netta's make-shift room where a lamp glowed under a canopy of curtains. Netta was feeding coal into the stove. She turned hearing Maureen's strangled sob. Maureen put her finger to her lips, and her lips to Netta's ear. Words jerking.

"Netta, Nils is here. He's come for his father's wallet, not for me."

"Child." Netta drew Maureen into her arms and patted her. "I will get the wallet." It was in the sideboard drawer. She handed it to Maureen. "Here, it is intact. The world isn't going to end for you although you may think so."

Maureen wiped her face with her sleeve and crawled away.

Nils was still standing by the roof door when Maureen returned with the wallet. "I hid it for safety. Sometimes drunks come up here off the street for shelter." She wouldn't give Netta away.

"You didn't tell me this," he said, opening his hands to embrace the roof.

"I left messages with your parents and your commanding officer."

"I didn't know. You must believe me." He was appalled at her living conditions and surprised that she accepted it.

"It doesn't matter now, does it? You don't want me." Her voice was sharp and cold, "And we don't want you," she placed her hand on her stomach, turning from him.

He gazed after her, full of guilt and self-loathing; she was lovely. How could he walk away and leave this girl with the child he knew in his heart was his? But he would. The threat of losing his yacht had made up his mind and joining the army had occupied him so he wouldn't have time to think of anything.

It had all been planned by his father. He couldn't turn back now. Everything was already ruined.

After Nils left, Maureen lay on Sarah's unmade bed staring at the ornate ceiling, at the bows and ribbons in the pressed tin. She felt so alone. A soft knock on the door broke through her thoughts. Could it be the police? If it was, she didn't care. She was rock bottom. She got off the bed and dragged herself to the door.

"I heard someone leave your flat and guessed you were alone. Is everything all right?" Netta said, concerned by the troubled face before her.

Maureen slumped into a kitchen chair and put her face in her hands. "I'm a fool. An idiot."

Netta came in and shut the door. "Tell me, child."

"He's gone." Maureen raised a sheet white face. "I mean really gone. Gone for good. You were right not to trust him. Why am I so naive?"

"My dear, you must think for the child now." It was good riddance to Nils, but she wouldn't tell Maureen that. She pulled a chair around and sat opposite Maureen taking her hands in hers. "Is he going to help you financially?" He could afford to.

Maureen shook her head. "I didn't ask him. I only asked him to give me back my money. He's looking after it in his bank account. He left me forty kroner." She picked up one of a few notes and dropped it back on the table. "This was all he had with him. He said he'd send the rest."

Netta looked at the shattered girl wanting to console her but not knowing how. Then she remembered the letter. "I forgot to give you this. Bernard had it. She put the letter from Australia in Maureen's lap and saw a flicker of hope cross her features. "Tomorrow I thought we might go to the Government charity shop. I have a coupon which I've never used. It will get you some maternity clothes." Netta paused, reticent to make a suggestion.

"You know, there's a Church of England church in Gothenburg. It's not too far from here. I used to go there. I would have suggested it earlier, but I let the church think I had gone back to England after Phillip died. I didn't want to have to explain to people about the newspaper scandal. I still want them to think I went to England." The congregation were mostly English people, married to Swedes or in Sweden on business contracts. "I'm sure you would find them very supportive. I remember the rector and his wife were a nice young couple. But I would ask you not to mention me."

It wouldn't have entered her head to mention Netta without getting her permission. Maureen didn't think she'd bother with the church. She needed Netta to go. She didn't want to talk or think. "Netta, I'm sorry I missed our lunch today, but I just want to be alone right now. I'm really tired." Without looking at Netta, Maureen walked over to the bed, lay down and pulled the doona over her head.

Netta didn't move. "Child it is Christmas Eve. I want you to come somewhere with me."

Maureen pulled the doona down. How could it be Christmas? Nils hadn't even wished her a Merry Christmas. Netta was looking at her expectantly. There was nothing merry or happy about it but she didn't want to spoil Christmas for Netta. "Alright." She sat up.

"I'll be back in a moment." Netta hurried out.

Twenty minutes later she returned dressed in a long white sheepskin coat with a circuit of luminous candles on her head and her violin case. "There's a taxi coming to pick us up. I organised it earlier."

"You are busking in this cold after being in hospital?"

"Not quite. You'll see."

The taxi drove them to the centre of Gothenburg. All the shop windows were full of Christmas scenes and fairy lights.

Why hadn't she noticed? Probably too busy trying not to slip over. They stopped outside the store where Netta had busked in the doorway the day Maureen met Bernard for the first time. Netta shook some coins from her purse and paid the driver.

"He will come back for us in an hour and a half," Netta said. They went into the shop. Next to the escalator was a raised platform covered in red carpet, a microphone and chair. A few rows of chairs surrounded the platform. "You sit in the front. I'm on the stage."

A suited man Maureen took for a floor manager, came over to Netta. They spoke, he shook her hand then motioned her towards the chair by the microphone. Netta removed her violin from the case, leaving the case open by her feet. The chairs filled. Netta put the violin under her chin, lifted her bow and closed her eyes. 'Silent Night' floated from her violin and into the hearts of her audience, soothing and uplifting. Tears trickled down Maureen's cheeks. At the end of her performance the store manager returned, giving Netta an envelope. The violin case was heavy with generosity. Netta tipped out the coins and put them in a tin she had brought with her. "Happy Christmas, Maureen," she said handing her the tin.

That night Maureen lay in bed and thought of her mother. Soon she would be dishing up Christmas pudding and custard to the family. Lifting her nose, she could smell Christmas at home. Hear Harry Belafonte singing 'Away in a Manger' and feel the surf as it folded over her new Christmas bathing suit.

15

Eden – A Second Letter
from Sweden

It was a lovely warm day. Lillian was feeling buoyant; soon she would sign a cheque for Maureen. A late Christmas present. She sat with Splinter and Johnny in front of the bank manager thinking what a pompous prig he was. She saw him look up at the wall clock and back at them as though they were a waste of his time. He glanced at the bank statement in his hand.

"I'm sorry, Mrs McKinley, this account was closed two months ago."

"Closed?" Lillian stared at the bank manager in disbelief. "Eric paid me for his washing three weeks ago and he gave Johnny money to bet on the races. Where did he get that money from?"

"Maybe he opened another account somewhere else? Ask his accountant, he will know." The manager shuffled some papers together and checked his wristwatch, making sure it was the same time as the wall clock. He didn't want to be late for the draper's wife. They were going to try a bit of bondage.

Johnny smacked his fist into his hand and turned to Lillian. "Mum, I forgot to tell you. I saw Quick Parker in the pub, and he said Kathy had done a runner with Dad's accountant."

The bank manager looked up, suddenly interested. "Well, that might need looking into."

"Do you think …?" Lillian bit her lip. Maybe Kathy had cleaned out Eric's account?

"I think you need to speak to the police or a lawyer, Mrs McKinley. I wish I could help you further but all I can do is have my secretary type up your husband's last transactions in this bank. However, to do that I will need a letter confirming your power of attorney."

"Power of attorney?"

"We need a lawyer, Mum," said Splinter.

The only one around was Peter Turnstile, otherwise known as Blinky, because he wore glasses. He had handled Aunt Maggie's will and her divorce. He was a good man. If it hadn't been for him, she might have lost her house. Trouble was, since her divorce he kept popping by to prune her roses (he had the best rose garden in the district and often dropped off cuttings for her) but once he had his foot in the door, he was hard to get rid of.

"I can make an appointment with the lawyer. We can see him after we visit Dad."

Lillian gazed at her daughter. If Splinter made the appointment with Peter Turnstile it would appear more formal and hopefully, he wouldn't be rushing around to examine her roses.

"That's a good idea," Lillian said.

The power of attorney paper was folded in Lillian's handbag along with Maureen's letter from Sweden. She would read the letter to Eric to help his memory.

A nurse had just finished feeding Eric when she entered the

ward. The nurse wiped his mouth and removed his plate to the trolley where she scraped and stacked the dishes. Lillian sat in the chair closest to Eric's bed. He squinted at her, trying to place her.

"I've received a letter from Bubs and I'm going to read it to you." She took a small photograph album from her bag and propped it in front of Eric. "Here's a photo of Bubs when she was fifteen and this is a photo of her now." She pointed to the photos she'd arranged in age order. Eric wrinkled his brow then he lifted his body on one side and farted, waved the sheet and laughed.

Embarrassed, Lillian looked around to see if anyone had noticed. No one had. She closed the album, placing it on his bedside table. This was a new Eric. He would never have done anything so childish before the stroke. In fact, he thought he was above farting. She opened Bubs' letter and began to read aloud.

Dear Mum, I'm so sorry but I'm in an awful fix. Nils has left me and I'm living like a squatter in the roof of the building where Sarah has her flat. I guess I'll be here until she gets back from her holiday. It's freezing. The restaurant I work at has fired me because Nils' father threatened to spread rumours about food poisoning.

Lillian felt the familiar squeeze of anxiety in her solar plexus as she continued reading aloud, unaware the clatter of plates had ceased, and the nurse was leaning on her trolley all ears.

The problem is, Mum, I gave the money you sent me to Nils to look after and now I can't contact him to get it back.

"You stupid, girl!" Lillian exclaimed, putting the letter down and looking at Eric who was grinning at the nurse, and not taking a blind bit of notice to what she was reading. Her eyes went to the nurse who was waiting by the trolley for Lillian to continue reading. She threw her a withering look. The nurse straightened, smiled at a patient on the other side of the room and guided the trolley towards him. Nosey parker, Lillian thought. Her eyes dropped to the letter and she began reading to herself.

Would you be able to send me some more money? Just enough to tide me over until Sarah is back. I'm sorry to ask you, Mum, but I will pay you back when I can. It would have to wait until after the baby is born though because nobody will give me a job while I'm pregnant.

The restaurant owner, Bernard, said I should go to a lawyer and see what the government will do for me because Sweden has a good social security system.

I eat once a day at Bernard's restaurant but not on Sundays when it's closed. The food is free, but I need the money to buy coal, toiletries and tram fares to the hospital.

Please give Dad, Splinter and Johnny my love and please write to me. I miss you so much. Maureen, alias Bubs. xxx

P.S. You can send the money to the restaurant. I've put the address on the back. Love to you all. xxx

At the end of the letter Lillian sat dazed. "It doesn't rain but it pours," she said.

Eric's eyes flicked towards her and he giggled. Lillian folded the letter putting it back in the envelope and in her bag. Somehow, she would have to find money. Her thoughts went to the letter she had written at the lake, telling Maureen the news of her father's stroke. It would arrive in Sweden soon. Poor girl, no home, pregnant and a father she will think is dying. How was she going to manage?

She hoped Maureen would heed what she had written and not entertain the idea of keeping the baby. She had asked her what she intended to do, but there was no accounting for that surge of love when a mother held her baby for the first time. Dear Lord, don't let her do anything stupid, Lillian thought.

No one in Eden need know she had had a child if it was adopted in Sweden. It would be ludicrous to think she could look after a baby in a foreign country. Her letter had been strong on that point. The best solution was for Maureen to come home. Selling the farm would pay for her fare. Lillian clucked her tongue. How could her family at both ends of the world be in such a mess? She opened her book, there was still an hour to kill before visiting hours were over.

Half an hour into visiting time Lillian shut the book. She hadn't managed to read a single page. The book went into her bag. "I have to go, Eric, Splinter is waiting for me." She leant over and pecked Eric on the forehead. He shrank back, child like, a puzzled expression in his eyes. Pity tugged at Lillian's heart, tempting her to stay longer, but she didn't want to keep Splinter waiting at the police station where they had arranged a meeting with constable PJ. It was important she find out where Eric had put his money.

The police station was at the end of the main street past the Fisherman's Club. The bees hummed among the spring flowers as they opened the picket gate. The garden was Constable PJ's pride and joy. Lillian put her nose in a flower, the perfume heavenly after the hospital. The red brick building was more like a cottage than a police station.

"G'day, Lillian." The constable stood as she entered.

"Your flowers are lovely, PJ." He gave her a proud smile and motioned her towards one of the two straight-backed chairs in front of his desk. On the wall behind his desk hung the Australian flag. It was the same one that had been draped over Aunt Maggie's coffin. Lillian made a quiet request to the flag that everything would turn out alright. Splinter came in, looking rushed.

"G'day, Louise." He waited for her to sit down.

"Hello PJ, I mean Trevor," Splinter said, sitting down and

looking pointedly at her mother. Her mother now called Bubs Maureen from the time she had left Eden, so why couldn't she call her Louise? Splinter hated her nickname.

The constable seated himself. "Now, how can I help?"

Lillian withdrew the lawyer's letter from her handbag and placed it in front of the constable. "This is a power of attorney that I believe gives me the right to speak for Eric. The thing is we need to find out why Eric hasn't got any money in his bank account. The bank manager said it was moved but we don't know where to and we need it to cover his expenses." She had said her piece well, despite the nerves in her stomach. Money matters weren't her thing, she had never handled money until after her divorce. Eric had liked to be in control. And since the pound had changed to the dollar she was completely lost. She rummaged in her handbag again withdrawing a bank statement. "Here's a copy of the bank statement."

"Perhaps he didn't have any money?"

"Not true," Splinter said, unable to contain herself. "She's a thief! It was Kathy." She turned a furious face to her mother. "Mum knows he had money."

"He did. He said the farm was doing alright. He bought a Buick, and that was after the date on this statement."

"There's nothing to show he paid for the Buick in this account." Constable PJ said looking at the twenty-five-cent balance on the statement.

"Well, he must have been getting money from somewhere otherwise how did they live? The bitch wasn't working." Splinter's eyes sparked.

"Could he have lost it on the horses?" The Constable knew Eric's weakness, had seen him hammering the bar and pulling at his hair on a few occasions.

"The account was closed two months ago and according to this," Splinter said, leaning over the desk and stabbing the bank statement with her finger. "He had nine thousand six hundred and fifty dollars, and then poof! All gone, along with Kathy and his accountant."

Constable Trevor Price-Jones's back straightened. He could have a dinky-di case on his hands which was far more interesting than arresting drunks. "If you think the money has been stolen then you could ask for an investigation on Eric's behalf now you have power of attorney, Lillian. In fact, I would advise it."

"How much will it cost?" She was trying to gather Maureen's fare.

"A police investigation doesn't cost anything. You sign a statement and I open a file." Constable Trevor Price-Jones face went pink with pride.

"Do it, Mum. Remember how she drugged Dad with those pills? Well, I'll bet you that's how she got him to move his account."

It was feasible. Constable PJ's efficient pen raced as he took down Lillian's statement. When he had finished writing he pushed the document towards Lillian.

"Please check everything is correct and then sign."

Together, Lillian and Splinter read the statement. "Where do I sign?" Lillian asked.

"Here and here," said Constable Trevor-Price Jones, pointing a serious finger at the allotted places and handing Lillian his pen.

On the way back to the house, Lillian was congratulating herself. She had started a case against Kathy on behalf of her children and had a power of attorney. She could sell the farm and help Maureen. All she had to do was write an advertisement for the farm, put it in *The Eden Magnet* and ask Mick the butcher to put one in his shop window. It was the only butcher shop in town, and everyone went there. Lillian considered what she would write. *Farm for Sale in Towamba. 125 acres, river flats with cottage.* What was its value? She'd have to find out what land was selling for. Maybe speak to the council? Her confidence was zinging. Aunt Maggie would be clapping in her grave.

16

Maternity Clothes

Maureen had slept like the dead. She yawned, reached up and pulled the curtain back to view the day. It was already light outside; an indication it must be around nine o'clock in the morning. Remembering Nils' visit yesterday, she was surprised she'd slept so long and without bad dreams. The baby booted her in the stomach as she stretched and sat up. "Naughty," she said, giving it a pat. It was like having a little friend to talk to. Someone to stop her dwelling on the bad things. They were a twosome, in this together and she would make it work. Her mother's letter was on the kitchen table. Maureen fetched the letter, returning to bed to read. She switched on the lamp next to her for added light and opened the envelope.

The letter was ten days old. If her father had died, she would have received a telegram by now. She didn't like to think of him in a coma or recovering as a cripple. She had been his little buddy until her boobs had started growing and he became suspicious of any boy who said hello to her. Following her in his car in case she had gone to meet boys instead of her friends to listen to Elvis records. Making her wear a cardigan up the street on a hot day, although once out of sight, she ripped it off and pulled out the lippy. It was no wonder she had left home at sixteen and moved to Melbourne to live with her aunt and uncle. By the end of the letter Maureen realised she probably wouldn't be getting any more money if her dad was in hospital. She had already worked out that her mother must have filched the last lot she had sent, otherwise she wouldn't have asked her not to mention anything if she wrote to her father. But the letter left her angry. Her mother wanted her to have the baby adopted. She put a protective hand on her stomach. She would manage somehow, she always did.

Hunger pangs. The baby was insisting she eat. Pulling the doona around herself, Maureen made her way to the kitchenette. The thermometer on the wall said two degrees. She turned on the gas heater and filled the kettle. It was nice having water and not having to cart it up from the downstairs toilet. She put the kettle on for a cup of tea, found the bread roll in her bag from yesterday's lunch, cut it into halves and placed it under the grill. There wasn't any butter, only a piece of mouldy cheese which she trimmed and placed on top of the halves to melt. The breakfast was satisfying. The tea minus milk warmed her up.

As hard as she tried to do up her bra, the hooks just wouldn't reach the eyes. Her breasts had become enormous and they hurt. She gave up on the brassiere, throwing it into her open suitcase. Two vests under her jumper and no bra would have to do. The struggle into her trousers helped to make up her mind to accept Netta's offer of the maternity clothes from the government store. Now she wasn't waiting for Nils to call, she couldn't get out of the flat quick enough. She didn't want to encounter the police if she could help it. Apart from folding the bed back into a couch, washing up and closing her suitcase there wasn't much else to tidy. Maureen surveyed the flat one more time to ensure it looked presentable if Sarah suddenly returned, then gathered her coat and bag and headed up to Netta.

Wriggling and crawling had become difficult as she wasn't as flexible with her pregnant stomach. She knocked on the underside of the table letting Netta know she was there before hauling herself to her feet. Soon her stomach might be too big to fit between the cupboards and crawl under the table. Netta was already up and dressed. She eyed Maureen as she stoked the embers.

"Merry Christmas, sleep well?"

"Merry Christmas, Netta." It didn't seem like Christmas as she stood with her arms hugged around herself in the chill. Her Christmas was sunshine and beach. "I did sleep. I thought I wouldn't after Nils' visit." Maureen sat on her appointed couch.

"Now you aren't playing the waiting wondering game and know where you stand you can move on and make some plans."

"My father has had a stroke. He's in a coma."

Netta's brow furrowed. The poor girl had a lot of worries. "How unfortunate."

"My parents are divorced, and he lives on a farm on his own. If I wasn't pregnant, I'd go back."

"You should have kept the wallet."

Maureen shook her head. Her father would have another stroke if he saw her like this. "I can't think about it right now. If anything happens Mum will send me a telegram. I thought I'd ask you to take me to get those maternity clothes today but I forgot it was Christmas Day." She lifted her jumper. "Look, my trousers won't do up and I can't wear my bras."

"You'll get a lot bigger than that," Netta said, looking at Maureen through the small mirror hanging from a nail on the side of the kitchen cabinet where she was brushing her hair and adjusting a Russian style fur hat. Dressed in her padded coat, scarf and fur-lined gloves, Netta collected her carpet bag. "You look alright. We are going to have Christmas lunch at the restaurant. The shop can wait another day."

The restaurant was decorated with gnomes and Santas. Candles in the middle of Christmas wreaths and apples lined the centre of three tables that Bernard had pushed together for the staff celebration. The waitress handed Maureen a glass of mulled wine and kissed her cheek. The happy faces of the staff lifted Maureen's spirits. Everyone raised their glasses and shouted "*Skol!*" She raised her glass and forgot about Nils.

It was another two days before the government community shop opened. The shop was down a corridor inside a single storey brick building. The room had a counter that stretched from one end to the other. Behind it were rows of cardboard boxes on numbered shelves. People were lined up in front of the counter, taking turns to present their coupon.

When it was Netta's turn she called Maureen over, explaining in Swedish to the receiver of coupons what Maureen's requirements were and handed him the coupon. Three boxes were taken down. One contained underwear, the other two were elastic waist woollen trousers and A-frame corduroy tops with long sleeves. The tops came in beige, blue, navy, white and red. The trousers, brown or black.

Maureen took a handful of brassieres that had button up cups for breast feeding, red top and black trousers and headed for a curtained cubicle with a full-length mirror. It didn't matter what view she had of herself in the mirror, she looked huge. Depressed, she left the fitting room wearing a bra that made her breasts look like soufflés under a red tent, and black pants that gave her a big bum. Her pregnancy was hidden and accentuated in one go, but she was warm and comfortable and trying to feel grateful even though she looked like a whale.

A sing-song exchange in Swedish passed between the shop assistant and Netta.

"They are giving out coupons for boots next month," Netta explained. "Usually you only get one item at a time but because I haven't used my yearly issue, we are allowed all three items." She looked pleased with herself.

"It's very good of the government to give clothes to people who aren't Swedish. I don't think they would do that in Australia," Maureen said. Visiting the hospital and getting new clothes had been easy. She had expected interviews and lots of paperwork.

"It's because the father of your child is Swedish." The brightness went out of Maureen's face. "Cheer up," Netta said. "At least for the moment you are legal. I feel like playing the piano today so let's go to Bernard's, see what he thinks of your new clothes."

On the tram to the restaurant, a man offered Maureen his seat. "Your outfit has some benefits," Netta said, kindly. Maureen smiled her thanks to the man and sat down.

"You can show me where the English church is on Sunday if you want to?" Maureen wanted to let Netta know she was grateful for her help.

Netta smiled. "I'll draw you a map."

They arrived at the restaurant. The waitress looked at Maureen in surprise. "You are soon having baby?" She hadn't noticed how big Maureen was on Christmas day.

The new clothes were like wearing a billboard. Perhaps Maureen should have taken the beige tent instead of the red one?

Bernard clapped his hands together and walked around

Maureen. "Ma chérie, it is sizeable. Today I will give you healthy food. Potato cakes with fish roe and pickled beetroot makes strong babies."

Maureen tried to look eager but she didn't like fish. She enjoyed catching them off the wharf in Eden but not to eat. Her mother had insisted it was brain food and made her eat it for breakfast with a fried egg on top before school exams. What she craved was spaghetti bolognaise. She had never bothered with spaghetti much until now. There was a packet in Sarah's cupboard she had her eye on for tonight. She would cook enough to have some for breakfast as well. They finished their lunch as the first guests were arriving.

Netta and Maureen disappeared into Bernard's office where Netta changed into her wig and glasses. Maureen left the door ajar so she could see and hear Netta at the piano.

Two men entered, one she recognised as Herr Classon. She sucked in her breath. Unaware of who they were, Bernard was showing them to a table. She needed to tell Bernard but couldn't risk being seen. In the corner of the office Bernard's overcoat scarf and hat were hanging on a stand, his outside boots next to it. Maureen slipped into them. The coat was long, big in the shoulders but fitted around her middle. With the hat on her head, muffled in the scarf and boots on her feet, Maureen went into the dining room. Without glancing in Herr Classon's direction she crossed the room and entered the kitchen. Bernard bristled in after her. His hand grabbing her shoulder. She pulled the scarf down and pushed the hat back.

"Maureen, what is this?"

"Bernard, the two men you have just seated, the bald one with glasses is Herr Classon. I don't know the other man, maybe journalist or health inspector?"

Bernard's face went red. "I will send them out."

"No. Give them the best food and attention so they can't

complain. He may be here to see if I am working illegally. You could get one of the waitresses to stand near them and listen to their conversation?"

Bernard bounced on his toes; fists clenched. Then he called the waitress over and spoke to her in rapid Swedish. She looked from Bernard to Maureen and back to Bernard, eyes sparkling. Armed with a notebook and biro she hurried back to the dining room and busied around the tables near the men.

Herr Classon signalled her over. He removed a photo from his wallet and some coins. He put the coins in the waitress's hand and showed her the photo.

She looked towards the kitchen, slipped the money into her pocket, examined the photo and shook her head. She turned back to the table she was clearing and stacked her tray with dishes.

"This is my fault Bernard, if you hadn't helped me, they wouldn't be here. I'm so sorry." Maureen's eyes filled with tears. She was causing trouble for everybody. His hand flicked her words away.

"He is bastard, Maureen. We fix!" Bernard's eyes hardened in his pudding face. Maureen suddenly thought of Netta's husband and hoped Bernard wasn't going to send Herr Classon off with a poisoned apple! She was glad Netta was wearing her wig.

"I need my coat, hat and boots from your office, Bernard." He vanished through the door while Maureen removed his clothes, hanging them over a chair in the corner of the kitchen. The waitress returned with the tray of dirty dishes. She gave Maureen a nervous look and put the tray near the sink. Bernard returned with Maureen's clothes and the waitress joined them. Her eyes were fixed on Maureen while she spoke to Bernard.

"Herr Classon asked if you work in the kitchen. He showed a picture of you. I told him, no. I said for a small while you did work but you leave, and I have not seen you since."

Maureen grabbed the waitress's hand in both of hers. "Thank you."

The waitress gave a shy smile and put her hand in her apron pocket and showed them the coins. "He give money," she laughed.

"It is good you get money from the merde bastard. Now we must go and work," said Bernard, giving Maureen's back a pat. "Chérie, you do not worry anymore." He pointed the waitress towards the dining room and rushed off after her.

Maureen pulled her beanie down as far as she could without impairing her vision, shrugged into her coat and boots and stepped outside into the chill, anxiety surging. Nil's father had spoiled her visits to the restaurant. She asked herself why his father was still trying to make trouble for her? Didn't he know he had won and Nils had left her or did he fear Nils would change his mind and come back after the baby was born? Would he take the photo to the police or newspapers?

17

Eden – More Trouble

Lillian brought the newspaper with the advertisement for the farm to show Eric. It had been running for a few days with no responses. Farm deals were usually a shake of the hand in a pub. She entered his ward and pulled back the curtain around his bed. He was seated on the bedpan.

"Mum!" His smile was childlike.

"I'm not your mother, Eric." The last person she wanted to be associated with was Eric's long dead mother.

"I think he calls you that because your children do. Stroke patients often use the wrong word," the nurse said. She whipped away the bedpan from under Eric, turned him on his side, parted his bum cheeks and gave him a wipe. The smell and the act revolted Lillian, mostly because she feared it may end up being her job. Wiping Eric's arse was all she needed after years of servitude and struggle to control her own life.

The doctor came in and leafed through the file hanging on the end of Eric's bed. "Making good progress." He smiled at Lillian. "You'll have him home in no time."

Lillian gnawed her lip and frowned.

The doctor looked ruffled. "You don't seem very enthusiastic, Mrs McKinley?"

The doctor was an imbecile if he thought she was eager to look after a man on a bedpan. "We are divorced."

The doctor's head wobbled like a pointing finger. "One never knows when the shoe could be on the other foot, Mrs McKinley." He put the file back and went to the next bed. Enamel flaked off Lillian's teeth.

A tidied, evacuated Eric sat up and grinned at her from one side of his face. Lillian opened the newspaper she had brought and put it on the bed in front of Eric. His eyes crossed trying to focus where her finger indicated.

"It's an advertisement for the farm. I've put it up for sale." She took a deep breath and sat back the way she had always done when having to approach him with a problem. His eyes blanked. "You won't be able to run a farm now you've had a stroke, Eric." His interest wandered to the patient opposite. Lillian gave up, folding the newspaper and putting it back in her handbag. Johnny appeared at her side.

"G'day, Mum. How's Dad doing?"

"Still not comprehending anything. I've just shown him the advertisement to sell the farm, but it hasn't sunk in."

Johnny tapped his father's knee. "Hello, Dad, it's me."

Eric turned his attention towards Johnny. The lines between his eyebrows became gullies of concentration. His teeth foraged his lower lip then his face brightened, and he waved the sheets. "Poo!"

Lillian touched Johnny's hand. "They said it would take time." How was she going to manage Eric?

"Quick Parker was down the wharf this morning. He said Kathy had telephoned to speak to the kids. She's in Bateman's Bay. Might be worth paying Constable PJ a visit?" Johnny said.

Lillian rubbed her forehead; she was feeling the strain of the past few weeks. "I'm not walking up to the police station for everyone in Eden to see me and know my business."

"I came here in the Buick. We could drive there together after we leave Dad?" Johnny had better not get too attached to the car, Lillian thought.

PJ was rocked back in a chair, feet on the verandah rail, a newspaper on his lap opened at Lillian's advertisement. He came up straight.

"Mrs … Lillian." He nodded to Johnny, "Johnny, how you going mate?"

"Yeah, alright PJ," Johnny replied.

"Well, better come in then." His day had suddenly gotten interesting. The constable went behind his desk and motioned Lillian and Johnny to sit. Lillian sat with her handbag on her knee. Johnny slouched forward.

"What can I do for you?" The young constable looked from one to the other. Lillian nodded to Johnny.

"Quick told me he had a telephone call from Kathy and she's in Bateman's Bay. I thought I'd let you know so the police could interview her about the whereabouts of Dad's money?"

Constable PJ wrote the information on a notepad. "I'll contact the Bateman's Bay Police." He stared at the note pad, tapping his pen then looked up at Lillian. "I saw your advertisement for the farm sale, Lillian. However, I'm told it was sold about the time Eric had his stroke?" The cry of seagulls filled the silence. Lillian and Johnny stared at each other like stunned mullets.

"That can't be. Eric would never sell the farm, he loved it. Where's the money then?" Lillian demanded.

"That thief nicked off with it!" Johnny yelled.

142

"Hold your horses, Johnny. You can't accuse without proof. You might try asking your old man first," PJ said, dropping his formal manner.

"He wouldn't know what you were talking about if you hit him with a dead dingo's donger," roared Johnny.

"Easy there, mate, I heard it in the pub. Word's out that House bought it."

"House? What would he do with it? He wouldn't fit through the front door!" Johnny's eyes beseeched Lillian. "Mum, tell him it's not possible?"

Lillian's mind was racing. She was an avid crime reader. A thought struck her.

"Eric seemed very sluggish before the stroke. Couldn't seem to keep his mind on things." She remembered the episode with his washing, giving her five dollars and not remembering the change. "The pills! PJ, remember we told you about the Valium pills Kathy had taken from the hospital and was giving Eric? What if he had been under the influence of those when he sold the farm? Wouldn't that mean it was against his will? Fraud, or something?"

The constable pinched his bottom lip between a thumb and forefinger. "If Eric wasn't in his right mind, we'd need a witness to the fact. I'll see what I can find out."

Lillian and Johnny left the police station in a daze.

"I'll take a drive out to the farm, tomorrow," Johnny said. He would clean up his Dad's stuff and pack it away. Make the bed, do the dishes. Make it look like someone lived there and looked after the place. Buy a proper lock for the door. "Maybe you should live in it for a while, Mum?"

"I've had enough of farms in my lifetime. You live in it!" Lillian snapped.

"I've got a job!"

"Well, I can't drive." Thank God, she thought. It put an end

143

to their conversation. They glowered in silence back to Lillian's house.

"Coming in?"

"No, I'm going fishing." He waited for his mother to get out of the Buick and jammed his foot on the accelerator, roaring off up the street.

Lillian watched him go. At least one member of her family had gotten something out of Eric's mess although for how long he'd enjoy it she wasn't sure. Biddy ran up, tail wagging.

"Hello girl. Bloody men," she said. She went inside and began preparing tea for her boarder. Lamb chops, mash, pumpkin and peas, rice pudding for dessert, she wasn't in the mood to cook anything fancy. Halfway through peeling the potatoes the phone rang. Lillian turned the tap off, put down the peeler and dried her hands. When she picked up the phone she heard the click that said the telephonist was on the line.

"Hello?" She always sounded nervous on the phone. Didn't quite know what to say, preferred seeing people's expressions when she spoke to them.

"Mrs McKinley, it's Frederick van Someren here."

Lillian squeezed her eyebrows together. "Who?"

"House." There was a sigh in the voice at the end of the phone.

"Oh! Yes?" She felt a tremor in her stomach and wished Johnny hadn't left.

"I saw the advertisement for the farm in the paper. Did you know Eric sold the farm to me a couple of months ago? I haven't been out there yet, but I paid eleven thousand dollars for that place."

The telephone became slippery in her hand. Lillian closed her eyes and counted to ten in an attempt to quell her nerves. She imagined the ghost of Eric's eagle-eyed Aunt Maggie peering at her, telling her, 'keep your backbone girl.' Palpitations.

"I find that hard to believe, Mr van Someren. As you probably know, Eric's had a stroke and he's in hospital. He never mentioned selling the farm to me and I doubt he would have sold it, he loved the place."

"I'm not in the habit of preying on the unfortunate, Mrs McKinley. You can come by the club and I'll show you the documents," he wheezed. House was a large man, loved his fish and chips, and he was a director of the Fisherman's Club. Not a man to be messed with.

"I'll do that Mr van Someren, after I've visited poor Eric." Poor Eric, that was a good one, he couldn't be poorer! Lillian's hand shook as she put the phone down. She hadn't even said goodbye. When Splinter was home from work, she'd phone her.

The oven door shut on the rice pudding and Lillian sat down to stare out of the kitchen window. It was a classic spring day, sapphire sea and cloudless sky. Waves slapped against rocks and the seagulls cawed, but her thoughts were not on the day and the view, she might need a lawyer again. But where would she get the money to pay him? Dare she ask Peter Turnstile to put it on account until she sold the Buick? How obligated would that make her? She had made an excuse not to go to dinner with him when he set up her power of attorney. There was too much to deal with. She got up and went into the lounge, to the decanter on the sideboard she had inherited from Aunt Maggie and poured herself a stiff brandy, then put her feet up on Aunt Maggie's chaise longue and rested her busy brain on the burn of the brandy.

18

Farewell

Maureen's mind was in a turmoil. Although outwardly she tried to look pleased at Netta's news, she felt sad and afraid. It was only a few weeks that she had lived with Netta, yet it seemed like they'd been together months. What was she going to do without her?

"I was lucky the place came up. If Bernard hadn't been diligent, I might have missed out." The splat from a pigeon landed on the book in Netta's hand. "Well, the decision's made on this one," she put the book in her discard heap. "Bernard managed to procure a list of the musicians who live in the home. Some I know from the orchestra." Netta had never sounded so excited.

"That's beaut." Maureen tried to sound enthusiastic. Netta's squint told her she hadn't succeeded.

"You can still use this place if you need to. Although if

anything goes wrong," she wagged a finger, "early labour for instance, you wouldn't want to be trapped up here."

A skipped heartbeat. Maureen didn't want to think about anything going wrong.

"Stop putting off attending the church and introduce yourself to the pastor and his wife, John and Molly." Netta's busy hands went still. "You may need them as character references if you are interviewed by the police."

There was a squabble in the rafters and Maureen looked up. The pigeons had been her only companions while Netta was in hospital. Her hours had been filled watching them. No, she wasn't going to give in to that lost feeling in her gut. She would knit and listen to the radio, write to her aunt in Melbourne, go to the library.

"If Herr Classon had gone to the police, I think they would have come by now," Maureen said, trying to feel positive.

"They wouldn't just call without doing an investigation first," Netta replied. Then seeing Maureen's look of concern, quickly added, "but if they do, remember you were in a panic at the time it happened. It's important you emphasise that. However, as the fellow didn't die, I doubt they could charge you with anything."

"I'd rather not think about the police right now," Maureen said, annoyed she'd mentioned them.

"Sorry, it was meant as encouragement." Netta surveyed the boxes she had packed with books and photographs. "Bernard will collect this lot and send it later." She closed her suitcase and locked it with a small key that hung on a chain around her neck. There was a scraping noise coming from the other side of their furniture wall. Netta put her finger to her lips. Someone was in the roof.

A bottle rolled across the floor. Netta leant towards Maureen and whispered, "It's the vagrant. He's been here before, sleeps on the old mattress near the entry. I don't know if he's aware of me

147

or not. The smell of the fire must make him wonder, although he's never bothered me."

Maureen's hand went to her mouth. She didn't want to share the roof with a man if Sarah came back. "How are you going to get your luggage past him without him trying to find out where we came from? If he finds out he might move in and I won't be able to come up here anymore." They sat and ponded their dilemma. Feet scuffed across the floor, stopped and a stream of liquid splashed against a wall.

"He's peeing! The dirty bugger." Maureen looked at Netta, appalled. The wind moaned through the loft. The intruder shuffled back and dropped onto the mattress making the floorboards creak. Fifteen minutes passed in silence.

"I think he's asleep." Netta said. "I gave the taxi driver Sarah's address, so I'll have to take my cases down there." She eyed her luggage, "It's going to be a problem doing it silently. Although everyone has left for work so it should be alright once we're out of here."

Maureen picked up the larger suitcase and violin while Netta collected the smaller one and her overflowing carpetbag. They crawled under the table pushing the cases ahead of them, stopping to listen if they'd been detected. Once on the other side they eased their way past the sleeping form on the mattress. Maureen peered at him. He was thin, about her height. It was hard to tell his age under the beanie and beard. He looked vulnerable and not too scary. She could probably handle him if he attacked her.

She thought about the street people, the vagrants. She'd never feel about them the way she used to. All she felt for Netta was respect. Who would have thought a squatter in a roof could be a famous musician? Perhaps the drunk on the mattress had a sad background or didn't have a work permit like her? Wasn't she homeless, a beggar, living off Bernard's meals and sleeping in a roof? Netta's luck had changed, maybe hers could too?

They stacked Netta's things by Sarah's door to wait for the taxi that would take her to the ferry and England. "We've got time for coffee" Maureen suggested, not wanting Netta to leave. Netta nodded. She put the coffee pot on the stove to percolate. They didn't speak as she set out the cups and poured the coffee. She handed a cup to Netta.

"It's your stuff on the landing this time and me giving you coffee," she laughed. "I will never know how to thank you for rescuing me, Netta." A sob caught in her throat. "My family don't seem to care. I'm going to miss you."

Netta patted her arm. "Everything has a time, child. I'm grateful to you too. Through your dilemma, I got to live again. We'll keep in touch via Bernard. Best not to have contact addresses until the police thing is over with." They finished their coffee to a rap on the door. Netta stood up. "That will be the taxi."

The air was still. Icicles dripped from windows as Maureen stood on the street with her arms hugging against the cold. She gave one final wave as Netta closed the taxi door. What now? Maureen swallowed the lump in her throat and exhaled, watching her breath frost in the air. If only …? She squeezed her eyes tight to block out her thoughts. Go to the library, sit there in the warm and read. Don't think.

Back in Sarah's flat, Maureen rifled through her clothes looking for something different to wear, a bit glamorous. She needed to feel good, but nothing fitted. She flung the tent and elastic waisted slacks back on, then her coat.

It was a long walk to the library. Maureen was conscious of the baby moving inside her. When it was born, she would write to Nils and let him know he'd had a son or a daughter. Perhaps if he saw the baby, he would regret dumping them? A woman came towards her wheeling a pram. She'd need one of those. She would need a lot of things.

The warmth of the library lifted her spirits. She hung her coat on a peg in the cloakroom and found a table and chair where she put her bag to reserve the seat while she perused the shelves. At the desk the librarian smiled. Her pink cheeks and blonde plaits made Maureen think of chalets with fireplaces and snow-covered fir trees.

"Have you got any books in English?"

"Ja, plenty. I take you." Halfway down an aisle of books, the librarian swept her hand towards the end. "It is all from here."

Maureen found a biography of Lenin; it was thick and nothing that connected with her life and worries. She settled herself at the desk she'd reserved and read until the hunger pangs started. Gathering her bag and the book she went over to the librarian's desk and waited while she finished with a customer. The librarian smiled up at her. "Yes?"

"I'd like to borrow this book." Maureen put the tome on the counter.

"Library card?" Maureen shook her head. "Student card?" The librarian put her hand out. Maureen handed her, her passport, face flushed. The girl looked at it, uncertain.

"You will wait. I must speak with bibliotek supervisor." She took Maureen's passport and disappeared down a row of books. Five minutes later she returned with another woman in her mid-fifties and wearing a badge. "This is supervisor."

The supervisor held out her hand and Maureen shook it. "You are not a Swedish citizen or international student, therefore we cannot let you take books from our library." The supervisor handed back Maureen's passport. "I am sorry." Her eyes went to Maureen's voluminous maternity top and to her right hand with the single gold band engagement ring. She said something to the young librarian. Maureen looked away. "We will put your book under counter and keep for you to read in our library."

Maureen looked up. There was acceptance in the supervisor's eyes. She drew in a wonky breath. "That's kind of you. Tusen Tuk." Her thank you in Swedish brought two big smiles.

On the way home she collected a cardboard box from the restaurant. Inside was a thermos of soup, a bread roll, a letter from Australia and a small parcel with a Gothenburg post mark. There was no return address. She'd open it at home.

Back in the flat she flung her coat on a chair and pulled the letter and parcel from the box. Then curled up on the couch bed and opened the parcel. Inside was a bundle of letters, all addressed to her, care of Nils' parents. All were in her mother's handwriting. They were dated from the time she'd moved in with Nils. There was a note inside in Nils' handwriting. *I am sorry, Maureen, my mother was keeping these. Please pardon her. Love Nils.* Six letters. All that time she had thought she'd been shunned by her mother. She felt a sob coming, wracking her. She put her arms around her stomach and rocked forward, winded.

It was the cruellest thing his mother had done to her. And Nils. How could he expect her to forgive his mother? Flurries of snow hit the window and dripped down the glass. The best thing for her was to be as far away from his family as possible. She put the bundle of letters to one side for later and opened the latest one.

It began with the good news that her father was improving although the problem with his bank account was concerning. "Bloody hell!" she exclaimed, reading about his involvement with Kathy. Her poor mum having to deal with that. Her sympathy for her mother got lost in the rest of the letter that was full of her mother's advice. The story of her mother's abortion and how it had affected her at the time. The suggestion for her to be sensible and have her baby adopted. How she wished Netta was here to talk it over with, although she knew Netta would side with her mother. If only there was someone her own age to talk to, like Nils' friends, but they had abandoned her. It was understandable, they were his yacht crew, and Herr Classon was one of their university lecturers. Heavy-footed she went into the kitchenette to pour a bowl of soup from the thermos flask and eat a bread roll. Tomorrow was Sunday and she needed friends.

A painting of the Virgin Mary and child was the first thing Maureen noticed as she entered the church foyer. It was comforting. Welcome smiles tagged her as she passed the small groups of people gathered by the door. Not wanting to draw attention to herself, Maureen slid into the empty pew at the back of the church and removed a hymn book from the holder in front of her. Church wasn't new to her. She'd been brought up a Presbyterian until she was fifteen, after that she had lived with her atheist aunt and uncle in Melbourne.

The church filled. A few latecomers slipped into the pew beside her. The organist hit a mournful note and everyone stood. She knew the tune but had forgotten the words so hummed along. The minister was young, he wore glasses and reminded her of Hiram Holliday, a detective in a television series she used to watch in Melbourne. For an hour she forgot her loneliness.

When the service was over, Maureen allowed herself to be carried along with the parishioners to the hall adjoining the church. Inside, a table with an array of cakes and cups set out for tea and coffee beckoned. Taking a plate, she filled it with a slice of chocolate cake and a jam tart and accepted a cup of tea poured from the biggest teapot she'd ever seen. Around her everyone was speaking English. She felt at home.

"I haven't seen you here before?" A hand extended. "John Toy, I'm the rector." Her hands were full, she looked for a spot on the table where she could put her plate.

"Don't put your plate down, Mrs Svenson made that chocolate cake, and someone will take it." His eyes twinkled and his voice smiled.

"I'm Maureen. Pleased to meet you, Reverend."

"John. We're a small parish and all on first names. Where are you from?"

"Australia. I know Netta. She told me to come here and introduce myself."

"Netta? The organist?" His eyebrows went up. Maureen remembered she wasn't supposed to mention Netta.

"She lives in England. I met her on holiday, and she said if ever I was in Gothenburg to come here." Maureen looked away; she hated lying.

"We are pleased to have you. Come and meet my wife, Molly." He led her over to a group of women and touched the arm of a sweet faced, dark haired woman. "Molly, we have a newcomer, this is, Maureen. She's from Australia."

"Welcome, Maureen." Her eyes went to Maureen's stomach and she gazed over Maureen's shoulder. "Is your husband with you?"

Maureen swallowed and looked away. "No, I'm … not married," she stammered. Molly's arm went around her shoulders. "Who are you staying with?"

"A friend. She's away, though. Visiting her husband on an oil rig."

"Why don't you come back with us for dinner tonight? Of course, you'll have to excuse my unruly children." She pointed at a group of children chasing each other. "My two are amongst that lot," she laughed.

"I don't want to be a bother."

"Nonsense, John can drive you home afterwards. It's only lamb stew I'm afraid."

"My mother makes lamb stew. I love it."

"If you don't mind waiting until we clear everything up?"

"I can help," Maureen said. "I've worked in hotels." She felt happy as she wiped down tables and washed cups and saucers, listening to the laughter and English voices.

19

Sarah's Phone Call

A key turned in the lock. Maureen dropped the cardigan she was knitting for the baby and rose to her feet.

"Shit!" Sarah stepped back at the sight of Maureen and trod on her three-year old. He yelled, then caught sight of Maureen and rushed towards her, arms wide.

"You gave me such a fright. What are you doing here? How did you get in?" Sarah's face changed from 'happy-to-see-you' to 'what-a-cheek', then her eyes fell to Maureen's round stomach.

Maureen crouched down and gave the child a hug. "Hello Mikey, you are so big."

She looked up at Sarah, at her open mouth. "Can we have a coffee while I explain?"

Sarah nursed her coffee, now cold, as Maureen went through the drama of her past few weeks. Distant was the noise of her child pushing his truck across the floor.

"It wasn't Nils' fault," Maureen said, when she'd finished the saga.

"Don't you dare make excuses for that rat. I've got a good mind to phone his damn mother up and tell her what I think of her," Sarah said.

"Don't. They might have me deported."

"How? You said you had a welfare officer getting you a place to live? They wouldn't do that if there was a risk you'd be deported." She pointed to Maureen's stomach, "In there is Fru Classon's grandchild. You were engaged to her son. That's like being married."

Maureen thought hard. What Sarah was saying made sense and she would like someone to speak up for her. Bernard had tried, but because she was working for him without a permit, Herr Classon had something over him. He didn't have anything over anyone now.

"If you think so, although I don't want to cause trouble for Nils."

"What? I don't believe you. Look what he's done to you? High tailed it into the army to hide. Hasn't sent you any money yet he knows you haven't got any. They are bastards, Maureen! You should have gone to the police after his mother attacked you."

"Their word against mine, a pregnant slut. Who would the police believe?"

"Let me phone?"

"I'll think about it." She wanted to speak to his mother, but the language barrier had prevented her. Sarah spoke fluent Swedish. It was tempting, although at the back of her mind was always the threat of the hitchhiking incident. She wasn't in a good situation and being deported to Australia was Maureen's biggest fear. She couldn't face the disappointment of her family and it would be harder managing on her own as an unmarried mother in Australia. There was also the other thing. Maureen wanted Nils to see his baby and be sorry for what he had lost. Could Sarah's speaking to Nils' mother make things any worse or could it help? She rubbed her forehead; she'd inherited her mother's stress headaches.

"I forgot to tell you; Dad's had a stroke. He's in a coma in hospital."

"Gee, I'm really sorry. What's your mum going to do?"

"I'm waiting on the next letter. Do you know Nils' mother kept my letters from me? Nils posted them to me. That was the last time I heard from him."

"God, and you make excuses for him?" Sarah gave her a look that told her she was a moron. Maureen was filled with guilt. Sarah had just come back from holiday and here she was burdening her with all her dramas.

"I didn't mean to barge in on you like this. When Bengt comes back, I'll move back to the roof."

"You can't if there's a drunk up there."

"I can avoid him." She didn't feel as confident as she sounded. "There's a woman at the church who is a social worker. She's trying to get me into a home for unmarried mothers near the yacht club, but it could take a couple of weeks to process."

"I want to see where you've been staying with this Netta person," Sarah put her coffee cup on the table. "Come on Mikey, we're going up to the roof to Aunty Maureen's."

"I'm sorry for the trouble, Sarah. Truly. I just didn't know where else to go."

"Nils is a snake. He should be helping you."

The roof was like a refrigerator. The fire had been out for two weeks. Bottles and empty tins of food were strewn around the stained mattress. A sign the vagrant had made himself comfortable.

"God, almighty!" Sarah said, when a disturbed pigeon flew overhead. Mikey ran around the roof pretending he was an aeroplane.

"It's through there," Maureen pointed to the cupboards behind the mattress.

The passage between the cupboards seemed to have become narrower. Maureen squeezed through and then dropped to her knees, crawling with difficulty under the table. She pulled herself onto her feet with the help of a chair. It was getting too hard.

Sarah opened her mouth to say something, then closed it, shaking her head. "Unbelievable!" she said, when speech returned.

Maureen gazed around, seeing it through Sarah's eyes. Jumbled furniture, a forlorn stove, threadbare mat and two couches, now without bed covers which were showing their holes. Everything was covered in pigeon splatters. "It was better when Netta was here. We had the stove going and a lamp …" She saw the expression on Sarah's face and her voice trailed. Wind moaned through the roof, furniture creaked and shifted, pigeons squawked.

Sarah clucked her tongue. "The weak spineless mongrel, leaving you like this," Sarah said.

"I've managed. It was better before Netta left." Maureen chewed the inside of her cheek.

"Let's look at my storeroom," Sarah said. "Stay here while I get the key." Maureen struggled through the furniture and waited by the roof door until Sarah came back. Mikey zoomed past her; arms outstretched. Children could be happy anywhere, Maureen thought.

Sarah returned and led Maureen to a rough plank door. A heavy chain held together by a lock, threaded through a metal ring on the door and a metal ring on the doorpost. She undid the lock and swung the door open. "It only locks from the outside so I'd have to lock you in at night and unlock it in the morning." She stood back for Maureen's inspection.

The storeroom just fitted the single bed and two tea chests that occupied it. In the rafters above the bed was a cracked skylight A carton of ski wear and a pile of skis lay on the bed. Sarah stacked the carton on one of the boxes and leant the skis against the wall.

"You can put candles on the box. Keep your pee bucket here. I've got three spare blankets and there's a floor mat that's made of wool you can use on top of the mattress as an underblanket. You'd be safer here. You would only be in the room at night because you can spend the days with us." She stood back arms folded. Maureen had to admit it would be easier than crawling into Netta's space and safer.

"I'll stay up here tonight, see what it's like."

"Why? You can share my bed until Bengt comes back."

"I've been living up here for weeks so I may as well stay here." She didn't want Sarah to think she was her responsibility. "You won't have to feed me. I have lunch at the restaurant."

"What about breakfast and supper?"

"I don't eat breakfast and I keep my lunch bread roll for supper."

"Crikey Moses!" Sarah shook her head.

"Yeah. Stone the bloody crows." Maureen laughed, putting her arm around Sarah's shoulders. It was so good to have her Aussie mate back.

The first night in the storeroom Maureen went to bed in Bengt's long underwear, socks and an old jumper and still she shivered. Tomorrow, she would look for Netta's hot water bottle.

In the morning, Sarah unlocked the padlock and removed the

chain. Maureen posed in her husband's clothes one hand on her hip. Sarah laughed.

"Coming down for breakfast? I've made porridge."

"Yum! There's a service at the Church of England church today and I wondered if you and Mikey wanted to come with me? They're really nice and you could make more friends." Sarah looked pleased at the suggestion. She missed speaking English.

"Have you thought about me making the phone call?" Sarah said.

Maureen's chin went up, determined. "Yes, we'll do it."

"Good! We can phone from the newspaper shop after breakfast. Bring your clothes and get dressed downstairs in the warm."

Maureen collected her things and wrapped herself in a blanket following Sarah downstairs. The bowl of porridge was a warm hug in Maureen's stomach, and she savoured every mouthful. While they ate, they discussed what Sarah should say to Nils' mother.

"I want you to tell her I understand that she was shocked. What she did to me was a terrible thing but I will forgive her." Sarah opened her mouth to reply. Maureen put her hand up. "I don't want her hanging up on us before you've said all I want you to say. She must know I genuinely love Nils and wasn't after his money, that I didn't know anything about him when we met. Tell her I am keeping our baby." Sarah's mouth pruned but she nodded in agreement. Didn't anyone want her to keep her child?

"Is that all?" Sarah said. Maureen scraped her bowl and thought.

"Tell her I would have listened to Herr Classon if he hadn't been so nasty to me. That I'm not the bad person he thinks I am, and I am not a whore."

The newsagent showed them the phone and Sarah handed

him the kroner and spoke to him in Swedish. He nodded, moving away from the phone to give them privacy.

Maureen handed Sarah Herr Classon's phone number. "Here we go," Sarah said. Maureen wrapped her arms across her body and held tight.

"Fru Classon?" Sarah looked at Maureen and nodded, then introduced herself in Swedish. She had only just begun speaking but stopped, her mouth tightening. Then she continued, raising her voice slightly, "Fru Classon ..." then she listened, started again... mentioned Maureen's name, "... baby, police ..." Police? A moan escaped Maureen. Sarah was shaking her head in disbelief. Then she held the phone away from her ear so Maureen could hear the disconnected buzz on the other end. She put the phone in its cradle. The room tightened around Maureen. Sarah stared at Maureen.

"She's an evil old cow. You are better off away from them."

"What did you say to her?"

"Only what you told me to. But the woman kept shouting me down. Said you are a liar. Said she didn't attack you and ..."

Maureen was already numb. "And what?"

"They will get the police after you." Sarah put her arm around Maureen. "She's not right in the head. I had no idea how bad she was. I thought speaking to her would help. Now I've made it worse." Sarah looked miserable.

Nils' mother clawed at Maureen's chest like a rat on a cadaver. She hated her and there was nothing she could do to change it. Had her own mother hated her mother-in-law as much? A wriggle in her stomach sympathised, her hand went to her belly.

"It was worth trying. I wanted you to, so don't be upset. It's not your fault. She's nuts, like you said." They needed cheering up. Maureen looped her arm through Sarah's. "Let's have afternoon tea at the vicarage, the sponge cake is delicious."

161

The phone call had flattened Maureen and she had to force herself to smile as she introduced Sarah to the church women. She stood back feeling disconnected from the people around her and let Sarah do the talking. There was a light tap on her shoulder and a gentle tug on her arm. The Reverend drew her aside.

"There's someone I want you to meet. This is Paavo Kihlbom, I hope you don't mind but I've spoken to him about your predicament. He's a lawyer." The lawyer dipped over her hand. Maureen bobbed her head in return. Swedes were so formal.

"How do you do," she said, uncertain what was expected of her.

"Very well, thank you." Herr Kihlbom was tall. His face was tanned from skiing, except around his eyes where his ski goggles had been. He reminded Maureen of a koala.

"John has told me of your circumstances, and I may be able to assist you with information. Of course, this is not the place for such talks. I hope you will have supper with my wife, Penny, and I next Sunday, if you are not busy?"

The invitation came as a surprise. Last week she had eaten at the Reverend's house and felt relaxed in their company, but this man's formality made her feel awkward.

"A taxi can pick you up and it will be my pleasure to take you home." He put his hands in his pockets waiting for her reply. Heat came into Maureen's cheeks, she tried to think of an excuse, but nothing came to mind. She looked to the Reverend for direction. He gave a small nod. He had arranged it.

"I would love to come for supper, thank you."

"Good. I will tell my wife. Penny is English." He laughed. "That is why my English is so good." Maureen tried to think of something to say. What had the Reverend told him about her? She looked for an excuse to leave.

"I must get back to my friend, she's new here and doesn't know anyone." She pointed to Sarah who was chatting and laughing and making a lie of her excuse. The lawyer gave her a soft look.

"Of course. It was nice to meet you." He bowed over her hand. Maureen bobbed her head respectfully, smiled her thanks to the Reverend and headed towards Sarah, conscious of her pregnant waddle and the two men behind her.

She nudged Sarah to get her attention and gave her sheep-dog eyes. "Do you mind if we leave?" Sarah was onto her.

"Yep. I was just thinking it's time to get Mikey home." They said their goodbyes and moved away from the women. "What's up?"

"I'll tell you on the way home." They sat together in the tram and Maureen briefed Sarah on the lawyer.

"But that's good! He might come in handy if Nils' father goes to the police."

"I don't want to tell him everything. He's expecting to talk about the welfare system."

"You need protection from those people."

Maureen gazed at the reflections in the tram window. It seemed impossible to believe that Nils' family would harm her. Their rejection ripped at her heart. Her mother had met that same rejection in Australia from her mother-in-law. How far the apple falls, she thought. "I wish I could just live in the roof and hide like Netta did."

"Well you can't, you're going to have a baby."

"I know." Maureen sighed.

20

The Good Samaritans

The snow sparkled under the city lights as Maureen got out of the taxi. Herr Kihlbom lived in the best part of town. His apartment, on the top floor of a two-storey block, curled under the eaves of a red-tiled, pitched roof. Two large bay windows overlooked a tree-lined street and a park. The door opened the instant she knocked, and the lawyer and his wife welcomed her with smiles, ushering her in.

"Welcome to our home. I'm Penny. It's lovely to meet you, Maureen." She was tall and elegant, her dark hair swept up in a ponytail. Maureen guessed she was in her thirties. "Paavo has told me all about you." Maureen lowered her eyes. "I haven't been to church because of this." Penny put out a leg covered in plaster. "Skiing accident," she laughed. Her eyes were the colour of cornflowers and crinkled when she smiled, and like her husband Paavo, she had the same white rings from ski goggles.

Penny helped Maureen out of her coat and hung it on a coat rack by the entrance. The house was warm. "This is the powder room if you are in need." Penny pointed to a blue door opposite the coat rack and raised her eyebrows.

"I'm alright, thanks." Maureen followed her hosts along a thickly carpeted hall into the sitting room. An antelope head looked down from the wall. The room smelled of leather and a fire crackled in a brick fireplace. Books lined one wall. Sculptures of animals sat on carved tables. It was a wealthy home.

"I've been looking forward to your visit. I do love having English company." Penny sounded like the Queen.

"I'm Australian," Maureen said.

"It's not too different if the language is the same. Where did your forebears come from?"

Maureen hesitated, unsure of what she meant. She was Australian. What did her heritage have to do with anything? "My dad's family came from Ireland and my mother was half English, half French. You're English, aren't you?"

"Pure English, a bit boring, I know."

Maureen nodded without thinking.

"I'm going to serve dinner early so the children can go to bed and you and Paavo can talk. I hope you don't mind?"

"No, I didn't eat lunch today." The supper invitation had worried her appetite away. "Would you care for a drink before we eat?" Paavo asked, holding up a bottle of wine.

"No thank you. I'll just have water with my meal."

Leaving Penny to her food preparations, Paavo led Maureen into the television room. Identical twin girls gave her shy smiles.

"This is Lotta, and this is Anna. Say hello to Maureen, girls."

The children giggled. "Hello, Maureen," they said in unison. The girls looked like their mother and were around eight years old, a similar age to the twins Maureen had looked after. "Can we finish watching Heidi, Daddy?"

"Of course, and you can have your supper in here while I speak to Maureen."

Penny was serving up slices of blood pudding with lingonberry jam, red cabbage and mashed potatoes when they returned to the kitchen. She handed two plates to Paavo. "Tell the children not to drop their food on the furniture, darling."

"Can I help with anything?"

"You can take a plate and serve yourself. It's a free-for-all on Sunday nights. Cook's day off."

Maureen put one slice of blood pudding onto her plate. It wasn't her favourite.

"Take more, Maureen, you're feeding two."

Wanting to show Penny her gratitude she added another slice and helped herself to vegetables. She hovered, waiting for Penny, feeling awkward.

"Follow me." Penny carried two plates into the small dining room where a table was set for three. "Please sit." She motioned Maureen towards a chair. Paavo returned and took his place at the table. Maureen picked up her knife and fork and waited for Penny to start eating. Penny reached across the table for Maureen's hand.

"We will say grace," she said, a tease in her smile. Embarrassed, Maureen put her cutlery down and took their hands. Heads bowed.

"Thank you for the food before us and bless our guest, Maureen. Thank you, Lord. Amen. Now while we eat, you must tell us about Australia," Penny said, filling her mouth with food.

Talking about Australia kept Maureen's mind off the blood pudding which she managed to swallow without tasting. When the meal was finished, they moved to the sitting room and Penny brought in a tray with coffee and Danish pastries. Maureen salivated.

"I'm going to leave the two of you to talk," she said, going off

166

to join the children. Maureen sat on the edge of the couch with her feet together, conscious of the silence and Paavo's gaze.

"We've asked you here because I would like you to tell me about your situation," Paavo said.

Maureen lost her appetite for the Danish pastry. Hadn't the Reverend said he'd told them about her?

"For instance, if you are going to keep the baby, you will need the father to pay maintenance."

That caught Maureen by surprise, she had never heard of child maintenance. "But we are not married, and he doesn't want the baby."

The lawyer lowered his head and peered at her from under his brows. "Under Swedish law the father has to help maintain his child, married or not. Have you thought about what you're going to do after the baby is born?"

"I have a cousin I can contact in England. We haven't met yet but she might help." Paavo looked surprised. "Why would you not return to Australia?"

"I don't want to embarrass my family."

He looked thoughtful. "In that case, if you live in England you can receive monthly payments from Sweden. However, if you moved to Australia there's no agreement between our countries so child support could not be relied upon. I don't think you have made a choice where you will live yet, so I suggest you ask for a lump sum. The amount you get will be judged on Nils' income. If he is a student that won't be much."

"I don't want any money from him, I just want him to send back the fifty dollars he was looking after for me."

Paavo tapped the ends of his fingers together. "It's something for you to think about, Maureen. Of course, we cannot approach Nils until after the baby is born. I will represent you pro bono when you decide." Maureen frowned. "Pro bono means free of charge. I take a couple of charity cases a year."

It was kind of him to want to help her. She hadn't given any thought to Nils paying maintenance. A headache started; she rubbed her forehead. She wanted to get away from the sympathetic eyes and questions and wondered if it would be impolite to leave so soon after dinner. She knew it would be either leave or embarrass herself and end up spewing.

"I'm sorry, Herr Kihlbom but I'm not feeling very well, would you mind if I went home now?"

He jumped to his feet. "Of course not." He called his wife.

"I'm sorry to leave so soon, Penny, but I have a really bad headache."

"You must take an aspro before you go, they always help me." She fetched a glass of water and a bottle of aspros. "Take the bottle with you I have more."

"Thank you." She felt bad running off when they had been so nice. "It's really kind of you to want to try and help me. I'm truly grateful for your advice Herr Kihlbom." She put her hand to her head, the pain was really kicking in. "The headaches just happen suddenly, sometimes they make me sick. My mother used to get migraines. I am sorry."

They didn't speak much on the way to Sarah's. Paavo parked outside the block of flats.

"Wait while I get your door," he said, eyeing the drunks loitering in Maureen's entrance. He walked around the Mercedes, opened her door and helped her out. "I will walk you inside."

He's a nice man, she thought. A lot of people had been kind to her; she shouldn't judge all the Swedish people on Nils' family. Perhaps she should tell Paavo about the staircase attack? See if he thinks she should go to the police. What did she have to lose? The headache lessened after leaving him. She lifted her hand and knocked on Sarah's door. The door whipped open. Sarah looked agitated.

"What's up?" Maureen asked.

She went over to the kitchen table where she had been playing a game of solitaire and picked up a newspaper. "Take a look at that."

Maureen stared at the Swedish newspaper, uncomprehending, and then gasped at the photo. It was her, posing with the Finnish truck driver who had picked them up after the kidnap attempt. Jane had taken the photo with her camera. How did the newspaper get the photo? Then she remembered. It had been in Nils' bedside table. Surely he wouldn't have given it to the press! No, it had to be his father. She remembered having written the date on the back of the photo. An avalanche rumbled in Maureen's head. Eyes fixed on Sarah; she handed the newspaper back.

"What does it say?"

Sarah began reading the article.

In 1965, two English girl hitchhikers left a man stranded in the snow in his car after hiding his keys. Was it an act of heartlessness or survival? The stranded man was Tristen Aaberg, recently arrested as a suspect for the vicious rape of Tove Persson. Twenty-one-year-old Tove Persson, had accepted a lift from Aaberg when her car broke down outside Gothenburg, the same place he was reported to have picked up the English hitchhikers two years earlier. The police want to interview the English girls.

Maureen dropped into the chair. "Shit! What am I going to do?"

"You might need your lawyer."

21

Eden – Eric's Outing.

After speaking to her lawyer, Peter Turnstile, Lillian put the phone down. He had been happy to agree to her paying off his bill. They would discuss her case over lunch. She felt bad for House, he had bought the farm in good faith, but Eric's signature on the deed of sale looked like a drunken scrawl next to his normal precise script. Eric had always prided himself on his good handwriting. Also, the witness to the sale was Kathy Parker. Lillian had a good case.

Lunch with the lawyer was at the Grand Hotel in Bega. It wasn't far from the hospital so Lillian had time to do some shopping in the co-op store before meeting Peter. Fortunately, she didn't meet anyone from Eden. It was the wrong day of the week for the Eden shoppers, as they preferred to shop on Fridays. She had arranged the meeting for Monday, the day most women did their washing. Lillian hadn't washed on Mondays since Aunt

Maggie's death and the divorce; she had changed her life as much as she could.

Under the table, Lillian felt the pressure of Peter's foot on hers. She stiffened, tucking her foot under her chair. "How's your wife, Peter?"

"She's in Sydney with my daughter," he grinned, withdrawing his foot. The light caught his glasses and flashed. Lillian lost her appetite for the plate of liver and bacon with mashed potato, usually one of her favourites, and rested her knife and fork. She picked up her handbag and removed a copy of the Deed of Sale to Eric's farm and put it on the table.

"This looks like it's either been signed under duress or is a poor copy of Eric's signature. I want you to prove that the sale of Eric's farm to Frederick van Someren is illegal. The Deed was signed in front of a Justice of Peace."

The local Justice of Peace was the chemist, someone Lillian had never heard of. "You can check Eric's signature against our divorce papers. I'd like you to write to Kathy Parker on Eric's behalf telling her of your findings and say he will ask the police to prosecute. She might try and blame House which will be our proof and the sale can be cancelled." Lillian attended to her plate of food, enjoying her Power of Attorney. Peter's look of respect made her glow with pride.

He scrutinised the signature and pursed his lips. "There's certainly something off here. I'll look into it." He tucked the deed in the breast pocket of his sports jacket. "Now, what would you like to drink?"

It was a hot day. Lillian would have liked a beer, but women didn't drink beer in public. "A shandy, please."

After lunch Peter gave Lillian a lift to the hospital. "Why don't you come and say hello to Eric since you'll be representing him?" Seeing Eric might make Peter more sympathetic to his cause.

He glanced at his watch. "I can give him ten minutes." It could earn him brownie points with Lillian.

When they entered Eric's ward, he was sitting in a wheelchair, head bowed, asleep.

Lillian touched Eric's hand. "Hello Eric." His head lifted and he gave her that puzzled expression he always did on first sight. "It takes him a moment to recognise people," she explained to Peter. "Eric, I've brought someone to see you. Remember Peter, our lawyer?" Hers actually, and Eric had wanted to kill him over their divorce settlement. Eric's eyes screwed up in thought.

"G'day, Eric." Peter put his hand out to shake. Eric stared at the hand then looked up at Peter with a lopsided grin.

Lillian turned to Peter Turnstile; she had an idea. "Peter, get him to sign his name on something and see if it looks the same as the signature on the deed." Peter took out a notebook and his pen and put it in Eric's lap. Eric picked the pen up in his left hand and made some jerky marks. "It won't work. I forgot his right side is paralysed and he's right-handed."

"Poor bugger." Peter felt a quiet fury that someone would take advantage of an incapacitated man. He would ask Lillian to lunch again after he had done some sleuthing to prove the sale was illegal. They could have it at his place rather than the hotel. He felt a stirring in his trousers at the thought. "I'd best be off. Hope you make a quick recovery, sport." Peter saluted Eric and focused on Lillian. "I'll let you know when I find out what's going on."

"It's very kind of you and thank you for the lunch, Peter."

A nurse entered the ward as Peter left. "Would you like to take Eric for a walk in the garden, Mrs McKinley?"

"Of course. Yes."

Sitting in the garden was much nicer than the ward. Lillian got behind the wheelchair and pushed. It wasn't easy to steer, and Eric was heavy. Getting him down the steps was a struggle. She was perspiring by the time they reached a bench where they could sit in the shade. A fountain recently opened by their local member of parliament was next to the bench. She whirled Eric around to face the fountain and sat down. Eric leant forward and vomited in the water. The swivel of the wheelchair had upset his balance. A nurse hurried over.

"He's been sick," Lillian said, wiping spew off the front of Eric's pyjamas.

The nurse took his pulse, smiled at Eric. "Just vertigo. A stroke often affects a patient's balance. He'll be right in a jiffy. I believe you'll be taking him home for weekends soon?"

Lillian looked up, startled. It was news to her. "No one's mentioned it to me."

"The doctor will speak to you when he does his rounds ..." she checked the watch pinned to the front of her uniform, "in about twenty minutes."

Weekend visits? How was she going to get him home, get him out of his chair into a bed? Get him on the lavatory? She lived on a hill with a dirt road. How would she manage to push him up the street? Lillian sat on the bench looking at Eric, his head back, face in the sun. She couldn't rely on Splinter or Johnny for help. They had their own lives. He shouldn't be her burden, yet she couldn't turn her back on him. Her body sagged.

The doctor motioned Lillian to a seat in front of his desk. "Eric is progressing well. We can trial him at home on Saturday to see how you go. Fetch him at nine in the morning and have him back here by five o'clock." He hadn't asked her; it was an order. "After that, all going well, he can go home for weekend visits until we have rehabilitated him enough for him to leave the hospital permanently."

"I don't drive." It was all Lillian could think of as a reply.

"He has a son?" The doctor gave her an indulgent smile.

"Yes, but he works on a trawler and he's often at sea."

"I'm sure you will find a volunteer." He pushed his chair back and gathered some papers.

She was speechless. That's it? Find a volunteer? Stunned, Lillian left his office. Bloody Eric, why did he have to have a stroke now when Maureen needed her?

The weekend came too quickly. Lillian hadn't thought about wheelchair access or lavatory requirements and Johnny was on his way to collect his father. She rushed around trying to organise the house.

With the help of two nurses, Johnny managed to get his father into the front passenger seat of the Buick. Eric's face shone with excitement. Johnny got in and started the car. "Whoopee," Eric shouted, his good arm out of the window banging the side of the passenger door as they left the hospital.

Everything inside the car caught Eric's attention. He wound the window up and down, opened and shut the glovebox then, bored with that, twisted in his seat and put his left hand on the steering wheel giving it a tug. The car veered; Johnny braked.

"Stop it! Dad, we'll have an accident," Eric giggled, switching on the headlights. "Dad!" The road was narrow. Johnny had to concentrate.

Eric wound the window down and put his head out, pulled it in. He did it a few more times. Sick of that he sat back and looked around the interior of the car and spied the handbrake. They were heading down Bellbird Hill doing seventy miles an hour, not fast for Johnny. Eric leant forward and pulled the handbrake. The car swung, wheels locking, tyres smoking.

"Jesus Christ!" Johnny punched his father with his left arm while he tried to keep control of the car now travelling sideways down the road. Eric let the brake go. Johnny fought the car to keep it on the road. When they screeched to a stop, they were facing back the way they had come from. "You, idiot! You could have killed us. I'm not fetching you from the hospital again, you can bloody rot there." Johnny banged his head on the steering wheel in fury, armpits wet, hands shaking. He got out of the car and tried to light a cigarette burning his finger. "Fuck!" His father chuckled in the passenger seat.

"Right old man, you asked for it." He removed the car keys, went to the boot of the car and grabbed the emergency tow rope. Pinioning his father's arms to his side, Johnny wound the rope around his father's torso and the seat, secured him and got into the driver's seat. Eric wriggled to free himself. A horrible smell filled the Buick. Johnny gagged and wound his window down. "You old bastard!"

"Never again, he nearly killed us." Johnny stamped around the kitchen, "and I think he's shit himself."

"No," Lillian wailed. "I've got the CWA ladies coming at two o'clock and he has to be ready."

There was the sound of a car revving next door. Johnny needed help with his Dad.

"Mum, can you fetch Tim next door to give us a hand getting him out of the car?"

Lillian ran for the neighbour, cursing Eric for side-tracking her from Maureen's problems. Bloody, Eric!

Johnny brought the wheelchair close to the car door. The neighbour leant in to lift Eric and pulled back hit by the whiff of Eric's backside.

"Sorry, mate, Dad's had an accident. You'll have to hold your breath." When they had him in his wheelchair. The neighbour stepped back, lifted his arm in farewell and hurried towards his house.

"I owe you a beer," Johnny yelled after him. He wheeled his father into the spare bedroom, tipped him onto the towels Lillian had spread over the bed and turned to go.

"We're not finished yet. I need you to help me undress him." Johnny looked like he was going to cry. "Pet, I can't do it by myself. You will have to keep an eye on him while I get soap and water." Lillian collected two buckets, one with hot water and the other empty for the soiled underpants. His dirty underpants weren't going in her prized washing machine.

When she returned with the hot water Johnny had a handkerchief tied over his nose.

Gagging and averting his eyes, he lifted his father up while Lillian pulled his underpants off. "Open your legs, Eric, I'm going to wash you." Like a lamb he spread his legs.

Johnny's eyes bugged. "Cripes! Look at the balls on him!"

"He has a hernia which he refuses to have seen to. He thinks they're manly," Lillian slapped a flannel around Eric's bum. "You can dry him off while I get rid of the poo." She shook the underpants out over the lavatory, dropped them into a bucket, poured a kettle of boiling water on them and added soap powder. She jabbed and stirred with her washing stick until they looked clean and without rinsing, flung them over the line to dry. He would have to go without underpants until they dried. All the rushing around had her heart racing by the time she had Eric presentable enough to meet the CWA ladies. How long would she be able to keep this up? He would never have done it for her.

The CWA ladies who had volunteered to help Lillian sat in her lounge with their cups of tea and slices of sponge fresh from the oven. Eric was asleep in his wheelchair at the back of the group. They cast sympathetic eyes towards him.

"We can work out a roster so there's someone on call if Lillian needs help." Everyone nodded in agreement and a notebook was passed around for their names and phone numbers. They discussed which weekend they would be available and listed names against the dates. Lillian was overcome by their kindness and put the precious bottle of sherry her mother had left behind on her last visit on the table with six glasses. Everyone accepted a glass with a gleam in their eye. Behind them, the wheelchair became active, squeaking on the wooden floorboards. All eyes turned to Eric. Sherry glasses remained inches from eager lips, motionless.

"God! Eric, what are you doing?"

"It's trapped," he said. The buttons on his fly were undone and his testicles, the colour of a ripe eggplant, protruded from his trousers. Lillian grabbed her serviette and rushed over, covering Eric's escaped member. He threw the serviette aside.

"I want a pee."

Lillian released the brake on the wheelchair and hurried him out of the room. The sherry glasses emptied in her wake. Stifled laughter came from the lounge room behind her. At least the women hadn't jumped up and left. She held a urine bottle for Eric while he relieved himself and then left him in the kitchen.

"Now you know what you will be dealing with if you help me," Lillian said, addressing the women. "I'm not holding any of you to your promise." She poured herself a sherry and gulped it down, close to tears.

"We have discussion," said her friend Ingrid. "It might be good plan for us to make trousers like pyjamas. Then easy for pee." All the women grinned and nodded. It was a great solution and Lillian wasn't being abandoned. She hugged her friends at the door, knowing that soon the whole town would know how big Eric's balls were. But for all she cared they could take a photo of them and put it in the newspaper.

22

Welfare Appointment

Maureen looked around the congregation and wondered if anyone else had seen the photo in the newspaper and recognised her. The lawyer came in with his family and sat at the front of the church. What would he think when he found out the police were looking for her? She felt miserable. When the news got out, everyone in the church would be looking at her with suspicion. It was bad enough being pregnant and unmarried but how were they going to judge her for abandoning an unconscious man? The Reverend began the sermon of the Good Samaritan.

"Jesus," Maureen dug Sarah in the ribs, "I can't tell the lawyer today after that sermon," she hissed.

Sarah snorted, then frowned. "You have to tell him about your kidnap because the police want you to give evidence in the trial of the Swedish girl, Tove Persson. They want that bloke to get a maximum sentence. You owe it to that girl."

When the service had finished Maureen followed Herr Kihlbom outside and stood behind him while he shook the Reverend's hand.

"Excellent service, John," the lawyer said.

Maureen decided it was definitely the wrong day to approach him. She started to move away.

"Maureen, how are you?"

Too late. Her smile was tremulous. "Well, thank you, Herr…"

"Paavo," his eyes crinkled, "This church wants informality."

"Paavo." She blushed. "I wonder if I could speak to you about something important?"

"Of course. I am delighted you have accepted my offer to help."

"It's not about maintenance for the baby." She looked up at him and wondered if he could see her heart beating in her throat. The decision to speak to him had plagued her for days and nights and now she had to get it over with. "It's about something I need to say in private." Her eyes held his. His face softened with concern.

"Let us get a hot drink and go in the church so there is no disturbance."

Maureen nodded, allowing Paavo to get their drinks. She noticed heads turn and eyes follow them as they left the hall.

The church was empty. They put their cups on the seat and Paavo nodded for Maureen to begin.

"First I must tell you he had turned off the highway and was taking us somewhere unknown. He was strong and my friend and I couldn't stop him attacking her. We were terribly afraid, and I didn't think the gun would harm him because it was loaded with blanks. Jane got out of the car with our suitcase while I pointed the gun at the man. He stood by the driver's door as I climbed out of the back seat. It was a VW Beetle, and I had to get out of the same door as he did. I kept the gun aimed at his face while I climbed out and then he went to grab me, so I pulled the trigger. I only meant to scare him. There was a flash from the muzzle and a huge bang that made my ears ring. He fell against the car and banged his head. I remember smelling something like scorched wool. I think it was his beanie. The snow was thick, and he was unconscious. We pushed him into the car and put the keys on the floor to give us time to get away. We ran until we reached a crossroad. A truck picked us up."

It was an eruption of words. The silence grew in the empty church.

Paavo looked at her, amazed. "Maureen, I'm not understanding. What are you telling me?"

She pulled the folded newspaper clipping from her pocket. "If you read this you will know. It's about me."

Unfolding the clipping he started to read. His eyebrows lifted, then knitted. He looked at Maureen in disbelief. "This is not good."

"I know." Maureen felt the tremble of tears. "I don't know what to do. Nils' father must have given my photo to the newspaper. Nils' father said that's what he would do if I told the police his wife tried to push me over the balcony. The breath she drew caught in her throat.

"What!" Paavo's hand went into his pocket for his handkerchief and handed it to Maureen without dropping his gaze. "You must explain everything and then we can see what action we have."

Telling Paavo was exhausting. He asked questions, took notes and when his wife came looking for them, he waved her away. At the end of an hour she felt so tired she just wanted to stretch out on the pew and sleep. To her relief, Paavo closed his notebook and put his pen away. He helped her up and led her out of the church, steering her by the arm. She felt unworthy of his help.

"I will drive you and your friend home," he said, face heavy in

180

thought. They joined Sarah and Penny who were the last people in the hall.

"What's the matter?" Paavo's wife looked from one to the other and reached for Maureen's hand.

"It's not something to discuss now. We will take Maureen and Sarah home. I have much thinking to do."

His wife didn't argue. She fetched her children while Sarah got Mikey and they piled into the Mercedes.

Maureen watched the windscreen wipers clean paths through the icy rain as they drove. When were her problems going to end? What was Nils doing? Did he think of her? They pulled up in front of Sarah's building and Maureen climbed out before Paavo could open his door. "Thanks for the lift, Herr Kihlbom." He didn't correct her. She wriggled her fingers at the children and turned to his wife. "Fru Kihlbom, if you would like a babysitter anytime, I would love to look after the children for you." They had a nanny, but it was important Maureen let them know she would repay them anyway she could. It was her motto never to owe anyone anything, but it hadn't been working very well in Sweden.

"I will contact you. Do not worry," Paavo said. His voice was reassuring.

"Thank you," Maureen whispered. Their eyes met and he gave her a wink of encouragement. She left without waiting for Sarah to finish her goodbyes, walking into the building as quickly as she could, eager to close out the day.

When Sarah came in, Maureen was slumped in a chair, head in hands at the kitchen table.

"How did it go?" Sarah had known what Maureen was going to discuss with Paavo but hadn't mentioned anything to Penny.

"God, Sarah, he was so shocked. He said I would have to inform the police and to be prepared for newspaper interest."

She banged her fist on the table. "It's just what Herr Classon wants. Nils will hate me. I'll probably be deported."

"They won't deport a seven months' pregnant woman, surely?"

"I don't know. I can't think straight; all I want to do is curl up and pretend this is not happening."

"Lie on my bed and I'll take Mikey for a walk."

"No. It's raining and too cold. I can have a rest in the roof. The vagrant only comes up at night, so you won't have to lock me in, just wake me up in a couple of hours. I'll take a hot water bottle with me." When Maureen crawled into her bed in the roof a blanket of black dropped over her.

The door chain rattled. Maureen woke. Someone was trying to get in the storeroom. There were men's voices. Maureen lay rigid, her heart banging against her rib cage. The inside of her mouth was dry. Had she been snoring, and the drunks come to investigate? Thank God the chain was on the door. Sarah must have come after she'd fallen asleep and fastened the chain. The door shook from the impact of a boot.

Maureen held her breath, afraid to move in case the bed creaked, thanking her lucky stars she was in the storeroom and not on Netta's couch. The feet walked away, and someone laughed in the distance. She exhaled. Her teeth began to chatter from fright and cold. She needed to pee. It would make a noise; the bucket might clang. Crossing her legs, she held on.

Someone was shaking her. She sat up with a start hitting at the air. Sarah stepped back.

"Whoa! Sorry I didn't mean to scare you. I've made porridge."

"It's morning?" Maureen tried to get her bearings, then the night came back to her. "Thank God you locked me in. Someone tried to get in here last night. I was so scared."

"There's no one up here now. Lots of bottles though."

"I heard a few voices, so it was more than one person."

"You can sleep with me tonight. Maybe your social worker has found a place for you?"

Maureen pulled a face, "Damn!" She'd forgotten about her afternoon appointment with the welfare worker from the church. She wasn't looking forward to living in a home for unmarried mothers. She'd heard stories about homes in Australia where babies had been taken away from mothers and put up for adoption. But she couldn't continue to be a burden on Sarah or live in the roof if it was going to become a refuge for the street drunks. She pulled on her coat and put her feet in her boots. The clothes she was wearing were yesterday's and her suitcase was in Sarah's flat.

"I feel like a scrub after breakfast. Mind if I boil the kettle and have a wash? I'm going to pop into Bernard's before I go to my appointment. There might be a letter for me." Perhaps her mother had sent her some money and she could hire a room in someone's house.

"Be my guest."

Maureen washed up the breakfast dishes then filled the kettle for her wash. When it whistled, she carried it into the lavatory and filled the basin. Stripping to the waist, she soaped the flannel and rubbed her skin until it was red. Cleaning off the problems that clung to it, making her surface new and ready for all the good things her day would bring. Then she did the same from her waist down. She stood naked, looking down on her body.

Her breasts had always been a comfortable thirty-seven inches, the same size as Marilyn Monroe's. She was proud of her breasts. Looking at them now, she wasn't proud. They had blue veins and were huge. Her small waist had disappeared. It was now a stomach that pushed beyond her breasts, and her belly button, which was once inverted, looked like another nipple.

She whipped the door open and posed. "What do you think?" Sarah's head went back; she was a modest person. She turned away and laughed.

Mikey looked up from the red fire engine Maureen had given him for his birthday.

"You are fat."

Maureen blew him a kiss closing the door. She peered at her face in the mirror. It was thinner, her eyes looked enormous and her cheekbones stuck out. The Mary Quant hairdo had grown into a thick mane nearly down to her shoulders. She looked like a waif. Wrapping a towel around herself she went back into the room. "Everything is skinny but my gut and tits."

"That's good. It's better to look like a charity case when you visit the welfare officer." Sarah tapped her lips. "You could put on some lippy and mascara, and put your hair in a French roll, there might be a bloke on the welfare board."

Sarah had always been blunt. The last thing Maureen wanted was an ogling welfare officer. "What am I going to wear?" she wailed. Her maternity clothes were still drying on the clotheshorse in front of the heater and the clothes she'd slept in stunk of sweat.

Sarah opened her husband's wardrobe. She was smaller than Maureen and her clothes wouldn't fit. She removed two polo necked jumpers from the cupboard and held them out. Maureen pulled a face but settled on the black one. It didn't look too bad, at least it fitted over her stomach and was made of wool. "Beggars can't be choosers, I suppose."

"Try this with it." Sarah handed her a corduroy skirt she had started sewing two days ago. It had an elastic waist and was a mustard colour.

"You finished it?" The skirt fitted and with the polo top, looked nice. "Thank you." Maureen gave her a squeeze.

"Your coat needs a dry-clean. Try Bengt's jacket, it's reindeer skin and warm." Apart from the shoulder width, it fitted. Wearing a scarf and beanie no one would recognise her on the street. At least she'd be warm. Some days it was so cold that the insides of her nostrils stuck together and her ears ached. No matter where she went, she always kept her eye out for Nils, she didn't want him to see her looking shabby. He had loved her look and style. He wouldn't love her now her stomach had become a beach ball. In spring she'd be back in stilettos and mini skirts.

"I might be late back, so don't worry about supper. Keep your fingers crossed I get a letter from Mum." Maureen had told her mother about the missing letters turning up and how she had thought her mother had abandoned her.

The social security building was as faceless as all government buildings. They had pulled down a beautiful Nordic style home to put up a brown brick box with a red tiled roof. Maureen presented herself to the receptionist. "I have an appointment with Fru Wellander. My name is Maureen McKinley."

The receptionist checked the appointments book and picked up the phone to announce her presence. "Fru Wellander will see you in second office down hall."

The office was small, well-lit with fluorescent lights. The Welfare Officer came around her desk and greeted Maureen. "You look tired," she said, taking Maureen's hand, eyes full of concern. Marion Wellander was born in Surrey, England and had lived in Sweden for twenty-five years. She was a horsey woman, who wore plaid skirts and brogues, and she had a heart as big as a horse and showed her concern for the abandoned Australian girl. She had tried to contact Maureen's boyfriend but had met a blank wall. She showed Maureen to a seat.

"I have good news. We have found a room for you in the home for unmarried mothers in Langedrag. It's a beautiful old house near the water. It used to be owned by a very important man. There are five girls and the staff who consist of a cook, two midwives and matron. I'm sure you will be well looked after. The home is soon to be closed down for development."

There was a sinking feeling in Maureen. She was used to being independent and it would be different at the home. She forced a smile. This lady had gone to so much trouble for her. The thought that her baby wasn't going to suddenly pop out of her in the roof or Sarah's apartment or walking to hospital was a comfort. They were concerns she had tried to bury. However, a new fear arose with the knowledge of the midwives. "Thank you for your help, Fru Wellander. I didn't know what was going to happen to me."

"You'll be able to stay there after the baby is born, at least for four weeks, all depending." She didn't say depending on what. "If you need assistance moving in, I can arrange a day and accompany you?"

"I'll be fine. My friend Sarah, will help me."

"There's also the matter of financial support. You will receive coupons to cover your needs. That will extend to after the birth, depending on circumstances and if you are still in the home." Fru Wellander didn't say what the circumstances were, and Maureen was too afraid to ask. "The welfare system in Sweden is excellent," Fru Wellander added.

In her heart, Maureen thanked Netta for insisting she go to the English church. If she hadn't, she would never have known how to get help.

"Have you any questions?"

Maureen stared at her saviour and voiced her fear. "Will my

baby be born in the home or will I go to hospital?" In the hospital they wouldn't take her baby away. The officer looked surprised. "It's just that there are midwives in the home so I thought, maybe that's where I would have my baby?"

"No, the midwives are there to make sure the pregnancy is progressing without complications. You will give birth in hospital, my dear."

Maureen relaxed for the first time during their interview.

"There is something else. Curfews. You will not be able to be out after ten o'clock at night. The doors lock. There's a daybook you must fill in if you go out. Where you go, contact names and if you are not in for meals."

Gaol! Maureen's shoulders drooped.

Fru Wellander came around her desk and sat on its edge in front of Maureen. "You must understand, the people who run the home are responsible if anything happens to you." Maureen nodded, she understood, but hated the idea she would lose her freedom.

23

Eden – PJ Interview

It was time for Eric to return to the hospital, but he wasn't going to be told what to do. He sat in the wheelchair, jaw stuck forward, green eyes harpooning Johnny. Lillian let go of the wheelchair, wincing at the stab of pain in her back as she straightened up. They had been trying to lift Eric into the passenger seat of the Buick. She threw her arms in the air, exasperated.

"I'm driving." Eric's lip came out, petulant. Somewhere in the shambles of his mind he knew his place was behind the steering wheel.

"Dad, you can't drive anymore, your licence has been suspended. I have to drive you back to the hospital." Gripping the arm of his chair with his good hand Eric flopped the other at Johnny. The wheelchair twisted and Johnny made a grab to stop it from tipping over.

"It's no good. We'll have to think of some other way. Maybe the ambulance?" Lillian said.

"Might take awhile to get here and I have to go baiting tonight. Why don't I see if I can borrow the boss's ute? Stick him on the back?"

"It's worth a try," Lillian was tired and her back hurt.

Johnny stared at his father. "If you won't get in the car then you're going in a ute." Eric turned his head away. "Right, that's it." It was strange, becoming the parent of your father. Johnny had always been scared of his Dad, often at the end of his razor strop. He shut the passenger door going around to the driver's side and sliding in behind the wheel. Eric's chair rocked in anger. Johnny started the engine and drove off. Lillian tried to push Eric up the bank into the house, but he was too heavy. She gave up and waited by the side of the road for Johnny's return.

Twenty minutes later Johnny was pushing Eric up the ute's ramp.

"You'll need to secure the wheels, so he doesn't roll about."

"I know, Mum."

"He looks a bit high up. He could fall over the side." Now Eric was on the back, Lillian wasn't sure the ute was a good idea.

Johnny reversed the wheelchair, wedged it against the rear window and tied it to the window guard. Using a separate rope, he tied his father to the chair. Lillian climbed onto the tray and checked Johnny's handiwork. It seemed secure. Satisfied, she gave Eric a peck on the forehead like she would have done one of her children. He smiled and held her hand. It was a different Eric to the one she had divorced. "Snug as a bug in a rug," she said. Eric grinned. The sun was shining, and the little hair Eric had ruffled in the breeze.

The ute made its way towards Bega with Eric lashed on the back. Johnny kept to the speed limit and Lillian sat in the passenger seat constantly checking the wheelchair through the back window of the ute. They drew up in front of the hospital. Johnny installed the ramp and untethered Eric's chair from the window guard. He wheeled him into reception. There were a few gasps from the nurses and Johnny realised his dad was still tied to the chair. He gave an embarrassed laugh.

"He's a menace in the car." Johnny undid the ropes that pinioned his father's arms and body under the grim eye of the triage nurse. She made a note in the day journal and phoned for an attendant to collect Eric.

"Well, see ya later, Dad. Splinter will pick you up next weekend." Eric gave him a blank look and Johnny left, hoping there wouldn't be a kafuffle over tying his father up.

They drove back to Eden with Lillian on the lookout for kangaroos and wombats crossing the road, mindful that sometimes kangaroos hit by cars had joeys in their pouches that ended up starving to death. Between the hospital and Eden, she counted eight dead kangaroos and two wombats, it wasn't many today.

Transporting Eric had knocked the stuffing out of Lillian. She collapsed on Aunt Maggie's chaise longue with a glass of sherry. To have the house to herself again was a relief. Next time Eric came home she would be more organised. Also, tomorrow she would mention his testicles to the doctor. Their purple colour concerned her, but that could have happened because she didn't know how long they had been caught in his fly. There was still the money to find for Maureen. Lillian wondered how Peter Turnstile was going with his enquiry. That was something else she had to do tomorrow. Also put the Buick up for sale. But the farm and Buick weren't going to give her the instant cash she needed. Poor Maureen was on her own. The belligerent ring of the telephone hauled her off the couch, the telephonist at the exchange must have known she was home. She picked it up and yawned a hello.

"Mum?" It was Splinter, "Constable PJ tried to get hold of you today and left a message for you to call into the police station. He has information on Kathy."

All Lillian's alert signals switched on. "Did he say what information?"

"He left the message at school, Mum. He wouldn't tell the school secretary what it was about." There was a huffy tone to Splinter's voice. Lillian guessed she'd had a slog of a day at school.

"Thanks, love. I'll let you know what it's about tomorrow when you drop your washing off." Lillian did Splinter's washing when the school exams were in progress because she had to work long hours marking papers. Teaching was a thankless job, especially knowing that Eden's talented children would end up working in the cannery, shops or on fishing boats. She put the phone down, grabbed her latest Agatha Christie and headed for bed.

The sun washed the sky with yellow and orange as it lifted from the sea, bathing the verandah where Lillian sat crunching cornflakes and praying for a good-news day. She'd spent a sleepless night worrying about Maureen. In the early glow she noticed how high the grass had grown and remembered the blades on the lawnmower needed sharpening. If the farm sale was resolved, she'd buy a Victa lawnmower. She was done with the sheep Eric had foisted on her when she'd first complained about the grass.

There wasn't a soul around when she left for the police station. The young constable lived on the premises so she knew he would be in.

He opened the door at Lillian's knock.

"G'day, Lillian. You're early."

"Keeping away from the nosey parkers, PJ." No reason to be formal when there was only the two of them. Besides, she'd kicked his arse for piddling in the teapot when she'd babysat him as a kid. He held a chair out for her. She sat and clutched her handbag on her knees.

"We've located and interviewed Kathy Parker," PJ said. He had driven to Bateman's Bay with his siren on to be at the interview when his colleagues brought her in for questioning. He was an avid fan of the television series *The Saint*. And this was his case.

Lillian listened intently while PJ read through Kathy's statement. "She swears Eric sold the farm but doesn't know what he did with the money or why his signature doesn't look authentic."

"We raised the question of his medication and the stolen pills." Constable PJ gave a crafty grin. "She couldn't come up with an explanation for the pills being stolen. I accused her of procuring them to drug Eric for the purpose of swindling him. That unsettled her. She became quite emotional and told us a cock and bull story about finding the pills in the hospital grounds. But, when I pointed out that she hadn't returned them to the hospital, she dobbed Eric's accountant in and suggested we interview him about the farm sale money." He tilted his chair back a smile on his young face. He'd make a good detective. The news brought a sigh of relief from Lillian.

"When do you think we can get the money back or have the sale cancelled?" Lillian said. PJ opened his hands.

"Who knows? Could be weeks. The signature has to be discounted which I think we can do because Kathy left the house the day your daughter accused her of feeding pills to your husband. Ex-husband," PJ corrected. "That's a sign of her guilt for a start. Which would mean the farm is still Eric's and the buyer …" PJ faded into the distance.

Although Lillian was pleased that Kathy would get her comeuppance it wasn't going to help her with Maureen's predicament. She was still stuck in a foreign country without any help. There was her younger sister, Audrey, she could approach.

Maureen had lived with her and her husband in Melbourne for two years before she had gone overseas. Perhaps Audrey would be able to send her some money? She knew she would if she could. She was a generous soul. The constable scraped his chair on the floor and Lillian looked up, flustered that she'd let her attention wander.

"Sorry, PJ, what did you say?"

"I said the buyer, in this case, House van Someren, would have to sue whoever received the money for its return, or open a case of fraud against them. I wouldn't pass that on yet though, until we have proved Eric wasn't in his right mind at the time of signing."

"I have Peter Turnstile looking into the signature on the deed and the wording of the transaction to make sure it's a legal document. He can compare the signature with the one on our divorce papers," Lillian said.

Constable PJ nodded. He had been out to Eric's farm and now he would interview the lawyer and check the documents before the Bateman's Bay cops got onto it. They weren't going to steal his case.

Lillian left the police station feeling more optimistic. Across the road was the Eden Whale Museum and the bus stop. She entered the museum and stood in front of Tom's skeleton. He was the town's famous orca, a betrayer of the innocent. He had herded the mother whales and their babies into the murderous harpoons of whalers. It was an appropriate place to think of Maureen at the hands of Nils' parents while she waited for the bus to the hospital.

Lillian followed the ambulance trolley until she reached Eric's ward. When he saw her, his face lit up like a child's. It didn't make her feel any love towards him. Pity, yes. He had his dick to thank for his situation. That flagpole of vanity he'd never stopped waving. It wasn't waving anymore yet it was still dictating their lives. She thought about that as she bent forward and pecked him on the forehead.

"Hello, Eric."

"Hello." There was something lost in his eyes when he looked at her. She felt sad for him.

"The nurse said I could wheel you up the street and buy you a bun." Eric beamed, he loved currant buns. She wheeled him to reception signing him out for an hour. They bumped along the pavement and up the street to the Bega bakery. The shop was well patronised. Lillian left Eric inside the door and stood in line at the counter. She was paying for her buns when a shout behind her made her turn. Eric was waving his good arm at her.

"I've got half a stiffy. Do you want to do something about it?" He pointed to the pyramid in his trousers. Lillian went scarlet. The shop went silent. She cast frantic eyes around the customers. They looked from Eric to her.

"He's had a stroke," she said. She snatched the buns and rushed Eric out of the shop. He waved his arm with a huge smile. He must be thinking I'm rushing him home to alleviate his stiffy, she thought, grimly. The hospital could forget her taking him anywhere in public after that.

24

Moving

The Rolling Stones were singing '(I Can't Get No) Satisfaction' on the radio and Bernard's kitchen staff were rocking at their stations, unaware Maureen had entered the kitchen. Maureen felt a twinge of envy at all the camaraderie.

"Hej," she called out. The chef looked up. His eyes went to Maureen's face and then to her stomach and back to her face. She lifted her hand in greeting and he gave an embarrassed nod, his hands busy filleting a large salmon. "Hello, Chef, how are you?"

"Your door is good?"

"Yes," she grinned at him, criminals in kind. He indicated her stomach with his head.

"Baby come soon?"

"Seven weeks." It wasn't far away. Her hands held her stomach.

The waitress hailed her. Maureen smiled a greeting and went over to where she was filling pepper and salt pots.

"Herr Classon not been back?" Maureen asked.

The waitress put up her finger. "One more time," she said.

He wasn't going to leave her alone. It was a message. "Is Bernard in his office?"

"He not so busy." The waitress gave her arm a pat and went back to filling pepper and salt pots.

Maureen tapped on Bernard's door and popped her head inside. He clapped his hands when he saw her and came around his desk. She kissed him on both cheeks.

"Where have you been, chérie, I am worried?"

"My friend, Sarah has been feeding me. I am still in the roof but leaving on the weekend. I move into a home for pregnant girls without husbands." She saw the worried look Bernard gave her. "It will be alright, there are nurses in the home."

"I have a special dinner for you. Tonight is duck à la mode, you must try." Maureen hesitated, she hadn't come for food, only to see him and collect her mail if there was any. "I will taxi you home." Maureen had the urge to kiss his round smiley face.

"I have never had duck à la mode."

"Australians eat bad English food," Bernard said with a sniff. Maureen didn't say she loved fish and chips, roast lamb dinners and apple pie.

"I haven't been to see you because I've been seeing welfare officers and lawyers. My picture was in the paper. Did you see it?"

The smile left Bernard's face. "I saw the photo; it is not so recognizable but the hitchhiking story you tell me I recognise. Chérie, how did this happen?" He clasped her hand in his.

"Herr Classon put it in the paper after my friend phoned his wife. She tried to help me like you did."

"Merde bastard!" He stamped his foot.

"I have a lawyer who is going to tell me what to do. He's not going to charge, something called pro bono."

"No need for lawyer I will get the chef onto him," Bernard glowered. A violin played, a man was dying from a food allergy on the restaurant floor. Maureen shook the image from her mind.

"Let's leave it to my lawyer," she said. A dead Herr Classon would be more than she could cope with. "Have you any letters for me, Bernard?"

"Oui, how I forget, ma chérie." He opened a drawer in his desk and took out two letters. "There is one from Netta, you must read it to me." He sat down and stared at her expectantly. Maureen wanted to read it to herself first but feeling pressured opened the letter and read it to Bernard. It was a happy letter. Netta sounded settled and well cared for. Folding the letter, Maureen felt disappointed that Netta hadn't commented on Bernard's phone call to Herr Classon and his appearance at the restaurant. Maybe she'd been put off by the threat that Herr Classon would go to the police and didn't want to leave any tracks that would lead to her? She put the letter in her handbag.

"Merci, Maureen. Now we will have the duck."

Maureen burped all the way home, unused to the rich food and the quantity she had eaten at Bernard's insistence. She used the key Sarah had given her and let herself into the flat. Mikey was asleep and Sarah was on the bed knitting a layette for the baby. She waved her mother's letter.

"It's from Mum. Dad's fine but thinks he's a young fellow and sometimes he doesn't recognise Mum." She didn't mention the problems with Kathy and his bank account.

"What about your meeting with the welfare officer?"

"She found me a room. I'm moving into the home on Saturday. Want to come with me to see what it's like?" It would be good to have some support.

"Sure," Sarah said.

On Friday afternoon, Mikey developed a wheeze and a cough. Sarah bundled him up and put him in her pram. "Would you mind watching our dinner while I take Mikey to the doctor?"

"Of course. I hope he's going to be alright." Mikey was such a good little kid, Maureen loved him. When they had gone, she pulled the couch bed out and set the table, stirred the lamb and cabbage stew, peeled and cut up potatoes and put them on to boil.

She would have dinner ready by the time they got back to make sure Mikey ate when he felt hungry and not too late that he couldn't sleep – her one criticism of Sarah's parenting. Watching Sarah with Mikey was giving Maureen some parenting skills.

Sarah came in looking like a laundry basket full of washing. She peeled off Mikey's clothes and then her own. "He's got croup, and a temperature. I have to dose him with aspirin and keep him warm. He can't go outside for two days." She lifted the sleeping Mikey from the pusher and laid him on her bed. His cheeks were flushed. Sarah looked up apologetic. "I'm afraid I won't be able to go to the home with you tomorrow."

Maureen shrugged, "Can't be helped. I will be fine on my own. I'll sleep in the storeroom tonight so you can have the whole bed. You might have to put Mikey in with you if he wakes up."

Sarah looked concerned. "You don't have to."

"Yep, no good both of us being kept awake by Mikey's coughing." She laughed, not meaning it, but wanting Sarah to feel good about her decision.

It was so cold when Maureen woke up, she thought if she moved, she'd crackle. Then she remembered today was moving to the home day. She heaved herself out of bed and picked up the rug to put around her shoulders and noticed a white splatter. A pigeon must have followed her into the storeroom last night. She rubbed her hand over her hair to make sure none of it was in her hair; thankful it didn't stink. Then she removed the ski pole propped against the door to stop intruders. Sarah had forgotten to lock her in, and Maureen hadn't wanted to worry her with Mikey sick. She picked up the pee bucket to empty in Sarah's lavatory.

There were no signs of the vagrants. No bottles lying around. It was possible they had been arrested by the police or found a hostel room for the night because of the plummeting temperatures. The radio had predicted minus 15 degrees. She let herself into the flat. Sarah and Mikey were both asleep in the couch bed.

Maureen crept around the room, collecting clothes to pack in her suitcase. She emptied the bucket, washed and cleaned her teeth, dressed, applied makeup and pinned her hair into a French roll. She thought about waking Sarah to say goodbye but decided not to, leaving her a note.

She used the coupon the welfare officer had given her and hailed a taxi. The taxi drove off leaving her in the driveway of her new residence. Everything squeezed inside her as she took in her new surroundings.

The home was imposing, two storeys and gable roofed. It looked bleak under the layers of snow, despite the pale blue sky. A group of girls lingered on the porch entrance observing her approach. Feeling shy, she hesitated at the foot of the steps under their curious stares and smiled, trying to look cheerful. The response was a sweep of eyes that rested on her stomach. She hunched her shoulders in an effort to lower the hem of the skirt that arched in the front and made her stomach look bigger. The doorway seemed a long way off.

Maureen climbed the steps clutching her suitcase and bobbed her head in greeting. One of her observers said something to her companion and laughed. The other two girls lowed their gaze.

"Do you speak English?" she asked the bold girl who had

laughed, hating the timid sound of her voice. The girl flicked her Nordic hair and gave a tight grin, blue eyes full of challenge. She moved away from the low brick wall she had been leaning on.

"Anya," she said, sweeping an arm towards the steps in a mock bow. Maureen noted the girl's stomach wasn't as big as hers. The smile Maureen offered stuck to her face as she passed the girls and crossed the threshold of the grand old house. In the foyer, strains of the Beatles latest song 'Hard Day's Night' drifted down the wide staircase opposite the foyer. The irony of it after last night in the storeroom. What a shocker!

In the foyer Maureen felt diminished, her reflection stunted in the high polished floor. A tall, full-figured woman in a crisp blue uniform walked towards her. She smiled and the snow melted off Maureen's shoes, leaving a puddle where she stood.

She extended her hand, "Matron Tilda. Välkommen. You are Maureen, yes?"

Maureen took the woman's smooth dry hand in her own cold clammy one and gripped it. "I'm sorry I don't speak Swedish, I'm from Australia."

"Ja, I speak English. I have your papers from authorities, come in my office and we sign them." She indicated with her head that Maureen was to follow her. They skirted a wide staircase, walked down a long hall, passing a kitchen where the smell of fresh baked pastry made saliva pools in Maureen's mouth. She hadn't been hungry at Sarah's. Now she was ravenous.

The room she was shown into had a large wooden desk stacked with files and a collection of lounge chairs. From the size of the room and the large bay window that looked out on a snow-covered garden, Maureen guessed it must have been used as a sitting room in past years.

"You sit here." Matron Tilda patted the back of an armchair in front of her desk. "You excuse me. I will get Inga to bring coffee and pastry." Maureen's stomach growled in anticipation as the matron left the room.

The view from the window was a Christmas card scene, blue sky and white-coated fir trees. This is going to be my home for the next three months at least, Maureen thought. Beyond that she hadn't considered. On the mantelpiece above the fireplace were framed photographs of girls holding babies. There was one girl with empty arms. Her eyes lingered on the childless girl. They were all smiling, Maureen noted.

A woman in her fifties, wearing a large white apron and carrying a tray, came in. She gave Maureen a sharp look from under her brows and put the tray on the Matron's desk.

"Hej," Maureen said. The woman gave her a blue-eyed stare and rattled off some Swedish. "I only speak English," she apologised. Having to admit not speaking Swedish had become an embarrassment when people were helping her.

The woman looked at her cold faced and left the room. Good start, Maureen thought. She'd have to try harder to stumble her way through what Swedish she knew which wasn't much. After a few minutes, the Matron returned.

"Sorry, I get delayed." She spotted the tray, "Ahh, good, the coffee is here. You speak with Inga?"

"I don't think she understood English," Maureen said.

"Ja, she speaks English," Matron said. Great! Maybe she was one of the Swedes who didn't like foreigners? Like Nils' mother who had called her a farm flicka and made it sound like she was a piece of cow manure. "Come, I will show you your room."

Matron led Maureen up the stairs. The landing at the top of the stairs was a large space the width of the building. Five doors opened onto the landing. They entered the last room on the right. It was a big room with two single beds separated by two bassinets sitting side by side. A wall of cupboards was at one end of the room and a large window at the other. The window looked out over the back yard to a clothesline and a snowed-in vegetable garden. A distance away a suburb of red roofed houses faced the sea. The room smelled of floor polish.

"It is room for two but is all for you. There will be no more girls coming because of closure soon. You must call if you need me." Matron pointed to a bell on a bedside table. "You must ring if there is emergency. If water breaks, paining or bleeding," she explained. "I show you bathroom and clothes washing."

The bathroom was large and white, the only decoration a line of flowered tiles around the wall. Apart from the shower and bath there was a cabinet for toiletries, and a cupboard full of towels and floor mats. Three clotheshorses strung with drying towels stood in front of an oil heater. The only things different from a normal bathroom were the two baby baths sitting in metal frames with wheels and the long baby change table.

"The girls take in turns to clean bathroom. Next to bathroom is lavatory and laundry. There is also lavatory down the stairs. I will leave you to unpack and then you come downstairs for lunchtime and I introduce girls. After lunch we have coffee in the lounge next to my office."

Maureen gave matron an anxious look. After the reception she had received on the porch she wasn't keen to spend too much time with the girls.

"Everyone will be good," Matron said, giving Maureen a smile that made her think of her mother. She was left to unpack and settle in. The bedroom was sparse, white and impersonal. It needed a picture on the wall. Something with a wharf, boats or a nice landscape with sheep, like her father's farm.

25

Eden – The Farm Visit

L illian and Splinter were driving to the farm to give Eric's memory another jog. They were travelling in Splinter's husband's delivery van with Eric in the back in his wheelchair. There were no windows in the back, and it had a strong smell of petrol. The dirt road was windy. Eric vomited. The stink filled the van.

"Damn! You'll have to pull over, Splinter, so I can clean him up," Lillian said. If she wasn't cleaning up pee it was vomit. Her future wasn't looking bright. They crossed a small bridge and Splinter stopped. "Leave the doors open and let the air in. It might help him feel better."

"I'll get some water from the creek to wash him with," Splinter said. She searched for a billy can but all she could find was a bundle of rags behind the seat. They would have to do. She grabbed the rags and clambered down the bank to the creek.

The water was clear as glass and mountain fresh. Using the rocks as a scrubbing board she cleaned the grime off the rags, wrung them out and submerged them again. She carried the sopping rags back to the van and gave them to her mother.

"How are you feeling?" Lillian asked. Eric was pasty, he'd never been car sick in his life, usually it was Lillian with the weak stomach. Eric used to curse her every time they went on a trip. He held out hands full of chunky spew. He'd had a good breakfast.

"Sick," he said. He wiped his hands down his pants before Lillian could grab them. Her gut heaved.

"When we're at the farm I'll give you a cup of tea. We're nearly there, only two more miles." She mopped Eric's face, wiped his hands, the front of his clothes, shoes and floor. She handed the rags back to Splinter. "Give them a rinse and I'll give him one more go."

Splinter looked at the rags, fat with vomit and screwed her face. "Yuck, Mum!" She held the rags with the tips of her fingers and dropped them over the bridge into the creek, climbing down after them.

"Are you feeling a bit better now, Eric?" Lillian patted his hand.

"I'm good," he said. He wasn't much trouble when he was away from the hospital, except when he fiddled with his willy.

With the freshened rags from Splinter, Lillian finished wiping Eric and the wheelchair. "All done." She climbed out of the van and swung the back doors a few times to get more air on Eric and went back to her seat. They drove the last two miles with the front windows down and their heads out.

Splinter parked on the flat so Eric wouldn't roll down the hill and wheeled him out of the van. She swung the wheelchair around to face the cottage. His mouth flew open and his eyes shone. He tried to get out of the wheelchair.

"He certainly recognises the cottage." Lillian was thrilled with his reaction. She put a restraining hand on his shoulder. "Your legs don't work properly, Eric, you'll have to stay in the chair." He settled back. "There's a dear," she said. She wheeled him to the front doorstep and stopped. A large sign was tied to the door handle. KEEP OUT, EDEN POLICE ENTRY ONLY.

"What's PJ up to?" Ignoring the sign, Splinter opened the door to let her father see inside. He laughed and slapped his knee with his good hand, eyes clear and full of recognition.

"It's your house, Dad." Splinter squatted next to him. "Did you sell the farm Dad?" He looked startled.

"I'm not selling my farm."

"You sold it to House van Someren, Dad?" They watched him closely. He frowned and shook his head in angry denial.

"I'll have to milk the cow," he growled.

"The cow's being looked after next door while you're in hospital, Dad." Splinter saw her father grind his teeth, a sign she had grown up with. He hated his neighbour, McKenna. "I'll wheel you around the back of the house for a look."

"While you do that, I'll set up the picnic," Lillian said. Their visit had turned out better than she'd expected. It was just a shame she hadn't thought to bring the constable with her. Eric's denial had been vehement. She went back to the van and lifted out the cardboard box with their lunches. It was another reminder for Eric. Lamb sandwiches with mint jelly, and boiled fruit pudding, something he loved on picnics. She had a jar of custard for the pudding. The thermos was full of tea; she didn't have to bother with boiling a billy. After spreading a blanket under the river gum and setting out cups and plates, she plopped on the blanket and watched the river ripple over the rocks.

It was the spot where they had picnicked when Eric had told her he was going to buy the farm. He had been so excited that day. She knew in her mind nothing would have made him sell it. Especially not a woman. During their marriage he had never considered what she had wanted. At that moment she felt deeply sorry for him knowing his dream had ended and he would never be able to live here again. They ate their lunch while Eric smiled at the river reaching for his memories.

"Remember the kids on the tires floating down the river, Eric? You had to rescue Bubs because she got marooned on the rocks."

Eric nodded. "She could swim," he said.

Lillian turned to Splinter. "A successful conclusion my dear Watson."

"A great idea, Mum. At least we know for sure he didn't sell it."

They had to wrestle Eric back into the van when it was time to leave and only got him in because Splinter said she was driving them over to McKenna's to get the cow. They drove in silence while Eric sobbed all the way back to the hospital. There was more writing in the nurse's journal when they wheeled him in still crying. "God! What must they think?" Lillian whispered to Splinter. "The last time we brought him back he was tied up!"

As they said their goodbyes to Eric, Lillian noticed he had reverted to the same blank stare he often had in hospital. She left him with a hollow feeling in her stomach.

The following day Lillian contacted PJ and reported Eric's reactions to the farm and how he had denied selling it. She also rang the lawyer to keep him informed. After that she phoned her sister in Melbourne.

"Audrey, I need your help. You know about Eric's stroke and finances?" She had written all that to her sister but hadn't mentioned Maureen's predicament. The fewer people who knew about it, the better they could keep the secret.

"I can't explain over the telephone because you don't know who is listening in. But I urgently need money to help someone. If you can cable me as much as you can spare, I'll pay you back when the farm thing is sorted." Lillian sighed. Her sister didn't understand country telephone exchanges, and how the telephonist could pull the plug halfway out and listen in to conversations without being detected. "Yes, it's family and I can't tell you over the phone. I'll write, but it is urgent." Lillian stopped winding the telephone cord around her fingers and pressed the phone harder against her ear.

"What, when?" Her sister was moving to England for five years, her husband had been transferred to the head office in London. Audrey had been pining for England since she had been shipped to Australia in 1945, leaving her father, sisters and brothers. It was a wrench she had never gotten over. Lillian felt sad. She would miss her little sister.

"I understand, thank you. Whatever you can do would be a great help." Lillian made smacking noises with her lips into the mouthpiece and put the phone down. It was bad timing. Her sister needed money for their move, she had children of her own, but she would speak to her husband.

When Audrey was aware it was Maureen in trouble, Lillian knew she would do her best to help. She always had. It was just that letters back and forth took so much time, five days to Melbourne if she was lucky. Hopefully her sister would cable the money without waiting for her explanation.

The phone rang. Perhaps her sister had just needed a moment to think it over? She picked up the phone and wished she hadn't. It was House. She felt a flutter of apprehension, didn't want to speak to him, but couldn't put the phone down having already said hello.

The anger in House's voice was contained by the telephone wire. "I have been informed by your lawyer that the ownership of Eric's farm is under investigation and I can't take occupation. So, I have a proposition until this fiasco is resolved."

A proposition? Lillian knew she had to keep her wits about

her if there was to be a useful outcome. "I'm sorry, Mr van Someren, I know what's happened isn't your fault. My beef is with Eric's accountant." She didn't mention Kathy in case she was perceived as a vengeful ex-wife preying on her defenceless husband to get his money. The farm money would be Eric's when it was returned. She had no claim to it. All she was doing was acting on Eric's behalf knowing he would have helped Maureen. Her chin lifted. "What is your proposition?"

There was hope in Lillian's heart as she replaced the phone. She checked the wristwatch she had bought herself after Aunt Maggie died. It was time to put the tea on. Her boarder would be home soon. She wondered what the boarding house for unmarried mothers was like in Sweden, but all she could see was the orphanage she had lived in as a child and prayed it would be nothing like that for her daughter.

26

The Girls

Maureen bounced on the bed; it was soft. Outside her window was a small balcony which she hadn't noticed during Matron's tour. If the girls weren't nice to her, she had plenty of space she could retreat to with a book. A light tap on her door brought her to her feet. A grey-haired woman in a nurse's uniform came in unbidden.

"I am Sister Vigdis, your midwife. I will examine you now." Maureen felt a rush of heat through her body. She hated examinations, the episode with the hospital stirrup chair not far from her mind.

"I'm Maureen." She stood by the bed not knowing what was expected of her.

"Lie on the bed and lift clothes for me to listen to baby." Maureen did as she was asked. Sister Vigdis knelt beside her and laid her ear on Maureen's bare stomach. Maureen squirmed inside. Where was the wooden hearing device shaped like an egg timer that the hospital nurses used? Sister Vigdis moved her head to the other side of Maureen's stomach, then pressed it with her fingers. She straightened up and Maureen took a deep breath. "I will feel your breasts now." Maureen felt the blood in her cheeks. The sister lifted her blouse and released the cups on her baby feeder bra then smoothed her hand across Maureen's breasts. She held a nipple and peered closely, moving it around in her fingers. Maureen jolted upright and pulled her shirt down. The sister stepped back, startled.

"I wish to see if there is dryness. Sometimes nipples crack when baby sucks." But there was something else in her eyes that made Maureen uneasy. "You are healthy. Baby heartbeat strong. I give cream to make nipples supple." She washed her hands at the basin and nodded to Maureen and left the room. Maureen was sticky with sweat. She's just doing her job she thought, but it reminded her of the dentist who had taken a long time to wipe his hands on her bib.

The sound of laughter led Maureen to the dining room where the girls were seated at a long table. Matron was at the head. All eyes turned towards her and the conversation suspended as she entered the room. It was an uncomfortable moment. Matron jumped up and put her hand out to Maureen.

"Girls, this is Maureen from Australia. Anna, Birget, Drachia, Eva and Astrid." Heads bobbed towards her, examining her from head to toe. Dark hair, brown eyes, tanned skin, she felt foreign in the blonde room.

"Nice to meet you," Maureen said, giving a polite nod. The girl called Eva patted the empty chair next to her. Eva was the last addition before Maureen. She had clear blue eyes, and short cropped blonde hair. Maureen sat down. Eva leant across the table and pulled a casserole dish over for Maureen, "Please," she said, smiling. Maureen felt a rapport. "You must come for a walk in the garden after we have coffee?" Her English was excellent.

Maureen could do with a friend. She felt a rush of gratitude. "Yes, thank you." She sat quietly, watching, listening and smiling not understanding much of what was said. Occasionally the girls looked in her direction but didn't offer any explanations. Only Eva tried to include her. After coffee in the lounge Eva excused them both and Maureen was able to fetch her coat and escape outside.

They walked around the garden filling each other in on their histories. Maureen spoke about Australia and only a little about meeting Nils in Norway. It was nice to listen to someone else's story. Eva had worked as a stewardess on the P&O line and had an affair with the Bursar on the ship. He was the father of her child. Eva had never told him because he was already married. The ship had docked in Sydney Harbour and Eva had visited Kings Cross. Maureen liked her.

"You've had the examination from Sister Vigdis?" Eva's eyes twinkled.

"I have." She waited.

"The sister is harmless. Her companion is the cook, Bettina, so don't speak badly of her."

It was good to have some inside information. Maureen didn't want to put a foot wrong especially knowing there was bound to be a police interview and publicity, which she had said nothing of.

The evening meal was fish soup and rolls; lunchtime was their main meal. The girls spoke in Swedish and Maureen listened, trying to catch words to follow the conversation. She noticed the girl called Birget didn't appear to be pregnant. She ate with her eyes down and didn't join in the laughter. After supper they went to the lounge and played records on a gramophone. The girls chatted in Swedish ignoring Maureen. Anya, the tough girl who had made fun of her on the porch when she had arrived, monopolised Eva, shooting an occasional glance in Maureen's direction.

Refusing to let it ruffle her, Maureen perused the bookcase. The books were all in Swedish, so she chose a travel book and pretended to be interested in the pictures. She sat in the lounge for as long as she felt it was polite before excusing herself. The silence behind her added to her feeling of isolation.

The following morning a big discussion took place at breakfast and the girls all turned to Maureen. What had she done?

"We are going to walk to the yacht club in Langedrag for a beer and we would like you to come with us," Eva explained.

"Ja, tuk, I would love to," Maureen said, eager to make friends with the girls.

"The walk is long," the tough girl, Anya, said.

"That's good, I need to lose some weight," Maureen patted her stomach. To her relief the girls laughed. They trouped off down the road, feet following their stomachs. The sky was a blue haze and the air a soft chill. Sun played on their faces, warming the only exposed skin on their bodies. The walk was invigorating, and Maureen noticed that away from the home the girls seemed to change. In the home, like at school, there was the top dog. Out on the street there was no role to play and they had blended back into life. Maureen became the focus of the girls' attention, each one trying out their English.

"You have boyfriend?"

"No, he dumped me and joined the army to get away from me."

There were growls of anger. "Swedish boy?"

Maureen nodded. There was an exchange of Swedish. The girls looked at Eva to explain.

"They want you to know that Sweden owes you welfare if your child is Swedish," Eva said. It was a surprise to Maureen to learn she had been resented because they thought she was a holiday worker using Sweden's welfare system.

The yacht club was attached to the wharf. Yachts crowded the small harbour. The girls chose a table outside the main entrance where they could sit in the sun. A waiter came over and everyone ordered a beer. Maureen lifted her face to the sun, listening to the buzz of voices and laughter, giving herself up to the moment.

Three men coming up the steps were arguing in low voices. Recognising one of the voices, Maureen opened her eyes. Nils was in the centre of the group. He wasn't in uniform. He had seen her and was trying to make a retreat, but his friends were insisting he go with them. She gasped and stared. It hadn't entered her head that Nils would be here. She wouldn't have come if she had known. Maureen pulled her coat closed. The girls looked over to see what had grabbed her attention.

Eyes-to-the-ground Nils drew level. He sidled a look in her direction. "Hej," he said quietly.

"Hej," Maureen replied, her heart in her throat, eyes ready to spill.

"You know him?" Anya asked.

"He was my boyfriend," Maureen said in a low voice. Anya called out to Nils and rattled off some Swedish. Her mouth set in a hard line. He turned away and rushed into the club.

"What did you say?" Maureen was angry. Anya had no right to speak to Nils.

"I tell him he is coward."

"You shouldn't have."

Anya shrugged a reply and pulled out a packet of tobacco and cigarette papers and rolled a cigarette. She had never shared her story with the girls.

If Maureen had known the way back to the home she would have left right then, but on the walk to the yacht club, distracted by the girl's stories, she hadn't noticed which way they had come. The beer had gone to her head. She hadn't had alcohol from the time she'd fallen pregnant. A chill wind picked up and whipped across the water. The girls went inside the club to get out of the wind. Reluctantly Maureen followed, trying to look as inconspicuous as she could. Nils was at the bar, one of his friends slapped him on the back and Nils laughed. Had that been about her? She shrunk into her seat and closed her eyes on the room.

Maureen didn't speak on the walk back, nor at lunchtime. Her room became her haven for the rest of the day, and everyone left her alone.

On Sunday she used her taxi coupon and went to church. There was no sign of Sarah. Mikey must still be sick, Maureen thought. Without a phone and a taxi coupon she would have to wait until the following day to see Sarah.

"You are well?" the lawyer asked, sliding into the church pew next to her.

"Yes, thank you. Have you heard anything?" They both knew she was asking about the police. Paavo nodded and looked around.

"We will speak in here with a cup of tea," he said. Maureen tried to concentrate on the Reverend's sermon but all she could think about was what the lawyer wanted to tell her.

Once again, eyes followed Maureen and Paavo carrying their teacups and jam scones out of the hall door.

"You will have to make a statement to the police. They want to charge your kidnapper with the abduction and rape of the Swedish girl. To get the maximum sentence they need to show he has attempted this before, and you are the prime witness. The newspapers will not be permitted access to your story at this stage. I have arranged a time for us to go to the police."

This was the worst news. Thoughts of flight filled Maureen's head. But where could she go? She was now eight months pregnant. The gun played on her mind. She had been given it by a friend who she and Jane had stayed with when they had started hitchhiking after the loss of her car. "Will the police charge me for firing the gun?"

"It was an act of self-defence and you were told the gun was legal to own, so I don't think the police will charge you. But you must make the statement."

"When?"

"I have arranged for Tuesday morning. I will collect you from your residence." An image of being escorted by a suited man into a Mercedes flashed in front of her. What would the girls think? Well at least it wasn't a police car.

"Will I be sent back to Australia?"

"If your child is born in Sweden then you can stay here, Maureen. But you will have to find work and a place to live. You must think hard how you can look after a child because you do not speak Swedish. The employment you get will not be worth much money.

"There is Nils to help if it is proved he is the father, but he is a student with no income. That is not in your favour."

All Maureen cared about was not being thrown out of Sweden, so she would have time to sort out her life.

Tuesday landed on Maureen like a dump of snow. She pushed her spoon around the bowl of porridge and noticed Matron's worried eye on her. Too full of the jitters, she had hardly eaten anything over the past two days. She excused herself from the table and went and sat in the entrance hall to wait for her lawyer. She hadn't explained who was coming to get her, just said a friend. The thought of going through all the explanations to Matron was beyond her energy. The car pulled up and Maureen opened the door to save Paavo from coming inside and being scrutinised. He opened the passenger door for her. He didn't look much like a friend with his sober face and businesslike manner.

215

She glanced back at the home and saw two faces at the lounge room window as she climbed into the car.

"Nervous?" Paavo asked. Maureen held her hands out, they were trembling. "It's going to be alright; I will be with you." She drew a shaky breath.

Inside the police station people were lined up in chairs in front of the reception desk. The room smelled of cigarettes, alcohol and unwashed clothes. A guffawing drunk was propositioning a woman in fishnet stockings and a mini skirt, attire too cold for Gothenburg. The woman's face was heavily made-up, and she looked bored.

The officer in charge signed them in and made a phone call. Minutes later a grey-haired man in a suit came through the security door, introduced himself and shook their hands. They followed him down a long hall. Panic glued Maureen to Paavo's side. The policeman's office was tidy; there were bookshelves and metal filing cabinets, just like on television shows. Aside from the desk were three lounge chairs and a coffee table. The detective waved them to the lounge chairs and sat down.

"Coffee for you?" He spoke to Maureen, his eyes reading her pulse. She swallowed and shook her head. The baby kicked and she put her hand on her stomach. The policeman's gaze followed her hand. He leant over to a tape recorder in the centre of the coffee table and switched it on. "You will not mind if I record?"

Maureen looked at Paavo. "We are happy for you to record," he said. The next hour went with hundreds of questions, all asking the same thing, but each phrased differently. Maureen told her story as she pictured the events in her mind, making sure she said how they had put the man in the car because they didn't want him to freeze on the snow-covered ground. That she thought she had placed the keys on the driver's side of the car floor where he would eventually see them. The policeman's questions about their actions with the gun and keys didn't seem to interest him as much as the attack on Jane. How he had turned off the main road, telling them he was taking them back to his place.

The officer showed Maureen a photo of the man. She couldn't be sure because he'd worn a beanie and a scarf. She pictured him in her mind and remembered he was unshaven, that he had a large space between his front teeth and his whiskers were red, also that he wasn't much taller than her. The policeman looked pleased, nodding at her description. She described the car, remembering a tear in the back of the driver's seat. He asked for Jane's full name and where they had worked in Jersey and Norway. She told him Jane had kept the gun. Paavo remained silent the whole time.

At the end of the session the policeman switched off the tape and leaned back. His face more serious than when he had introduced himself. Maureen's body stiffened. "Thank you, for coming forward," he said. "I understand this must be difficult," he looked at her stomach, "but this is a dangerous man and we will make sure he goes to gaol." He stood up, shook her hand and then conversed with Paavo in Swedish. Their eyes went to her a few times during the conversation. She tried to read their faces. Paavo wasn't looking worried.

"We will go," Paavo said, at last. Maureen melted with relief. The chair was deep, and she had difficulty getting up. Paavo offered his arm. The policeman escorted them to the exit door, shook their hands and went back to his office. Maureen held Paavo's arm until they reached the car.

"You did well," he said when they were inside the car. "The commandant was impressed with your honesty. They want to charge him with your attempted abduction as well." Why did he have to tell her that when she had thought it was all over?

27

Eden – The Luncheon

Constable PJ was peeved. He had put the 'keep out' sign on the door of Eric's cottage to make sure the Bateman's Bay coppers wouldn't come nosing around. They would have to see him first. He was pissed off that they had interviewed Eric's accountant without notifying him in time for him to be present at the interview. Fortunately, he had managed to get the accountant's address and tomorrow would drive to Bateman's Bay and do his own interrogation. Now Lillian wanted him to remove the sign so she could rent the place.

"Are you sure that's what you want to do?" He thought it was a mistake to rent the farm out until ownership was proven.

"It's a sensible alternative and I think it's legal," Lillian said.

PJ tapped his fingers on the desk, he wasn't happy. "Have you checked that with Blinky?" There was a battle of stares. Lillian raised her eyebrows. "I mean your lawyer," PJ said.

She'd consult the lawyer when she got home. It was obvious she needed to show the disgruntled constable her appreciation for all his hard work. Put him in a good mood. "I'm grateful for all you've done, Constable PJ. It's just that, if I have to look after Eric, I will need to cover his expenses. He's going to have an operation soon which means frequent trips to the hospital and that's costly. And taking him to familiar places to help his memory improve is also expensive. I'm paying for my daughter to have a window put in the back of her van so we can transport Eric in his wheelchair. He gets carsick otherwise. The van is the only way we women can manage him on our own." Lillian gave PJ a helpless look. She was sick of all the negotiating.

"What operation is he having?" PJ said, sucking in his cheeks.

Lillian went pink. "He has a testicular hernia." She saw PJ's hand cover his mouth. The aubergine between Eric's legs was the talk of the town, just as she'd expected. The doctor had made her sign as Eric's power of attorney giving him permission to operate, but the operation wasn't going ahead until Eric was strong enough to cope. In the meantime, Lillian had made a cushion for him from her collection of sea sponges; they were better than feathers. She had tried feathers, but they had a habit of working through fabric and causing a rash, which meant Eric was always scratching. She was using Eric's incapacity as an excuse to get the sign removed from the farm cottage. If there was one good thing about Eric's stroke, it had taken the town's attention off his affair with Kathy.

"I suppose there's no harm in removing the sign, but I would like to know what a lawyer thinks."

"I'll give him a call when I get home." If only Maureen knew the trouble she was going to.

The first thing Lillian did when she got home was to pour herself a brandy from her inherited crystal decanter that had kept an old lady happy for years. She had a long sip before lifting the phone to call Peter Turnstile. The telephone operator blasted his phone a few times before he answered.

"Peter, it's Lillian. I've just been to see Constable PJ and he asked me to discuss the renting of Eric's farm with you."

Peter rattled off advice and then asked her to wait while he consulted his law books. The information he told her about removing a tenant who had purchased a farm and then found it to be fraudulently sold was unsettling. Lillian sipped at her brandy, her mind on selling the Buick and facing Johnny's disappointment.

"Are you there, Lillian?"

"Yes, Peter." There was dust on the plaster deer head in the hall archway. She should give it a wipe.

"It's an unusual request and as long as there's a written agreement between you, I don't see why van Someren can't rent the farm while waiting on the ruling. If he ends up with the farm, the rent money would have to be repaid, of course. You understand? It will be in the agreement I draw up. You're asking seven dollars a week including the stock, equipment and furnishings?"

"That's right." She would send the rent to Maureen until the baby was born and after that she must come home or manage on her own.

"You will put it on tick, Peter? You know I can't pay you until there's money coming in." She wondered how much her lawyer's bill was going to be and prayed the farm would return to Eric. If not, her plans might end up like a hole in a fishing net.

"Don't worry we'll sort something out. Would you like to come to lunch at my house and I'll have the agreement ready for you?"

Warning bells. Bloody hell, why had she brought up owing him money? Did he think he was going to get a roll in the hay now? But she needed the agreement and soon. Think, woman. Think.

"I could bring Mr van Someren too, then we can both sign the agreement in your presence." There was silence at the other end of the phone. She threw him a lifeline. "Or, why not come to my place for lunch?" She needn't tell him she would ask House and maybe Ingrid? The more witnesses the better and Peter Turnstile couldn't try his luck with her. She would word Ingrid up in advance. "My roses need some pruning?" Peter wouldn't be able to resist the roses.

"When were you thinking?" Her roses would take a while to prune. Although it was a bit late to prune roses.

"Day after tomorrow?" Lillian patted herself on the back for finding a solution and not causing a problem between them.

"Hang on while I check my schedule." There was a rustle of paper. "I'm free for lunch and I'll bring my secateurs; they're sharper than yours."

Lillian had inherited hers from Aunt Maggie. She wondered if his were a metaphor!

After they'd made their arrangements, Lillian phoned House and Ingrid. Ingrid would bring apple strudel and Lillian would make steak and kidney pie. Pastry was her forte.

The day arrived. Wedgewood china and crystal glasses inherited from Aunt Maggie graced the dining room table. Ingrid arrived with the strudel still warm from the oven and a jug of cream fresh from the cow's teat this morning, according to the milko. The door knocker banged twice. Lillian tweaked the curtain in the front room. It was Peter Turnstile. House was coming up in the rear. She smoothed her dress and opened the door. Peter didn't look pleased to see House, or Ingrid who was standing behind Lillian, a glass of sherry in her hand.

"Come in, gentlemen. Ingrid, do you know House?"

"Frederick van Someren, if you would be so kind." He lifted

his nose and sniffed the aroma of steak and kidney pie floating down the hall. His fat cheeks wobbled with approval.

"This is Ingrid Kasbauer, Mr van Someren. And I'm sure you both know Peter Turnstile, my lawyer?" They all shook hands.

"Frederick and I have had a few telephone conversations. Nice to meet you," Peter said tersely. He handed Lillian a box of Cadbury Roses chocolates. "For later," he winked.

Lillian blushed and grabbed the box putting it on the sideboard. "Ingrid will pour you a sherry or beer, whichever you prefer, while I dish up the meal." She hurried into the kitchen.

The steak and kidney pie was a great success. House had mopped every trace off his plate, while Peter, having devoured his meal, started a boring monologue on legal cases that he had won which were mostly to do with real estate. Then he mentioned a case where he'd succeeded in reducing a fine for proving his client wasn't wearing shoes when he had kicked his boss's arse. "His feet were like iron. He never wore shoes." House and Ingrid laughed; Lillian had heard the story before. She cleared the dishes, taking them into the kitchen, pleased everyone was enjoying themselves. Lips smacked when she returned with the strudel and cream.

"This is Ingrid's specialty," Lillian said. She served the strudel and passed around the cream. House didn't wait for Lillian to start, he hoed straight in, face radiant.

"Simply delicious." He turned appreciative eyes on Ingrid. "I must ask how you make it?" Ingrid went pink and giggled. Lillian shot her a look. Ingrid ignored her and began to explain the art of strudel making.

House's hand went up. "I think I should come to your house for a demonstration or perhaps bring you to my farm?"

Ingrid fluttered her eyes, blushing. It was time for Lillian to get to the guts of their luncheon.

"I'm sorry, Mr van Someren, but it isn't your farm," Lillian said.

Peter Turnstile pushed back his chair. "Since we're talking about the farm, I'll get the rental agreement I drew up."

Lillian motioned Ingrid to the brandy decanter. Ingrid floated towards the men's glasses with the decanter, giggling at House who was rubbing his hands. Lillian couldn't believe her eyes. Her friend was flirting. "Ingrid!" Lillian hissed. Ingrid smiled at her and poured House a whacking serve of brandy, then filled Peter Turnstile's glass. It was good quality brandy and it didn't take long for the men to empty their glasses. Ingrid refilled them at the same time putting the last piece of strudel on House's plate. His chubby cheeks trembled with delight as he savoured the strudel, casting her looks of appreciation.

Meanwhile Peter Turnstile read out the agreement and passed it to House to sign. He signed without reading it through, too occupied with swilling the brandy around his teeth to remove bits of strudel.

The agreement was passed to Lillian. On the pretext she hadn't turned the oven off she took it into the kitchen and quickly read the document. It seemed to be in her favour. There was no mention of the rent being repaid if Eric lost the farm to House. Nor was she tied into a time limit. It could be cancelled anytime she wanted. Was it an oversight on Peter's part? She didn't waste time signing and returning it to Peter. Ingrid witnessed their signatures and Peter folded the agreement putting it in his briefcase.

"When will you move in, Mr van Someren?" She wanted the rent as soon as possible. House reached into his coat and removed a cheque book, flipped through the stubs and wrote a cheque in her name for fifteen dollars.

"Two weeks rent," he said, presenting the cheque. Lillian couldn't believe her luck. She would bank it as soon as Peter left.

The men had a smoko while Ingrid and Lillian cleared the table and washed the dishes.

"Thank God that's over. It went well, Ingrid. I think another brandy might get rid of Peter before he starts on my roses and makes excuses to hang around." The women giggled. Their plan had worked. "What are you going to do if House visits for his cooking demonstration?"

"Ja, I will show him." It was sixteen years since she'd cooked for a man, especially one that appreciated her. If he walked up her hill enough times, he might lose some of that tractor tyre around his stomach. Her uninteresting life was looking up.

By the time the women had cleaned up, the decanter was empty and the men were engaging in a slurring debate. To Lillian's relief, House checked his watch. He had another appointment. He bowed over Lillian's and Ingrid's hands and trundled down the hall. Roses forgotten, Peter Turnstile followed him, still arguing the merits of Australia's involvement in Vietnam. She saw the men to the door and watched them get into their cars. The door had hardly shut when the telephone rang.

It was the hospital. Lillian felt like singing after she put the phone down. "Guess what? Eric's walking with the aid of two sticks." She wouldn't have to push him around in a wheelchair. He could get himself to the toilet. Splinter didn't have to put a window in the shop van.

"That is good news. Maybe he gets better enough to live on farm?"

Lillian looked at Ingrid. Somehow, she couldn't see it happening. Not for a while anyway. "I was going to put an advertisement in the butcher's window for the Buick today."

"But what if Eric drives again?"

Lillian tapped her teeth with her finger. She didn't want to jump the gun on the Buick but then she didn't want Johnny to think he could take over the car. The car would sell faster than the farm. But now she had House's cheque for fifteen dollars she wasn't so desperate. "After we've had a cuppa I'll walk up the street with you. I have a cheque to bank."

Lillian waved Ingrid goodbye from the bank steps. Since her divorce she'd had her own bank account. It felt good going into a bank to do her business. She filled out the deposit slip and a withdrawal slip for the same amount and handed it to the teller.

"The cheque will take two days to clear before you can withdraw the money, Mrs McKinley," the teller said. Embarrassed, Lillian picked up the withdrawal slip and shoved it in her handbag. She still had a lot to learn about finances. Fortunately, there was no one in the bank to witness her ignorance.

Quick Parker pulled up outside the bank as Lillian made her exit. She pretended she didn't see him, feeling awkward that it was Eric who had broken up his marriage. She put her head down to walk past him.

"How ya goin', Mrs?" Quick said, stepping towards her. A smell of fish clung to him. Since his farm had failed, he'd been working at the cannery to support his kids. Lillian looked up, pretending surprise.

"Oh! Hello, Mr Parker. I'm well thank you."

"Just want ya to know, I'm sorry for what me wife did to Eric. Runnin' off with his accountant like that. She was doin' it with the accountant fella when we was together. I reckon they was still doin' it when she moved in with ya husband." He shuffled his feet.

His sad face tugged at Lillian's heart. "My ex-husband was also to blame, Mr Parker. He's had a stroke you know?"

"She'd give anyone a stroke, Mrs."

"Nice talking to you, Mr Parker. Sorry, I have to rush." Lillian didn't want to hear anymore, afraid Quick might go into details on how Kathy was capable of giving Eric a stroke. He lifted his hand in a salute as Lillian walked away. She mulled over what

Quick had said and wondered how the town gossips had missed Kathy's fling with the accountant since it had happened before Eric? If Kathy and Eric's accountant had been together before she moved in with Eric perhaps the two of them had planned to dupe Eric into selling his farm? It might be worth passing the information on to Constable PJ. What a scandal. Thinking back on all the scandals surrounding Eric, Lillian couldn't understand how he could have been such a hypocrite to cut Maureen off the way he had.

It was time she let Maureen know what was going on with her father and the farm. It would help Maureen understand why it was taking so long to send her the money. She would include the advertisement for the farm in her letter.

28

New Life

A hand rested on Maureen's shoulder. Startled, she whirled around to see who had stopped her.

"Excuse me. My name is Lars Eriksson." His hand came forward and she shook it without thinking. "I'm a reporter for the *Göteborgs-Posten*." He showed her his identification card. "I have information that you are one of the English hitchhikers that left a man in the snow?"

It took Maureen a minute to gather her wits. "No, I'm not. I don't know what you are talking about. You must be mistaking me for someone else."

He gave a superior smile and shook his head. "Your English is perfect, and I have been informed this is true."

His English was good. He had caught her out. Why had she answered him? Who had sent him? The police said it wouldn't get in the papers. Whoever it was had given him Sarah's address.

The police knew she was living in the home for unmarried mothers so it could only be Nils' father. He was trying to frighten her out of Sweden.

"The suggestion is the man you abandoned was the same one who kidnapped and raped Tove Persson?" he pressed.

Maureen shook her head. "I'm not who you think I am. I'm Australian not English. Now go away." Unnerved she pushed past him and went into the building, hurrying up the stairs, the baby heavy in her stomach. The journalist was a dog on her heels. His informant had mentioned one of the girls was Australian.

"I won't take much of your time," he insisted.

Maureen held her stomach in her arms as she tried to put distance between them. It hurt to breathe. She heaved herself up the last two steps and fell against Sarah's door.

The journalist stepped back looking apologetic. "I'm sorry, I didn't notice you were pregnant. I didn't mean to scare you. I'll leave you my details if you want to talk to me." He pushed a card into her hand then raised a camera that was hanging from his neck and took a snap before she could cover her face. It reminded her of the Petrov case in Australia when a Russian woman had been chased by journalists and lost her shoe.

"What's up?" Sarah said as Maureen fell through her door out of breath. "Are you in labour?"

"Someone's told the newspapers I live here, and a journalist chased me up the stairs to ask about the kidnap." She put her hand over her mouth, rushed to the lavatory and vomited. "God! I need to lie down." Everything inside her shook.

She lay on Sarah's couch while her heart settled into its normal beat. "I bet his parents have done this because one of the girls from the home insulted Nils at the yacht club. I think it would be safer if I just stay at the home until the baby's born and you come and visit me." How was she going to manage with a baby if all this was to continue? Should she give it up for adoption like everyone wanted her to? At least it would grow up with lots of opportunities in a proper home. She didn't even know what country she would live in. Certainly not Sweden if Nils' parents were going to harass her like this.

She thought of her mail. It wouldn't be wise to go to the restaurant in case Bernard was brought into her mess. She was the reason Netta had to move to England. Thankfully, Netta had sounded happy in her letter. Probably another thing the kind woman wanted to let her know so she wouldn't feel guilty.

"Sarah, if you're near the restaurant at any time would you ask Bernard if there's any mail for me? I'll phone and tell him why I can't visit." The baby was heavy and walking was difficult. She was feeling too pregnant to make a long journey on public transport. Matron had been right to worry about her going so far today. She didn't have a taxi coupon and it was a long way back to the home on a tram. And a good walk from the tram stop. There was also the prediction of snow. It was possible the journalist wouldn't want to trudge after her in the snow so she would wait until it started snowing before she left Sarah's.

It was dark and wet when she arrived back at the home. Matron flew down the hall at the sound of the front door closing, grabbed Maureen's coat, pulling it off at the same time scolding her in Swedish.

"It's five o'clock," Maureen said in self-defence. "I said I'd be back at five."

"You are close to baby birth. Snow is slippery. You fall and have baby in snow. Bad girl." She wagged a finger. Then squeezed her arm. "Come, I make a hot coffee for you."

She was sorry she had alarmed Matron and was grateful for

the hot soup and coffee Matron put in front of her. It had been an exhausting day.

"There is message for you," Matron said, putting a note on the table. She gave Maureen a quizzical look.

The message was from Paavo. He'd made an appointment for her for ten o'clock tomorrow. A taxi was picking her up. "I have to go out in the morning for an hour," Maureen said folding the note.

Matron tutted. "This person cannot come here. It is not good so much running around. Too much worry is not good for you also."

"They're sending a taxi for me. I won't be gone long, and it will be the last time I leave the home until my baby is born, I promise." She didn't want to upset Matron after today's panic.

Matron put her hands in her pockets and paced. She turned to Maureen with her decision made. "In the morning Sister Vigdis will check baby's heartbeat. Now you have early sleep. I must go home. It is a long day of worry for me." She looked pale and tired. Maureen lowered her eyes at the reproof. Shrugging into her coat, Matron collected her small case then went into the lounge to say goodnight to the girls.

Maureen heaved herself up the stairs. The bedroom facing her at the top of the stairs was Birget's. Her door was open. A closed suitcase stood by the door.

Exhausted moans came from the curled form on the bed. They echoed the pain of mothers down the ages and stirred a deep emotion inside Maureen. Following her instinct, she went into Birget's room, crawled onto the bed and curled around her. She didn't ask what was wrong, just rocked and stroked Birget until she lay quiet in her arms. They lay together in silence until Birget whispered, "I go back to Norge without him. The family I give him to are nice."

"You are a heroine." It was all Maureen could think to say or trusted herself to say without crying. Holding all that pain in her arms, Maureen knew what she'd said was the truth. Would she be able to give her baby up if she had to? Birget was in her thirties, she wasn't married, she had a sick mother and no one in her village had known she was pregnant. The father was married. He was her boss and had sent her away. All this she had gleaned from the others, who had combined their pieces of knowledge to satisfy their curiosity. Birget had not mixed with the girls while she had been in the home.

"When are you leaving?"

"When the doorbell rings," Birget said. She sat up. "I will give my address for you. You must tell me what you do."

She scribbled her address on the bottom of the Rules and Instruction notice that hung on the wall in all the bedrooms and handed it to Maureen. A bell rang in the distance and Sister Vigdis appeared in Birget's doorway. Birget clung to Maureen. There was an exchange of words between the sister and Birget and then the sister picked up the suitcase by the door and left. Maureen walked to the stairs with Birget. They hugged. A low animal sound came from Birget's throat as she pulled away from Maureen.

Maureen flung herself on the bed crying tears of mourning for Birget. Was this what it would be like for her? Deep inside, she felt as though something had changed within her. She felt older. She was twenty-two, a grown woman, soon to be a mother and she had to prepare herself for what was to come.

The next morning Maureen was ferried by taxi to Paavo's office. The driver opened her door. She swung both feet out of the car, making sure she missed the pool of slush and pulled herself upright using the door for leverage. She adjusted her beanie to cover her ears against the spring bite, then said a quiet prayer as she entered the lawyer's building.

"How long to go?" Paavo enquired, showing Maureen to the chair in front of his desk.

"Sister Vigdis thinks between two and three weeks. First babies are usually late, she said." Maureen wanted it to happen right now. She was fed up with being pregnant.

Paavo sat on the edge of his desk and spun a small globe, watching the world go around. "That's what I want to talk to you about," he said.

Maureen gave him her full attention.

"Nils is requesting a blood test to prove the child is his." Her eyes flashed and she was about to say something when Paavo's hand went up. "I believe it is his baby. But you must understand we have to comply with his wishes." Maureen's face flushed with anger. "We have a problem, however. Nils is going to Canada for three months. He leaves in seven days. And, of course he has to have a blood test himself, which if it's not done before he leaves, will delay everything. He insists on having a test only after the baby is born in case there's a stillbirth or you put it up for adoption. If that occurs, he won't be financially responsible."

Maureen choked with fury. "That's awful. He knows when the baby is due. Why would he do that to me? Go away before the child is born? What have I done to them to make them hate me so much?" She sat white-faced, eyes glistening with tears she refused to spill.

"It is his right to make that request, Maureen. You must remember his father is a lawyer." He held out a handkerchief. She shook her head, her heart needed more than a handkerchief. "I will order us some coffee."

"No, I'm alright," she wiped her hand across her eyes and shifted to get more comfortable. Her back ached. "So, what am I to do?"

"You could give birth this week?"

Was the man serious? He wasn't smiling. Maureen laughed

to cover her confusion. "How can I do that? Tell the baby to pop out?"

"I can speak to the hospital on your behalf and have them induce the baby. That way it will be born before Nils leaves and he will be forced to give a blood sample."

It was so unfair. Nils hadn't suffered through any of this. He wouldn't know if something went wrong with the birth or the baby. He wouldn't be there to wrap his arms around her like she had done with Birget. Whatever happened, Nils would not be affected. Why had she always jumped to his defence? He was weak and uncaring. Now she had to think about bringing on the birth of her baby, and she was scared. Could anything go wrong? No more willy-nilly decision making.

"I must speak to Matron and see what she thinks before I decide on inducing the birth."

"You must act quickly." Paavo stood up, impatient for her decision. "Go back and speak with Matron."

On her arrival Maureen went straight to Matron's office. The door was open. "Matron could I see you for a moment?" Matron waved her hand at the armchair by her desk and Maureen closed the door behind her.

The story came out in a series of events with no interruptions apart from aghast looks on Matron's face as Maureen told her everything that had happened to her in Sweden, including the hitchhiking incident.

"Stackars flicka." The word *flicka* sounded very different coming from Matron. Nils' mother would never have clucked her tongue and said 'poor girl'. Matron tapped a pencil on the desk, brow crinkled, gazing at Maureen. "I think you can induce baby. It is due anytime so should not be problem." She pointed to the telephone. "Call your lawyer. Nils should not get away with this."

Within four hours Maureen was in hospital hooked up to a drip and wishing her mother was with her. White gowns came and went and with them the pain in ever increasing spasms that left her breathless. She had never felt anything like it. It went on and on. Two minutes apart for twenty-three hours. Emergency bells went off, doctors collected around her bedside, conferred. She understood nothing. Terrified. With the next contraction, she fainted. The baby's heart rate had increased. The drip was closed off and they left her to rest for an hour before starting it up again. She was soaked in perspiration, exhausted and had paid for every bad deed in her life by the time her eight-pound four-ounce, healthy son was born. Nils could get ready to have his blood test while Maureen had a well-earned sleep after twenty-four hours of torture.

A gentle hand shook her awake. "Your baby, Maureen." The nurse handed her a bundle of white blankets. "You must feed."

A pink bald baby with a wrinkled fist in its tiny mouth mewed. It was the most beautiful creature Maureen had ever seen. She thought she was going to burst with love. The nurse put the baby to Maureen's breast. Its tiny mouth hunted for her nipple, latched on and Maureen's breasts caught fire. Although she winced with pain, she was full of pride that her body could keep this gift alive. If only her mother could see them now.

"What are you going to call him?" the nurse asked.

Maureen didn't take long to decide. The name just popped out. "Henry Bernard." The name would always remind her of Netta and Bernard."

"When feeding is finished, we must make blood test for you and baby."

"Will it hurt him?" She couldn't bear the thought.

The nurse looked away. "We must take phial of blood from his arm and foot. Babies have little veins," she said.

Maureen felt sick. They were going to hurt her child. No! Nils was hurting his child. She hoped Nils' veins were small and the syringe blunt.

The nurse came for the baby after she had finished feeding and picked him up. "I will bring him back for cuddles," she said, cooing to him as she carried him from the room.

An hour later the nurse returned and laid Henry Bernard in Maureen's arms. His face was red and damp with sweat. She opened the blanket and showed Maureen his foot. A band-aid the length of his foot was wrapped around his heel. "He cry a lot that is why his face so red." Maureen felt her own tears coming. How could Nils be so cruel? The baby squealed in his sleep. She clutched him close.

The doctor arrived with the welfare officer. Fru Wellander smiled at Maureen, putting a box of chocolates on her bedside table and pulling a chair close.

"I hear you had a difficult birth. Lots of stitches. But now you look glowing." Maureen was propped up with pillows the baby nestling in her arms.

"Have you seen him?" She opened the blanket for the officer to admire. They have taken a blood sample and it hurt him." She clenched her teeth and held the tiny foot up to show the officer the band-aid. "I want you to tell Nils he caused his baby pain." The welfare officer considered Maureen and the baby thoughtfully.

"It had to be done. I am here to see what you have decided. It's not good for you to have contact with the baby if you are going to have him adopted." Her voice was soft and her eyes kind. Adoption? Why did she have to think about it so soon? The bundle in her arms squirmed. Her mind went to the devastated girl in the home. She could feel Birget's shuddering body in her arms and knew she could not do what Birget had done.

"I'm not having him adopted," she said with conviction. She waited for the welfare officer to tell her she was being silly, that she should think of the baby's future. Instead Fru Wellander leant over and took her hand.

"I hope you have a happy life together. You have six weeks in the home until we have to find other accommodation for you. We will discuss it after you leave hospital." She peeked at the baby. "He is beautiful." When her visitor had left, Maureen fell asleep smiling.

The blood test results came through two days after the birth. Nils was declared the possible father. The news coincided with a journalist visiting new mothers for their birth notices to go in the newspaper. She came to Maureen accompanied by a nurse.

"This lady is asking if you want a notice in her newspaper."

Maureen was thrilled. She was a proud mother and Nils would learn his baby's name. She hoped his parents would read the announcement and be full of regret for what they had lost.

"Yes. I do." Maureen thought hard. She wanted to get it right. "You must write it in English and large letters. *A son, Henry Bernard Classon-McKinley, born to Maureen McKinley of Australia.* She paid for the announcement with Netta's busking money. It was the only announcement in the paper from a single mother. And, as it turned out, the newspaper was the same one the journalist who had pursued her worked for.

29

Eden – A Grave Happening

Lillian opened *The Eden Magnet* for a quick peruse while she ate her porridge. This morning she was going to visit the police station to discuss her suspicions with Constable PJ. The spoonful of porridge dropped back in her bowl and she shot to her feet. She grabbed her coat and bag and the newspaper.

An hour later, Lillian charged into the police station and slammed *The Eden Magnet* on Constable PJ's desk.

"Have you seen this?" He shook his head. "I want to know who ratted to the editor. I've been to see him, but he refuses to dob them in. Stuff and nonsense. I'd like you to read the article."

PJ read aloud. "A debate rages over the ownership of Mr Eric McKinley's Towamba farm. Said to have been sold to Mr Frederick van Someren before Eric McKinley suffered a stroke and lost his memory, the sale of the farm is now being disputed by McKinley's ex-wife, Lillian McKinley."

His lips pushed forward in thought. "I did advise you not to rent the place until the ownership was resolved."

"It doesn't mention rent. It infers I want ownership and makes me look like a mercenary ex-wife out for my own gain. It's so unfair. Bugger, shit, bugger!" Lillian's expletives reddened the young constable's ears. She hardly ever swore, but this was too much. She couldn't speak up in her own defence and admit her unmarried daughter was pregnant in Sweden and desperately needed money. People had short memories about how Eric acquired his farm in the first place. If it hadn't been for her there would be no farm.

"Bugger, shit!" The expletives in her head worsened. "I bet House said something in the club after he'd had a few. We need to clear this matter up, PJ," she said firmly.

PJ had a lot of admiration for Lillian. He'd heard about the way she had manoeuvred House into signing the rental agreement and he didn't want her bad mouthed in the town. He leant on his desk deciding to discuss his findings with her. "I paid a visit to the accountant in Bateman's Bay a couple of days ago." Lillian's hands stopped twisting in her lap. "I told him Eric's signature wasn't going to be accepted on the deed. That the farm would be returned to Eric and he was under investigation for fraud. He's as slippery as an eel. Tried to make out Eric had invested the money without his knowledge. I told him our experts were checking to see who had managed his investments. I also said House was after him." PJ gave a satisfied grin. He was enjoying his job. When this was over, he was going to apply for a transfer to Sydney's vice squad.

"Good on you, PJ. What did he say?" Lillian moved to the edge of her seat.

"The mongrel was cornered. Tried some bullshit that Kathy had the money, said she'd bought a place in Bateman's Bay and that they weren't together, never had been. Turns out the place she bought is in both their names. Couldn't pull the wool over my eyes."

"Thank God," Lillian sat back. "Now Eric can sell the farm with my power of attorney."

"Not so easy. The mongrel's getting himself a lawyer. However, I hit him up with the nine thousand that vanished from Eric's bank account. He said Eric had owed him three grand and the balance Eric had put into another account that only Eric knew about. I said we were checking, and Eric's memory was improving." PJ tapped his head with his finger. "He's not going to outsmart me. I reckon I left him with a stain in his pants."

"Do you think we could let the newspaper know all this, so it doesn't look like I'm trying to get the farm back for my own ends?" She was still a Pommie immigrant to some people in town.

"Wait until we get the ruling that Eric wasn't sound of mind at the time of the sale." His eyes widened at the way he had expressed himself. No doubt about it, he was meant to be a detective.

Lillian bit the inside of her cheek. "I hope it's not going to take too long." Maureen needed her fare home. She got up to leave, then remembered why she had called in to see PJ. "I'm not sure if this is relevant or anything, but Quick told me the accountant and Kathy were having a relationship before she moved in with Eric. He seemed to think it had been going on for a while, so I was wondering if they had planned to do this to Eric from the start? I'm not a policeman though, you'd have more idea about this sort of thing."

PJ stroked his chin, something he'd copied off a detective show. "I'll drop by and have a chat with Quick," he said.

Good. Lillian thanked her lucky stars she had such an obliging assistant. When she got home there were a couple of people she needed to have a chat with. Everything going well, the telephonist on duty would have read the newspaper and be listening into her phone calls to her advantage.

Her first telephone call was to Peter Turnstile. She read him the article and he suggested she sue for defamation of character in the event of gossip. Happy with the outcome of her conversation with Peter her next call was to Ingrid.

"Hello, Ingrid. Yes, I did, that's what I'm phoning about. Would you know if House van Someren spoke to the newspaper? Well, it's a pity the newspaper didn't mention Eric was being drugged by Kathy Parker at the time he was supposed to have sold the farm. And they never mentioned his cheque account having been cleaned out of nine thousand dollars … Yes, it's a lot to just vanish into thin air." Lillian smiled as Ingrid went to town on the accountant. They planned a morning tea and said their goodbyes. Lillian heard a small click on the line after Ingrid hung up and gave a thin smile before replacing the phone.

She checked the clock; Johnny would be here with Eric soon. She did a quick tidy-up. The CWA roster had started, and Judy Thompson was coming to give her a hand with Eric.

Aided by one walking stick and Johnny's arm, Eric entered the kitchen. His eyes latched onto Lillian and he beamed. He was wearing a short-sleeved white shirt, khaki shorts, long socks and black lace-up shoes. Lillian hadn't seen the shorts before. Eric usually wore long pants, but it was a hot day and the hospital often had leftover clothing after a death. Perhaps that's where his shorts had come from. He looked quite smart.

"Hello Eric, it's good to see you walking." He wobbled over to the window with the aid of a stick and the stove and looked across at Aunt Maggie's old place.

"How's Aunty?" he said.

"She's dead, Eric. Died eleven years ago." For him to remember Aunt Maggie was progress. She saw him worry at a memory. His poor brain was a mix of negatives that she would have to constantly develop. It was a loss for all of them. Perhaps when all the farm and money issues were resolved she could help him return to the nice young sailor she had met in England. She looked at Johnny standing with his hands in his pockets frowning at the linoleum. "Would you like a cup of tea, son?" She switched the electric jug on.

"I've got to go, Mum." Johnny was taking Reidun to the pictures. She was Norwegian and her family were new to Eden. Her English wasn't good, but she was pretty and had great tits which she didn't mind him exploring. "I'll pick Dad up tomorrow arvo." Lillian gave him a distracted nod, her eyes on Eric as he opened and closed cupboards and pulled out drawers.

"What are you looking for, Eric?" He stared at her blank faced. "Sit down," she said, holding out a chair. "We're going for a drive later. Judy Thompson is taking us to the wharf and the cemetery for an outing in her car. She should be here soon." It was to be a memory lane trip for him.

Johnny placed a hand on his father's shoulder. "I'll be off then, Dad, I'll see you tomorrow." Eric looked up at his son.

"Can I come?" His eyes begged. Johnny cast his mother an imploring look. She was about to distract Eric when a thought struck her.

"Johnny, why don't you take Dad up to the Fisherman's Club for an hour? The horse races are on and he can watch it on television. It might be good for his memory. Perhaps he'll want to place a bet and remember where he put his money?" Johnny pulled a face. "Just for an hour?"

"No, I'm meeting my mates."

"Pity, because if he doesn't remember I'll have to sell the Buick." She sighed and turned to the sink, filling it with water to wash up the scone tray she'd used, to make Judy a nice afternoon tea after their excursion. Johnny moved from one foot to the other, frowning.

"Righto, just an hour, then. Come on Dad. I'll take you up to the club." Eric's face lit up like bonfire night. Lillian helped Johnny get him to his feet and gave Eric his cane. They looked sweet stumbling off to the car together.

In the club, Johnny found his father a chair close to the television set. "What do you want to bet on, Dad?" The vacant look Eric had greeted his well-wishers with when he'd entered the club was gone as the horses lined up for the race.

"Put a fiver on McKinley Park, number ten," Eric said.

Johnny checked the horses. "There's no McKinley Park, Dad."

"Yes, number ten."

"Have you got a fiver, Dad?"

Eric slapped his pockets looking for his wallet then scrunched his face. "She's pinched it," he said. He looked like he was about to cry."

"Who, Dad?"

Eric screwed up his eyes then shook his head. "McKinley Park."

Johnny shrugged. "It's alright. Dad, I've got a fiver. I'll put it on number ten."

They watched the race sitting side by side, Johnny grinning at his father riding his chair, whipping it with excitement. Eric whooped with joy as number ten crossed the finish line in first place. His face was pink, and his eyes gleamed with animation. Johnny welled up. It was a pleasure to see his dad so happy. When they left the club, Johnny was seventy dollars richer and Eric had ten dollars in his pocket. He would take his Dad again. He was a good luck charm.

They entered the kitchen with a swagger. Lillian knew from the grins on their faces that the club had been a success.

"Dad backed number ten and won a tenner," Johnny laughed. "He thought he'd backed a horse called McKinley Park, but it didn't exist. He said McKinley Park had stolen his money." He gave his dad a good-natured nudge and Eric tumbled into a chair.

"Careful, Johnny, he's not very strong you know."

After Johnny had left, Lillian mulled over the name. Perhaps Eric had remembered it because of his own name, or perhaps there was a park called McKinley? She would look into it. In the meantime, Judy Thompson had arrived to take them out.

It was a struggle getting Eric into the front of Judy's Holden, but together they managed. Lillian settled herself in the back. "This is so good of you, Judy."

"I'm happy to help poor Eric," Judy replied. Lillian thought about all the people that were helping poor Eric and thought poor Eric was doing alright. If he hadn't had his stroke and lost the farm, he probably would have kicked her door down and taken up residence.

He had always thought her house was his, regardless of his aunt's will. But now he was there at her invitation because what else could she do? Poor her!

The first stop was the wharf. The sea was as flat as a stingray, hardly a boat at the wharf or a soul in sight except for a couple of kids leaping off the wharf and bombing each other in the water. Lillian preferred it that way. She didn't want people gawking at them. Getting Eric out of the car was a chore.

"Put your feet on the ground and swing your body around, one hand on my shoulder and hold the top of the door with the other one. When I say one, two, three, try and lift yourself on three." A sore shoulder later and a lot of grunting from Eric, Lillian had him on his feet. They hadn't gone far up the wharf when Eric started puffing.

"That's probably enough for him, we still have the cemetery to visit." On the way back to the car they stopped next to where the kids were jumping in the water so Eric could catch his breath. He leant against a pylon and tried to pull his shoe off.

"No, Eric we don't have time for a swim." He dropped his chin on his chest and shuffled between Lillian and Judy. They hadn't long left the house and already Lillian was feeling exhausted.

At the cemetery she showed him Aunt Maggie's grave. His brow furrowed and he kicked a few stones, nearly over balancing from the effort. His lips tightened and an old look came into his eyes. He turned to Lillian. Her heart skipped a beat.

"Aunt Maggie left you money to buy your farm and you sold it to Frederick van Someren or House. Remember, Eric?"

"I didn't sell my farm," he said, agitated. Lillian put a calming hand on his arm. He looked at her clear-eyed. She was pleased Judy was there to witness his denial.

"I saw the deed you signed, Eric. What did you do with the money? It wasn't in your bank? Did you open up another account, maybe in the name of McKinley Park or McKinley Parker?" It was a long shot.

"She bought McKinley Park."

Lillian's hope ebbed. He wasn't following her. "Where is McKinley Park, Eric?"

"Training," he said. Suddenly the penny dropped.

"Is it a horse? Did you buy a horse with the farm money?" She looked at Judy to see if she was taking this in. Judy was wide eyed and watching Eric.

"I'm not selling the farm," he shouted. His face was white with fury. He started to lash the air with his walking stick.

Lillian grabbed his arm. "It's alright, Eric. You didn't sell the farm. We know that. I just don't know how you bought a racehorse."

"With the money in the bank," he said.

At last, she had a picture of what had happened. She turned to Judy to see what she thought of Eric's declaration.

Eric watched the waves tumble on the beach with a distant look in his eyes. He would like a swim. Using his stick and the headstones he wandered over to the wire fence that separated the cemetery from the road next to the beach. He lifted his leg to climb over, managing to get it the height of the wire where he rested it for a moment, then he tried to lift it higher to clear the wire, but it wouldn't budge. He was stuck on the fence like a dancer holding an arabesque. The wire cut into his poor herniated testicles, dividing and pinching them to the side.

"Jezzzuss!" screamed Eric, incoherent with pain. Lillian and Judy rushed towards him.

"My goodness!" Judy said.

"Try and hold the fence down while I lift his crotch and maybe I can flip him over." Judy pushed the fence down while Lillian got her shoulder under Eric's buttocks and heaved. He flipped over the fence, rolling onto his back, bellowing, hands clasping his crotch. The women clambered after him. A trail of saliva hung from his lips; his nose was bubbling snot. "You must try and get up, Eric." He kicked his legs in the air like a naughty child then rolled onto his knees and dry retched. "If you can't get up, I'll have to call an ambulance." Judy ran for her car to bring it closer to Eric. Lillian wrenched his weak arm away from his crotch and hung it around her neck but couldn't loosen the grip on his other hand.

"Hold onto the fence and help me get you up, Eric." A camper heading for the caravan park pulled up beside them. A hefty bloke got out to see what all the commotion was about.

"Need a hand Mrs?"

"Please," Lillian said, eyes weeping gratitude. "He tried to climb the fence, but he's had a stroke and couldn't get over and ended up stuck halfway."

"Mee ballls!" sobbed Eric.

"He hurt his, um, testicles in the process." Lillian went pink. "I'm trying to get him into my friend's car so I can take him to the hospital."

"Move away, ladies." The tattooed camper, recently returned from Vietnam, lifted Eric into the back of Judy's car. Eric curled up on the back seat, groaning.

"Thank you, so much."

"Not a problem, Mrs. Now get him to hospital as quick as you can." The camper could feel Eric's pain. He waved them off.

"Is it alright with you if we take him straight to the hospital, Judy?" Lillian could picture the look of disbelief on the triage nurse's face as she filled in her journal with the state Eric was returned in. She gave a deep sigh.

"Happy to," Judy replied.

On their arrival at the hospital, Eric's condition was treated as an emergency. Lillian held his hand while a nurse packed his scrotum in ice. His willy had shrunk to the size of Lillian's pointer finger. She stared at his once well-endowed member. Considering all the vaginas it had been into, it wouldn't even stop up Aunt Maggie's decanter she thought. The ice pack must have frosted his privates to the point of discomfort because Eric started to writhe around. A nurse tried to settle him down. He called her a cunt. A needle went into his arm and he passed out.

Lillian tossed up whether to stay with Eric or return with Judy. She decided there was no point staying while Eric was sedated.

30

Lawyer Appointment

Maureen arrived at the home for unmarried mothers with her baby. Standing by the front door eager to greet her arrival were the girls. They took it in turns to view the baby and compliment her on its looks. None of them asked her what the birth was like. Matron came out of her office with a bunch of flowers and a card.

"That's so nice of you, thank you," Maureen said.

"It is from outside person." Maureen blushed at her mistake. "There is a card. I will help you settle your baby."

The cot was already made up in her room. Maureen laid Henry Bernard down and tucked him in under Matron's watchful eye. Matron pulled the baby wrap away from the baby's face while Maureen put the flowers in a vase. She opened the envelope to read the card. A chill ran down her spine. She had thought they were from Bernard or Sarah, but the journalist had sent them. He knew where she lived. Alarmed, she turned to Matron.

"What is it?"

"The flowers are from the journalist who followed me to my friend's flat wanting to interview me about the hitchhiking story."

"You will phone your lawyer. Get advice. We do not want him here. The girls here must be private." The girls were matron's responsibility as was the safety of the babies. She couldn't have Maureen risking the girls' identities. Maureen wasn't the only one in hiding here. Anya, the one who put on the tough front, was hiding from a violent husband who had punched and kicked her in the stomach when he learned she was pregnant. Matron held fears that the child Anya carried would be born with brain damage. She couldn't risk her being found. "It would not be good for anyone if you leave the home."

"I must visit my friends. There are letters from Australia I have to collect. There could be money in them. Please, I have to go out?"

"How can you take the baby without a pram?" It was better to create an obstacle than veto an outing.

"I saw one in the storeroom." It was a battered old wooden framed pram with a carrycot that lifted out.

"No. I must ask you to stay here for four weeks without visiting. They are rules. Baby can't go out, he is too young. I will get messages to your friends. They must come here. If you choose to leave you cannot return, that is also rule. You will phone your lawyer." There was no moving Matron; her kind face was resolute. Maureen felt trapped. She couldn't stay with Sarah; her husband was back. Henry Bernard began to cry.

"He sounds hungry," Matron said. "Why don't you feed him and then bring him to the lounge so we can all see him? We have cake for afternoon tea. It is made for your welcome back." She smiled at Maureen.

Maureen didn't return her smile. She checked the baby's napkin. He was soaked. "I'll come down later." Maureen closed the door behind Matron. She laid her baby on her bed and watched him squirm, his tiny sparrow legs bending and stretching, arms punching the air and himself. His hands were miniature old man's hands, pink skinned and peeling. His week-old eyes were sightless dark orbs. He smelled of talcum powder and milk. She changed his napkin and singlet, swaddled him and cuddled him close. He was a good no fuss eater, guzzling and gulping. His burps were so loud even he looked amazed. Maureen adored him. After an hour she laid him in his cot, asleep and satisfied, and went downstairs to join the girls.

The lounge had been decorated with streamers. On the table was a cake surrounded by cups and plates, tea and coffee pot. Sister Vigdis, the cook, Matron and the girls clapped as she entered. Maureen smiled through tears. The girls looked pleased for her. They weren't just putting on a show for Matron's benefit. For once she didn't feel like an outsider.

"Look, you are thin," Eva said standing next to her. She was due in a week. "I do not know you. I want to be thin again," she moaned. Maureen remembered the painful price she'd paid to get her figure back. She wasn't going to tell them about the birth. They would all find out and it would be mean to scare them. She twirled and laughed.

"You look like film star," Anya said. Maureen did feel good in her old body shape, breasts larger, but still in proportion. At last she had a wardrobe of clothes that fitted, no more voluminous tents and elastic waist pants. She felt like partying, or going to the movies, except they were all in Swedish and she couldn't get a babysitter while she was breastfeeding Henry Bernard. Drachia, the Yugoslav girl, picked up a banjo she had brought to the celebration.

"You will enjoy a folk song," she said. Her voice was sweet

and lilting, the tempo like a gypsy dance. They were soon tapping their feet, lifting teacups up, calling *skol* to each other, saluting their future. It fed Maureen's resilience. She was a mother. Nothing was going to beat her. She forgave Matron for forbidding her outings and she would play by the rules.

When the afternoon tea was finished, Maureen phoned Paavo, telling him about the journalist and her banned outings.

"I will inform the police inspector of this intrusion," he said. "It could be we will have to make a statement for the newspapers. I will call the matron and discuss this with her. It is necessary we have an appointment in the privacy of my office. We can make it between baby feeds so you can leave baby at the home." Maureen didn't want to leave her baby with anyone, even for twenty minutes, but she would follow Paavo's advice.

Three days passed. Three days of constant advice from Matron and Sister Vigdis on how to look after her child. They stood behind her when she bathed the baby, told her when he should be changed, usually at the moment she was about to do so. Told her he should go in his cot when she was enjoying a cuddle and told her when to ignore his crying. Maureen was fed up. She knew she could manage on her own given the chance.

It was on her mind to ask Matron and Sister Vigdis to leave her alone when she fell asleep with the baby still attached to her breast. She woke up flat on one side and bursting with milk on the other. Alarmed, she rushed through Matron's door.

"Something's happened to me. Look!" In a panic she pulled her jacket open, showing Matron her deformity. Matron laughed.

"It is because you did not change sides when you fed baby. It will become normal. Next time you feed on fat breast first. You can squeeze milk out with a breast pump." She went to a cabinet and took out a breast pump. "Show me your breast." Maureen opened her jacket and Matron placed the glass end of the pump over her nipple and squeezed the rubber end. Milk streamed out filling the small glass bulb in the middle. She removed the pump. "Like cow. Take it to your room."

Maureen knew how to milk a cow and it wasn't the same. "Thank you, Matron." Relieved that she wouldn't be lopsided for the rest of her life, she took the pump back to her room. She wouldn't ask Matron and Sister Vigdis to leave her alone just yet.

Paavo telephoned Matron and they made an appointment for Maureen to visit his office. Maureen was annoyed she wasn't making her own arrangements, but Matron was monitoring her phone calls in case the journalist tried his luck again.

Bernard phoned, receiving the third degree from Matron before Maureen was allowed to speak to him. "I 'ave two letters from Australia for you."

"Can you re-address them and send them here, Bernard?" She frowned in Matron's direction. "I'm not allowed to leave here, and I am expecting money from my family."

"But it is not a prison? You can come here for dinner. I will send the taxi for you."

"No, I'm sorry, I can't come for dinner. There's a journalist looking for me. He wants to put my story in the paper." There was silence at the other end of the phone. Maureen knew Bernard was thinking about the publicity. She lowered her voice. "I will never mention you or Netta, Bernard."

"Merci, chérie."

"I've named my baby Henry Bernard. What do you think of that?" There was a wail on the end of the phone.

"You make Henrietta and me very 'appy. I will bring letters tomorrow so I can see him."

"I have a lawyer appointment tomorrow. Come when you aren't busy, I will be here." She grinned as kisses were blown down the phone. The money could wait.

The taxi arrived to take her to Paavo. Maureen stood over

the cot, straightening the blankets, not wanting to leave Henry Bernard.

"You must go. The baby will be fine. I can give him a bottle if you have delays," Matron said. Maureen had pumped her breasts in case she was late.

She was full of anxiety as the taxi drove through the city. Every slip of the car wheels on the wet road filled her with fear. If something happened to her what would happen to Henry Bernard? She gripped the seat as the taxi wove through the traffic and sighed with relief when it pulled up outside Paavo's office.

"Come in, Maureen. His eyes appraised her figure and glossy dark hair that reached her shoulders. She wore make-up, heels, black stockings and a mini skirt. He cleared his throat.

"I have news for you." It was good news. The police had located Jane in England. She had verified Maureen's story. Jane had kept the gun and handed it over to Interpol.

"Your friend will not have to come to Sweden for the trial. They have her statement. But you are in Sweden so you will be called upon to be a witness against Aaberg in the Tove Persson trial." Maureen's pulse quickened. "We cannot protect you from the newspapers when the trial starts. The date is three weeks from now. That is also the time when you have to leave the home by law. I have contacted your welfare officer. She has found temporary accommodation for you. It is a flat in a building close to the city centre and public transport. The building is to be pulled down for new development. The accommodation is free."

Maureen felt her heart soar. How good Sweden was to her. Much better than her own country would be.

Paavo continued, "I hope to receive some payment from Nils to help maintain you until you get work. I must warn you though, he will not pay enough for you to live on." He paused. "There is another problem we have." Paavo looked at his desk and shuffled some papers. "In your situation you must prove you can support yourself and your baby by the time he is six months old or he will be taken into care." A bomb went off in Maureen's gut. Her baby could be taken from her. She stared at Paavo, stricken. What was she going to do? She couldn't keep asking Bernard for help. Through the kindness of people things had worked out for her without much planning on her part. She had been lucky. But this could be catastrophic. She bit the inside of her cheek tasting blood.

"Paavo, could I use your telephone and ring a friend?"

"Of course. While you do that, I shall bring us coffee." He left her alone in his office.

"Bernard, it's Maureen. I'm at my lawyer's but I will be home in an hour, and I was wondering if you are still able to visit me today? I need my letters." Replacing the phone, she wiped her eyes, grateful to know such a lovely man. She was glad she had named her son after him.

31

Eden – Harvest Time

Lillian had to find out the name of the horse. She'd worked out that Eric must have bought it with the lump sum that had gone missing from his bank account. She pondered the prospects while Judy drove them back to Eden from the hospital. The horse could be another avenue for Maureen's fare. It was a pity Eric had damaged himself on the cemetery fence otherwise she could have taken him straight to the police station while he had some clarity of mind, but at least Judy had heard what he'd said and could back her up.

The car jolted around a bend threatening Lillian's stomach contents. Judy was a cautious driver, braking constantly and creeping down the hill. The slow pace worked on Lillian's nerves, and if Judy didn't drive faster Lillian would be too car sick to attend to her business.

"Would you mind dropping me off at the post office, Judy?"

The public phone box was next to the telephone exchange where she could see which telephonist was on duty. Her daughter's friend was trustworthy. "You won't have to wait for me. I'll walk home."

"I can do that," Judy said, her eyes never leaving the road.

"Can you go a bit faster? I want to phone the police station."

"Bellbird Hill is dangerous. Log trucks can come around those corners on the wrong side."

"Well I can smell your brakes and if you keep riding them, they'll burn out," Lillian snapped. She had listened to Eric telling Johnny when he was teaching him to drive.

"I'm the driver and when you learn how to drive you can criticise. I'll drive faster once we're at the bottom of the hill."

There was nothing Lillian could do but stare out of the window and concentrate on the magnificent gum trees and flowering clematis. The smell of eucalyptus trees and the tinkling of bellbirds filled the car. She rested her head on the open window and breathed in the bush, trying to forget her nausea as the car jerked down the hill.

Judy stopped outside the post office, gave a sniff of annoyance and stared straight ahead. She hadn't spoken to Lillian since her driving had been criticised. Lillian knew she would have to try and make amends. Judy had ferried her around all day without complaint. She put her hand on her friend's arm.

"You have been a wonderful help, Judy. I don't know what I would have done without you today." Judy's miffed expression softened. "And, actually, I was wondering if you would give me some driving lessons when you have time? I want to learn, but only from a good driver."

Judy wriggled in her seat and beamed. "I'm happy to. We could do it on the footy ground." She gave the accelerator a professional rev. "We'll work out some suitable times." They squeezed hands and Judy drove off smiling.

Satisfied that the telephonist was Splinter's friend, Lillian made her call to the police station to discuss her theory. The phone rang a few times before PJ answered. She rattled off her greeting and PJ asked after Eric, saying he had seen him at the club with Johnny.

"That's what I want to talk to you about." Lillian went over her day with Eric and told him what Johnny had said about McKinley Park. The silence on the end of the line indicated PJ was thinking.

"If he bought a racehorse, that's not a crime," PJ said at last. She knew that, but Eric's missing winnings could be a crime.

"He backed number ten," Lillian said. She could hear the tick of PJ's brain.

"What was the horse called?"

"Johnny didn't say."

"I'll check with Bookie Joe. I should catch him at the club if I go now."

"Thank you, PJ." Lillian put the phone down satisfied she had raised the constable's interest.

PJ entered the Fishermen's Club and cornered Bookie Joe. He was a slimy little skunk who was an SP Bookie and PJ had been itching to put him away for his illegal activity. He'd made a fortune out of the constable's father with his bogus tips.

"G'day, Constable." Bookie Joe's eyes darted around the room.

"I'm hoping you can give me some information, Joe?" PJ used his official voice, right hand bunching at his side.

"Sure. Why don't I shout you a beer, Constable?" He flashed a gold front tooth, hair stiff with Brylcreem.

"Sounds good," PJ said, even though he wasn't meant to drink while on duty. The bastard owed his father a truckload of beers. Bookie Joe blinked, then ordered two beers at the bar. Two schooners appeared before them, golden and with just the right amount of froth. "Cheers." PJ lifted his glass, swallowed and leant an elbow on the bar. He peered at Bookie Joe over his glass. The bookmaker's eyes flicked away, and he took a nervous swig that left a wave of froth on his upper lip. It melted into the pores of his skin.

"I'm enquiring about a horse race that Eric McKinley laid a bet on this morning. I believe it was number ten, but I would like to know the name and origins of the horse. Know anything about it?" He saw the bookmaker relax a little.

"Yeah, it's called Harvest Time. A Sydney horse. Owned by a syndicate."

"And who's in the syndicate?"

A sly look crossed the bookmaker's face. His tongue flicked across his lip. He didn't want to dob any Fishermen's Club members in. The club was where he did his best business.

"You might have to find that out yourself, Constable," he smirked. "Although, I doubt Eric McKinley could tell you much by all accounts." He winked and tapped his head.

PJ set his jaw. How he'd love to sock the little bastard. "Thanks for that, Bookie. I might have another beer for the road since you're buying. Off duty, you know." He drained his beer and belched.

Bookie Joe's face sharpened. He lifted one finger at the barman. "Put it on the tab, Pete." His eyes glinted into the Constable's. "Afraid, you'll have to drink on your own, Constable, I've got some business to attend." PJ raised his glass as Bookie Joe scuttled off.

After her chat with PJ, Lillian arrived home to a letter in her post box. It was from Maureen. An aerogramme. She hastened inside to find a knife and slit the flap open making sure she didn't tear through any of the writing.

The writing was small, and lines cramped to get as much on the single page as possible. Lillian fetched a magnifying glass making it easier to read. She read it three times and sat back, winded.

A grandson! Maureen was keeping her child! A court appearance as a witness for a rape trial! Lillian was stunned. She had been careful not to mention Eric's police drama to Maureen and yet there she was, on the other side of the world, going through her own police drama. What was the likelihood of that? How was she going to manage with a baby on her own? She should return to Eden. It was the sensible thing to do. She would spread the word that Maureen had married, then she would say her husband had died in a car accident. There were ways around things. Lillian rummaged through the sideboard for her writing pad and pen. The time had come to tell Maureen what had been going on in Eden.

It was nine o'clock the following morning when the telephone rang. Lillian answered, thinking it might be the hospital giving her information on Eric's condition. Instead, it was PJ. He gave her a cryptic description of his meeting with Bookie Joe. She felt a glow of confidence. Her theory had been right.

The syndicate, or 'business venture', in PJ code, was called McKinley Park! Everything was above board and any enquiries about the business would have to come from someone acting on the plaintiff's behalf. Lillian thanked PJ for his assistance and hung up.

She hadn't thought about the syndicate being legal and therefore not a police matter. She would have to act on Eric's behalf and prove theft. That meant using her power of attorney. If the newspaper learned of her involvement, they might point the finger at her again and say she was after Eric's money as well as the farm. She stared into the distance. The kids would have to come for tea and have another discussion. PJ had asked how her children were, indicating she should get them involved. It made sense. No one could blame Splinter and Johnny for looking after their father's interests.

"They're swindlers," Splinter said, after Lillian had finished telling her what PJ had found out. "I can write to the registrar of businesses and find out who belongs to the syndicate. I'll say my father has had a stroke and can't remember how to get hold of his partners and I need the information. I'll get a justice of the peace to witness my letter. I'll register the letter, so it gets there quicker." Splinter's eyes flashed in her lovely face. Her father was ill. She had forgiven him for humping a girl she went to school with. It wasn't his fault. Kathy was a fat randy tart. An adulteress, a thief, a murderer. "I bet Kathy's a member of the syndicate and they're all laughing because they think Dad doesn't know he owns part of a racehorse."

"There's something else," Lillian said, handing Splinter Maureen's letter. She watched her daughter's face as she read the letter.

"Holy shit!" Splinter said, looking at her mother aghast. "Is Bubs mad? She always was impulsive. Jumping into things without thinking about the consequences. I mean, she went overseas on a one-way ticket. Runs off with a bloke she hardly knows?" Splinter shook her head. "We have to help the little idiot, Mum. God, I hope she's going to be alright."

"Your Aunt Audrey has sent her money and I sent her the rent money House paid me for the farm. She should have received it by now, although she didn't mention it."

"How long will that last her in Sweden?"

Lillian shrugged, she didn't know anything about cost of living or money exchange. "If we can prove your father's been swindled, we can sue and afford to bring her home. We'll tell the town she's a widow so there won't be any talk."

Splinter nodded, eager to avoid the knowing looks from her students' parents on interview days. Exonerating her father's sexual behaviour with a young woman and turning him into a victim of a crime would remove the humiliation she felt. Also, it might stop the jokes about his knackering. "I'll get cracking on the syndicate. Send Bubs my love when you write." She grinned, "I'm an aunty!"

32

Two Letters

Bernard was coming to see the baby. Maureen stood at her bedroom window watching out for him. She saw his car pull up and ran downstairs to meet him.

Bernard bounced through the doors of the home, making quite a stir in his sealskin coat, fur hat, paisley cravat, jodhpurs and fur-lined boots. He kissed every available hand and bowed to Matron as Maureen introduced him. She showed him into the lounge. He twirled, eyeing the beige drapes and mismatching furniture with pursed lips.

"It is warm and comfortable, I suppose. Better than ..." he hesitated and looked around at Anya and Drachia sitting in the alcove by the window. They were the last two girls left in the home apart from Maureen. Eva had left the hospital after the birth of her baby and returned to her parents. Drachia and her baby were leaving tomorrow to move in with her boyfriend. "Better than your last abode," he said.

"It's so good of you to come and visit me, Bernard. Wait here and I'll bring Henry Bernard down." Bernard preened when she said the baby's name.

Maureen unfolded her tiny powdered baby like a prize. It amazed her to see him growing all because of her milk. Bernard leant over the foreign object. He touched its hand and the baby's fingers closed around his. Bernard turned to Maureen.

"Mon dieu, he likes me."

"Do you want to cuddle him?" She picked the baby up. Bernard shrank back.

"It is too small, chérie. I will just look." Maureen put a blanket around the baby and cuddled him.

"Did you bring my letters, Bernard?"

"I have them." He reached into his pocket and brought out two letters, which he handed to Maureen. One was from her mother and the other her aunt. She tucked them under the baby's blanket for later.

Their afternoon tea arrived. The girls sat at a distance from Maureen and Bernard, sneaking looks in their direction. Getting Bernard alone wasn't possible, bedrooms were out of bounds to visitors. Maureen learned the chef was buying Netta's share of the restaurant and that he wanted to change the restaurant's name to distance them from the past. Bernard shrugged.

"If he wants it, I will do."

Maureen felt guilty. They wouldn't have thought of changing the name if Bernard hadn't phoned Nils' father on her behalf. And, although the chef had helped her, she doubted he would want her hanging around his restaurant. The baby screwed up its face and began to cry. The cotton pads lining Maureen's bra moistened.

"I must feed him, Bernard. Do you want to wait? It will take an hour." Bernard stood up.

"No, there is much to do at the restaurant. I will say au revoir."

Maureen walked with him to the door. The sky had cleared. Birds chirped. The air was crisp, not bitter. She felt reassured for a reason she couldn't identify. Bernard kissed her on both cheeks, and she watched him climb in his car and drive away.

In her room she read her mother's letter and unfolded the fifteen-dollar postal note. How she longed to show Henry Bernard off to her family. Fifteen dollars wouldn't get her home though and from the sound of her mother's letter she wouldn't be able to help her until the farm business was sorted. In her Aunt's letter was a twenty-dollar note. Her aunt was moving to England in two months, and she said Maureen and the baby were welcome to stay.

She threw her head back and yelled, startling Henry Bernard who had been asleep at her breast. Family! She would have her family again. So far she had been lucky, receiving help from strangers, immigrants and a government that thought about its people, but through it all she had felt alone and homesick. Then it dawned on her: no one could take her baby away if she left Sweden. A dreadful fear lifted. She folded her Aunt's letter and thought about the flat Fru Wellander had arranged for her to move into in two weeks. What was it going to be like managing her baby on her own without Matron to help her when Henry Bernard cried with colic? Matron had said she'd manage fine. Said she was a good mother. She just had to prove it to herself.

Spring was showing itself in the garden. Plants sprouted, bees carried pollen and birds were building nests. The days were longer. Maureen wheeled Henry Bernard in the pram donated by a parishioner, her thoughts on her move. Sarah and Mikey walked beside her. Sarah helped her lift the pram up the church steps. Reverend John came over.

"I heard you're moving into a flat, Maureen?

"Yes, as soon as I can get some furniture." He stroked his chin. "I'll see what we can do." He moved off to welcome new arrivals.

Maureen parked the pram behind the back pew where she could sit and rock the baby if he woke up. Sarah sat beside her. At the end of the sermon the Reverend gestured towards Maureen.

"We have a young lady who is moving into a flat and is in need of furniture. Anyone with a spare bed, chairs, table, kitchen equipment and time to help move it, please see me in the hall. The congregation turned towards Maureen, nods and smiles coated her embarrassment. She raised her hand to them and made a fast exit from the church. How she hated being a charity case.

Paavo cornered her in the hall. "We must speak again. The trial is soon."

Fear gnawed. "I'll call Matron and organise a time." She didn't want to think about the trial.

Reverend John came over and Paavo moved away to join his wife. "We have enough furniture to get you started," the Reverend said.

"Gosh, so quick?" She had to get the flat key from the welfare officer. Arrange for Sarah to look after Henry Bernard while she was moving. Her stomach had butterflies.

"Yes, and we have the loan of a van and some help to install the furniture. I'll telephone you when it's organised."

It seemed like most of the calls that came to the home were for her. There were always curious eyes following her into Matron's office. "I'll have to tell Matron you're going to call. I guess I'd better start packing?"

Reverend John smiled his pleasure.

After the Reverend left, Paavo cornered her to make an appointment for her to see him. He wouldn't be able to contact her after her move, so it had to be done now. They arranged a date. This time he didn't offer to send a taxi. She wished he had. It wasn't so easy with the baby. The pram was heavy and difficult to get on trams and up flights of stairs. But it wouldn't be right to ask him to send a taxi, not when he was helping her pro bono. There was so much to think about.

She was leaving. Her feelings see-sawed between happiness for her independence and sadness to be leaving Matron, who had taught her so much and been caring and kind. Matron gave her a squeeze of reassurance and Maureen kissed her cheek. Now Anya was the only girl left at the home. Her baby was in an incubator in hospital and had been for three weeks. Anya wasn't the same cocky girl who had given Maureen the once over when she had first arrived at the home. She was subdued, pale and thin. There were dark shadows under her eyes. Maureen's heart filled with pity. She put her arms around Anya and gave her a hug.

"I hope your baby gets well quickly. Come and visit me," she said.

"I will try," Anya replied.

She handed the taxi driver her last free coupon and sat in the back with Henry Bernard. As the taxi pulled away, Maureen waved goodbye to Sister Vigdis and the cook, watching her from the porch, then settled back in her seat with a sense of relief as well as nervousness. No more curfews or filling out a daybook to say where she was going and when she would be back. She was in charge of herself again.

Maureen left the baby with Sarah while she collected the key to her flat from the welfare officer. From there she went to her flat to meet Reverend John and the parishioner who was bringing the furniture. A kitchen table, two chairs, a wardrobe, a large couch that opened into a bed, a box of linen, blankets and a duvet. Everything she needed to start her new life.

The flat was on the second floor. The staircase, narrow and

steep. At the top of the stairs she opened the door for the first time and stepped inside.

It had a good-sized entrance with hooks on the wall for coats and a long shelf for boots. The kitchen had a two-burner gas stove and walk-in pantry. In the middle of the ceiling was a clothesline that could be lifted or lowered by a rope. Curtains divided the kitchen from a second larger room that had a tiled fireplace and a window looking over a courtyard. There were a few chips and holes in the walls where previous tenants had hung objects but the flat was clean and the first home Maureen could call her own.

The Reverend and the parishioner volunteer carried her furniture up the stairs. Arranging it was easy. Even furnished, the rooms looked bare and the wood floor, cold.

"I haven't done any shopping yet so I can't offer you a coffee," Maureen apologised, wishing she had something to show her gratitude.

"Can't anyway," Reverend John said. "Molly's going out and I have to look after the kids." He hadn't taken his overcoat off and was sweating from exertion or he might have noticed how cold the flat was. "We are going past Sarah's so we can drop you off to pick up your baby."

Maureen locked the door and followed them to the van. She didn't stay long at Sarah's. There was shopping to do, a tram to catch and the baby to feed. And she wanted to get back before dark.

It was three o'clock by the time she got back. It was a struggle to climb the stairs with shopping and a pram and she was looking forward to a nice cup of tea.

The strange quiet hit her as she walked into the flat. This was where she was going to live. There was no one around to help her, no telephone for emergencies or advice. No friends in the neighbourhood. It was like being in the roof after Netta had left. A snuffle from the pram reminded her she really wasn't alone and would never be alone again. Maureen removed her coat and sat down to feed Henry Bernard. Goose flesh covered her breasts, it was freezing.

The only heater was the fireplace and she didn't have any coal. When the baby had finished feeding, she put the carry cot inside the big wardrobe, dividing her clothes up to hang both ends of the carrycot to act as insulation. He looked warm; his cheeks were pink. She knew she couldn't manage a bag of coal with a baby and pram. There was nothing else she could do but duck out and buy a bag of coal before he woke up.

Out on the street in the sleet, Maureen stopped people and asked directions to where she could buy coal. None of those she asked could speak English. She entered a food store asking people until she found one who spoke English. Her heart had started hammering. What if Henry Bernard had woken up and was screaming already? It seemed like ages before she was directed to a petrol station that sold coal. She bought a ten-kilo bag. The petrol attendant loaded it in her arms, and she staggered down the road towards her flat. When it became too heavy, she put it on the ground and dragged it.

People turned and stared as she puffed past them, driven by the thought of Henry Bernard screaming in the flat all on his own. Damp from the street, the bag of coal left a wet black trail as she hauled it up the stairs. She was too frantic to care.

Her chest was heaving and her nose leaking by the time she reached her door. She wiped her soot-caked hand across her nose and noticed the blood. As a child she'd had a lot of nose bleeds but none since. Terror gripped her as she entered the flat. Had her clothes fallen off a hanger and smothered Henry Bernard? Had he cried himself into a convulsion? The silence was astounding. She edged towards the wardrobe sick with anxiety and peeked inside. He hadn't moved since she had left him. The relief was so great she sagged against the cupboard.

The fireplace was stacked with coal. Maureen hunted for matches. There weren't any. She cursed her stupidity. Unable to face leaving Henry Bernard again, she wrapped herself in blankets and waited for him to wake so she could take him with her.

After the protection of the home, Maureen felt like a bird that had flown inside a new cage and didn't know its way out. Her nose bleeds continued, always starting after she had carried the baby up the stairs in the pram. Her money was running out. The baby was growing; he needed clothes. She had to buy disposable nappies because the cloth nappies wouldn't dry in her cold flat. When she lit the fire, smoke poured into the room and the baby developed a cough. There were panic trips to doctors instead of a lengthy excursion to a free hospital. Sometimes there wasn't enough money for food, and she had to make do with a boiled egg and toast for dinner. Breakfast was a bread roll and a cup of tea. Lunches were often skipped. Her milk started to disappear, so she had to buy baby formula. Maureen lost weight: she was seven stone eight pounds, a stone lighter after living three weeks on her own.

Visiting Sarah wasn't easy with a pram. Getting on the tram was awkward, the footpaths narrow and then there were Sarah's stairs. Without a telephone she couldn't let Sarah know she was visiting and often she wasn't home so it was a long return trip. Her trips to see Bernard became fewer. The restaurant was always busy which meant Bernard was busy and although he greeted her fondly, she felt she was in the way. In her flat she felt lonely having nothing to occupy her when the baby was asleep. When he was awake, she would do a reconnaissance of her area, wheeling the pram around the streets. Then she discovered the library. What a relief. It was warm, a place she could sit with

Henry Bernard and read books while she waited for Sunday, when she would show off Henry Bernard to the church crowd.

Sunday arrived with sunshine, blue sky and flowering pot plants on windowsills. Maureen dressed Henry Bernard in his best clothes, a matinee jacket and matching hat knitted by Sarah. She put her hair in a French roll and applied make-up. She stood on a chair to see what her dress looked like in the half mirror that was attached to the inside of the wardrobe door, gave herself a pass and left the flat for church. She was looking forward to showing Henry Bernard off, although not keen to see Paavo. It was two weeks since they had discussed the hitchhiking episode and no matter what he thought of her she had to face him sooner or later.

Molly and Penny lead the rush of women who came to greet her. Maureen felt shy from all the attention. Henry Bernard was passed from arm to arm around the women. They commented on his huge eyes, pert nose and petal lips. Maureen removed his hat to show the fuzz of blonde hair that now covered his once bald dome. He smiled and waved his arms at all the peering faces.

Paavo came over, greeted Maureen and tickled Henry Bernard. "Congratulations," he said, smiling at the baby. He turned to her and his smile changed into a worried frown. "You are looking thin, Maureen."

"Lost a bit of weight," she said not wanting to talk about her financial difficulties. He led her away from the women and lowered his voice.

"You know the court case is in four days?"

"Yes." How could she forget? Her nails were bleeding from being gnawed.

"My wife and I think it would be easier for you if you stayed with us the night before you are to be a witness. We can go to the trial together. That way I can ward off news reporters. It could be that Herr Classon might try to defame you. He has newspaper friends."

"If he does, I will tell them he locked me out of my fiancé's flat while he was away and left me on the street with nowhere to go." They weren't going to intimidate her.

Paavo narrowed his eyes. "With your permission I might pass that message on to Herr Classon. He has been making it difficult for me to get maintenance for you. He is keeping his son out of the country to delay us."

A fire lit in Maureen's gut. "You can tell him I know how he fiddles his taxes." Nils had bragged about it. "His father leases flats from the housing department under family names and sublets them at high rents."

Paavo looked grim, there was a five-year waiting list for apartments. He hated cheats. "I will enjoy passing your message on."

"I would like to stay with you before witnessing if you don't mind. I won't be so scared."

"Penny and the children will delight in taking care of your baby."

Maureen frowned. "Can't I take him to court with me?"

"We do not want your character to be questioned. Having your baby in court might raise questions."

Maureen blushed. Why was she constantly being looked down on while Nils was being treated like a victim?

"I know you are a good person, Maureen. All who have met you say so. Many girls have babies without being married and most times it is why they marry. However, we cannot have you discredited as unreliable. The victim, Tove Persson, was left close to death by this man. You must help put him in gaol for her sake. It will also exonerate you for using a gun and leaving him unconscious in his car."

Maureen thought she would be happy to put any man into gaol right now.

33

Eden – The Syndicate

Grim-faced, Splinter folded the letter from the Business Registrar's Office. She would put all the swindlers in gaol. She couldn't wait to show her mother the letter.

They sat around the kitchen table. Johnny mopped up the last of his lamb stew with a piece of bread.

"It's won a packet," Johnny said.

Splinter finished her mouthful and dabbed her lips with a serviette. "Well, where's the money?"

Lillian stared at the names associated with the syndicate. "It's not up to me to query this. Any business deals your father made after our divorce has nothing to do with me. You kids will have to make the enquiries or press charges if there's been any skulduggery."

"But you can act on his behalf as his power of attorney, Mum.

I mean, he can't think for himself. My two-year-old has more brains," Splinter said.

Lillian was aware of what she could do. Peter Turnstile had made sure she understood, but it might look like she was manipulating Eric for her own ends. "I'm not starting the enquiry." She gazed at Johnny. "This should be up to you. You were the one who placed the bet with your father and became suspicious." Lillian had enough to deal with. Eric would be placed in her care soon and there was the farm issue as well as Bubs' predicament. Her children had to sort this out. "You're the man about the house." Her lips twitched when Johnny squared his shoulders.

"Fair enough. I'll go out to the farm tomorrow and have a sniff around." The cottage hadn't been cleaned out completely and there was still a trunk full of photographs and letters and a few silver trinkets of his great-grandmother's. House had said he wouldn't be moving in immediately. The coast should be clear.

"You do that, and I'll go and see PJ," Splinter said, clearing the table and stacking the sink.

"I'll leave you to it then."

There hadn't been any arguments, Lillian was pleased. She wasn't looking forward to catching the bus in the morning. It was a bloody nightmare with the endless mail stops and deviations down farm roads. She usually arrived at the hospital feeling carsick. The return was just as bad because of all the school kids. But Eric couldn't leave hospital while he was recovering from his hernia operation. And according to the nurses he kept asking where she was all the time. They thought it was sweet. What they didn't know was he had been a heavy-handed, mean, philandering shit and she didn't know why she was still putting up with him. If it wasn't for the children … Lillian looked at Johnny and Splinter's determined faces and wondered if they realised what they were doing was partly because of Maureen.

Johnny stood and Splinter dried her hands. "We'll meet here for tea tomorrow," Splinter said. They left the house on a mission to find their father's money.

The farm cottage was still locked and there were no signs that anybody had broken in. Johnny unlocked the new Yale lock he'd put on and went inside. Everything was as he'd left it. He tried picking up the trunk in his father's bedroom and decided it was too heavy to carry. Bugger unpacking it and doing a lot of trips to the car. If he brought the car closer to the verandah, he could lift the trunk into the boot. What he needed was a sack to put under the trunk so he could drag it out, and he was pretty sure there was one in the barn.

The barn was dark and smelled of manure. Johnny propped the doors open to get some light and was startled by the sound of a snort. He peered into the darkness and waited for his eyes to adjust after the bright sunlight. Then he saw the horse. The shed had been converted into a stable. Johnny gaped at the horse. It was a beauty. Sleek, majestic, reddish-brown. It rolled an eye at him, tossed its head.

"Whoa, boy." Johnny put out his hand, palm flat for the horse to smell, then slowly stroked the side of its neck. He knew who the horse was. It was Harvest Time, the one he had backed a few days ago. His father was in the syndicate that owned the horse. And the horse was on his father's farm unless House van Someren could prove he owned the farm. Who had brought the horse here? Not his father, he was in hospital so it had to be one of the other syndicate members. Johnny's brain ticked away. What would his father do in this situation? A memory of his father rustling a cow came to mind, and the thought that the horse could be picked up any day by the person who had brought it to the farm. Possession is nine-tenths of the law; he'd heard that somewhere.

Bugger the trunk, he could get it tomorrow. Johnny walked

back to the Buick and drove it to where a bush track met the road. He turned down the track and edged the car into a small clearing surrounded by wattle, taking care not to scratch the duco. Satisfied it was out of sight he ran back to the cottage. In his father's bedroom he found a shirt and a bush hat and put them on. He went to the barn and saddled up the horse. The saddle was meant for jockeys, not tall Johnny. His knees were under his chin and he felt unsafe perched so high off the ground, but he knew how to ride. The horse was skittish, shying at passing cars, so Johnny left the road wherever he could, riding through the bush, out of sight. He wondered how Splinter was going with PJ. They didn't really need him now.

It had been a disappointing result for Splinter. There wasn't enough evidence for Constable PJ to investigate the syndicate finances nor did he have the expertise. He'd failed arithmetic at school. Her only consolation was he would make sure the syndicate was bona fide. It was only after Splinter had insisted the disappearance of her father's winnings could be robbery that PJ promised to discuss their findings with the fraud squad in Sydney. It was an opportunity for his future career.

The information from PJ was hardly worth the meeting with Johnny and her mother but she couldn't risk a phone call. Her husband would have to look after Olivia again. Why was it always so easy for Johnny?

Bum sore, face bleeding from being lashed by low-hanging branches, Johnny rode the horse into his mother's shed. Wincing with pain he swung himself off the horse and gave its neck a pat. "Good boy." He removed the saddle and bridle and put a halter on the horse, then led it into the back garden to dine on his mother's rose bushes.

When he entered the kitchen, Lillian and Splinter looked up from their cups of tea. "What in God's name happened to you?" Lillian said, looking at Johnny's bleeding dust covered face.

"I found the racehorse at the farm and stole it."

"You've done what?" Lillian and Splinter shrieked in unison.

"What else could I have done? They might move it tomorrow and then we wouldn't have any bargaining power."

"Bargaining power?" Lillian's eyebrows drove towards each other and parked. Johnny grinned. "I have a plan." He eased his saddle-sore bum into a chair.

Lillian poured him a cup of tea while he outlined his intention. Splinter frowned into her cup. "I can't be part of that, I'm a schoolteacher. My husband has a business in Eden."

"Mum could do it," Johnny said.

Lillian looked at her two children. If she was going to help them then they could return the favour. "If I do this, there's one condition. When your father comes to live with me, you will have to help. I want you both to give me a break when I need it and I don't mean a day, I mean maybe two weeks so I can go to Melbourne. Your father can't be left on his own to fend for himself. There's to be no arguments. I know that's not going to be easy for you, Splinter, but you and your family could move in here if I'm away. And Johnny, you will have to find someone to keep an eye on your Dad if you go away fishing. That might mean paying someone to take care of him."

"Hang on a minute …"

"No, you'll hear me out. The money you are after isn't going in my pocket. The two of you are going to benefit, and I hope, Maureen. She needs her fare to return to Eden."

Johnny picked at a moth hole in the tablecloth.

"If you can't help me then I won't be making any phone calls." Lillian folded her arms and waited. Splinter and Johnny looked at each other and nodded their agreement. "Good. Now after you shut that horse in the shed, Splinter can drive you to the farm to collect the Buick. And make sure you bring back a load of hay and the trunk."

"It's too late to get the car now. I have to get home to Olivia."

"It won't take more than an hour and we can't risk the car being found. Everyone knows the Buick." She was glad she had read so many 'whodunnits'. After the kids had left, Lillian stayed up late, making notes in preparation for the next day.

In the morning Lillian added a weak shot of brandy to her cup of tea to give her some Dutch courage and armed with her notepad, picked up the telephone.

"Hello, Mr van Someren. I'm phoning because I'm afraid I'll have to renege on our agreement. I've decided not to continue renting the farm. Eric's memory has improved, and he was very upset when I told him I'd rented the place. The doctor has advised me to keep him calm to prevent another stroke so I'm pulling the plug on our agreement." She lowered her notepad. Her eyes widened at his response. She had expected him to be angry but not threatening. She referred back to the note pad. "Eric wants me to take him out there this weekend, which is what I'll do. I'm sorry, but that's how it is. At least you haven't moved your furniture in yet so there's nothing for you to move." She held her breath as she listened to the tirade on the end of the phone. Her mouth tightened and her words became clipped. She knew this part by heart. "The agreement we signed didn't have a time factor, Mr van Someren. Which means I am at liberty to cancel anytime I like. We have witnesses to that agreement. A lawyer and my friend, Ingrid, if you remember our luncheon." She held the phone away from her ear again and waited. His voice echoed down the hall. "I'm sorry you feel that way, Mr van Someren. It wasn't my intention to cause you any grief." The phone banged down at the other end. Lillian waited, heard the click and put her phone back on its cradle.

She was shaking. He had threatened to sue her and Eric. He was going to drag the sale of the farm saga out for as long as possible. She hoped the telephonist had heard it all because now she was going to call PJ.

"He threatened me. He said he didn't care about Eric's state of mind when he signed over the farm, it was his and he had paid for it. He's so angry, I'm scared. Is there any way you can keep him away from me? I'm hoping the telephonist might be able to prove he threatened me. I heard her click on the line to see if I was getting through so she could have heard him shouting threats?"

Minutes after she had hung up, PJ phoned back. He'd spoken to the telephonist and yes, she could verify Lillian's conversation with Mr van Someren. There had been a problem with the connecting plug, and she'd had to stay on the line. He was going to replace the sign on the farm door and take out an order to keep Frederick van Someren away from her house and the farm. Lillian was delighted.

The horse could stay hidden for the time being. Any future negotiations with van Someren would be done through Johnny at the Fishermen's Club with Lillian behind the scene pulling strings. She doubted the other members of the syndicate, Kathy and Eric's accountant, would be game enough to return to Eden, which meant they would only be dealing with House. And House was proud of his reputation as one of Eden's leading citizens, which was a bonus for them. What worried her was the time it was all taking and how Maureen was managing. She thought about the rape trial and what an ordeal she must be going through.

An hour later Ingrid phoned, sounding confused. "I have a message from someone I cannot say ze name of. They were at lunch with me at your place?" Lillian knew exactly who Ingrid meant and was angry that House had used her friend to make contact.

"I'm sorry you had to be drawn into this, Ingrid. You can tell that person Johnny will meet him at the Fishermen's Club when his boat's back in. That's the end of the week. And he isn't to contact me through you again."

"I have made strudel if you have time?"

Lillian knew Ingrid was keen to know what was going on, but the fewer people who knew, the better their chances were of pulling off Johnny's plan. "Save me a piece. I have to visit Eric today. You are a good friend Ingrid, thank you."

After she'd hung up Lillian stood by the phone thinking. She didn't give a stuff about Eric's race winnings, just recuperating what had been stolen from him in horse flesh and the farm. She wouldn't be able to keep the horse hidden for long, eventually the neighbour would ask where it had come from. Maybe House didn't have to wait for Johnny. She picked up the phone and was put through to Ingrid.

"It's me. As much as I don't want to involve you in this, I'll ask you to do me one favour. Tell your caller he can meet me at the hospital for a discussion. I'll be there this afternoon."

"I bring strudel to you tomorrow morning." One good turn deserved another.

"Alright, see you then." Lillian rushed into the kitchen and made herself a strong cup of tea. What had she done? Self-doubt brought on her reflux. She chewed a Rennie's indigestion tablet and sat down with her writing pad and pen and wrote down what she thought would be House's counter arguments to her deal. Fingers crossed he would meet her at the hospital.

Eric crab-walked on his walking sticks beside Lillian to a seat at the edge of the hospital garden. They hadn't long been settled when Frederick van Someren puffed his way towards them, face puce with anger. Lillian removed her thermos from the picnic basket, poured herself a cup of tea laced with brandy and downed it, preparing herself.

House didn't greet Eric or sit. He towered over her, glaring. "Where's my fucking horse?" he said.

Eric looked up eyes bright. "You're taking it to my farm."

"It's my fucking farm now, you brainless coot." He wrapped his knuckles hard on the top of Eric's head. "Some bastard's stolen the horse."

Lillian's eyes became black holes. She leaped to her feet. "Keep your hands off him or I'll have you for assault. Your horse or Eric's horse and the rest of your thieving friends in the syndicate, is safe for the moment, although I can't guarantee for how long. It could get sick and die." House jumped as though he'd been bitten by a bullant. Lillian hated threatening the horse's life, but this man was dangerous. "If you want that horse, then you have to hand back Eric's farm and pay out his share of the syndicate. You can keep the winnings." The colour of House's face changed from red to white.

"I'll see you in court before I do that," he snarled.

Lillian's reflux burned. She fought her fury and relaxed her face. "No, you won't. I can prove Eric's accountant and Kathy Parker and you were in cahoots. That the drugs Kathy stole from the hospital were intended for the purpose of swindling Eric. Money is traceable. All your transactions are being looked into by the police."

The bullying tactics of House disappeared. His eyes darted around to see if anyone else was in earshot. He spread his hands. "Look here, I didn't know about the drugs. I wasn't present when Eric signed. But if you believe that's what happened then I'm willing to tear up the deed and hand the farm back. Also, I'd like to personally buy Eric's share of the horse because I want to dissolve the syndicate. I prefer not to be associated with crooks." His status in the town meant a lot to him and he needed to distance himself from his partners. They could dig themselves out of their own shit. A wave licked the sand.

"I would like a cheque for this amount now, made out to cash," Lillian said. "I have an agreement you can sign." She pulled an envelope from her bag and removed the two pages she had written up and handed it to House. "You can sign this at the reception desk because I'll need someone to witness your signature."

House opened his cheque book, stared at the figure on the paper and swallowed. He signed the cheque, ripped it out of the book and handed it to Lillian.

She waved it in the air to dry the ink and slipped the cheque into her handbag. "Time to go, Eric." She helped him to his feet. "I'll see you at the reception desk, House."

He grimaced at the use of his nickname and waddled ahead of her.

On the bus, Lillian hummed all the way back to Eden. She made the bank just before closing time, opened up a family trust account with herself as signatory and deposited the cheque.

Constable PJ looked at her like a woebegone dog. "You're asking me to drop the charges?" The disappointment on the young constable's face was touching.

Lillian leaned across his desk and clasped his hand. "Yes. Thanks to your enquiries, Frederick van Someren has dropped his claim to ownership of the farm. He signed a document to that effect today. And he has bought Eric's share of the horse, which means Eric is no longer in the syndicate." She didn't mention he'd paid her a considerable amount more for the horse because she had realised that the race winner was worth more. The horse money was safe in a family trust account. "We couldn't have gotten this result if it hadn't been for all your hard work, PJ. Your investigation scared the pants off him. I know you want to become a detective so I was thinking I could pay for you to spend a week in Sydney. You can investigate the possibility of a transfer into a detective unit?" PJ's eyes widened. "I'll write a letter to the Police Department telling them how helpful you were finding Kathy Parker and the accountant. They are still being investigated for those pills I believe?"

The constable squared his shoulders. "They are. Theft of a dangerous substance and drugging a man with the intention of stealing his property."

If House had actually paid Eric's accountant for the farm and not been bullshitting, then he might get his money back! Lillian hoped the court would be lenient with Kathy, she had three children to take care of. Lillian didn't want the children to be without their mother.

34

The Final Decision

A shudder went through Maureen as her kidnapper was seated in the court room. He glanced around then his eyes settled on her. She flinched and looked away. His lawyer leant towards him and spoke. The kidnapper put his finger in his mouth and picked his teeth, nodding. His lawyer stood and addressed Maureen.

"Are you sure this is the man who gave you a lift when you were hitchhiking?"

"Yes." Her hands were shaking and her throat felt like it was full of mashed potatoes. "He had a big space between his front teeth and one tooth was brown." The kidnapper pulled his finger from his mouth and clamped his lips shut.

"Please tell the court what happened on the night you were picked up by him."

"At first everything was fine. We had travelled for nearly an hour when he started to grab at my friend, forcing his hand between her legs. She tried to fight him off and the car slid all over the road while they were struggling. I couldn't reach him from the back seat. We shouted for him to stop but he laughed and said he was taking us to his house, that he had a big bed to share with us. We were terrified so I pointed the gun at his head and told him to stop the car, and he did. We got out. He tried to attack me then, and being so scared, I fired at him. It wasn't a real gun. It only shot blanks. I didn't think it would hurt him other than make him go a bit deaf. We thought he had fainted from shock, so we bundled him in the car. We were petrified he would follow us when he woke up, so we put the keys on the floor of the car, to buy a bit of time and ran as fast as we could to get away. It was dark and snowing and we didn't know where we were. When we finally got to a road crossing, we saw headlights and just ran on the road and waved our arms until a truck stopped."

The judge's face was expressionless. "Why didn't you report this to police?"

Maureen picked at her nails. She and Jane had talked about it. It was only later when it had gotten into the papers that they found out their kidnapper had reported it first, so he could make a case against them and accuse them of theft. Sarah had posted the article to her with a translation.

"We were on our way to Norway and didn't want to be delayed in case we lost our jobs in the ski lodge. We don't speak Swedish, so we didn't know the story was in the paper until a long time later. But by then we were too scared we might get into trouble for having the gun, even though it was a fake.

"You were scared of being arrested because of the gun and not because you stole money?" the rapist's lawyer asked.

Maureen jumped to her feet. "We didn't steal anything. All we wanted to do was run. The man was strong. My friend couldn't keep him off her even though he was driving. That's why I pulled the gun out."

"You have a baby and are living on Swedish welfare, I believe? I have a character report from a Herr Classon."

"I was engaged to Herr Classon's son, Nils. His parents didn't want us to marry so they forced their son to abandon me." Maureen turned to the Judge looking him straight in the eye. "I am very grateful to the Swedish Government for its compassion. After the trial I shall return to my own country." She held his stare, her chin high.

"Thank you, Miss McKinley. I find you to be a reliable witness in this trial. You are excused."

Maureen didn't know how she managed to walk back to her seat next to Paavo. She was trembling from head to foot. Paavo took her hands in both of his and gave them a squeeze. He leant towards her and whispered, "You were excellent. So much courage."

The rest of the proceedings continued in Swedish and Maureen wasn't quite sure what was happening, until Paavo elbowed her and signalled her to stand up alongside him. The judge spoke slowly and sternly, looking directly at her kidnapper who continued to fidget and pick at his teeth. It was only when the court officials came to lead him away, to a chorus of his protests, that she realised he was going to be incarcerated.

Outside the court, the parents of the girl who had been raped and beaten came over to Maureen and introduced themselves. On shaking her hand, cameras flashed.

"We want to thank you. He will get maximum sentence. If we can help you, please contact us. My address," the mother said, pushing a piece of paper into her hand.

"He deserves to stay in gaol forever," Maureen replied. She allowed Paavo to steer her away towards his car.

"I will be informing the tax department to investigate Herr

Classon. I think he will regret what he's done. Now it is all over we will pick up your baby and Sarah and go out to dinner to celebrate. It will be my pleasure."

Paavo took them all to Bernard's for dinner. Bernard seated them at his best table, his cheeks pink with delight. He personally waited on them and gave them a bottle of his best champagne to toast the success of the trial. Maureen's relief was enormous.

"It's all over," Maureen said, collapsing on Sarah's couch after dinner. Sarah handed her Henry Bernard and she cuddled him close. "Mummy's got to think about what we are going to do next," she said, smiling into his chubby face. His baby arms shot out of his blanket and punched the air. His eyes locked onto hers and he smiled. "Look, he knows what I'm telling him. He's so clever." All the mums at church had told her he did things ahead of his age. "It's just about you and me now, Henry Bernard." Whatever she did would be for him.

"I was thinking of taking Mikey to see the boats at the yacht club tomorrow if you want to come?" Sarah looked at Maureen, remembering the story of her last visit to the yacht club with the girls from the home.

"Sure." Maureen was grateful to have somewhere to go. Her flat was depressing. She put Henry Bernard into the pram and wheeled him to the door. "See you tomorrow."

She returned to her flat with a lot on her mind. Although the trial was over, her struggles weren't. She didn't have enough money to live on and if it hadn't been for Paavo, she would have had a cheese sandwich for dinner. Baby formula and nappies were expensive. There was so much to think about, but the day had exhausted her. She was grateful to climb into bed.

Maureen woke to the sun and melting ice. Thrusting her feet into a pair of Bengt's old slippers, she went into the kitchen to heat milk for Henry Bernard's bottle. The last slice of bread in her cupboard was edged with mould. She put it into the toaster that one of the parishioners had loaned her. When it was done, she added the last of her pot of jam. After cleaning up, she fed Henry Bernard and got ready to visit Sarah.

It was a struggle through the slush to the tram. The whole time she couldn't stop worrying about how she could get work. She had tried to get jobs as an au pair, but no one was interested in a girl who had to bring her baby to work and who couldn't speak Swedish properly. The thought that she might have her child taken from her and put into foster care was like an approaching bushfire.

The tram pulled up as she reached the stop. A man put out his arm and helped her lift the pram on board.

"Thank you," she said. There was a perk of interest around her. Some passengers were staring at her and muttering to each other. She wondered if she had baby glug on her face, then remembered her picture had been in yesterday's newspaper under the heading 'Australian hitchhiker, secret witness in rape trial, was abandoned by boyfriend'. She had become a news item. She got off the tram a stop early and walked the rest of the way to meet Sarah and Mikey. They were taking Mikey to the wharf to see the boats. The sun was shining, air cold but pleasant, flowers were blooming along the walkway and the sky was an unbroken blue. Seagulls swooped and cawed. Boats creaked at their moorings. It reminded Maureen of Eden. She turned to Sarah.

"What do you think I should do? Go back to Eden? They want to pass me off as a widow."

"Someone would find out eventually," Sarah said. "You might have a couple of beers and, oh dear!"

A white Volvo sports car scooted past them. Maureen drew a breath.

"That's Nils and he's with another girl." The girl's long hair was whipping in the breeze. "He didn't see us," she said, relieved. The car pulled up in the parking lot near the wharf and Nils got out, went around the back of his car and opened the door for the girl.

She was pretty with a nice figure. The pram Maureen was pushing seemed to take her towards them. Nils heard the squeak of wheels and turned. He looked horrified when he saw her. He tried to place himself in front of the girl to block her view and stumbled against the car. Maureen felt a hardening in her chest.

"Hello, Nils," Sarah said. "Fancy seeing you here." His mouth hung open. Maureen was glad she'd put on makeup and was wearing a jumper that clung to her curves and a skirt that showed her legs off. She knew she looked good. Maureen pegged Nils with a look. He flushed and his eyes went to the pram.

"Would you like to see?" She pulled the blanket back. The girl with him put her arm through his and cocked her head at Sarah and Maureen.

"Your friends?" she spoke German and Maureen understood.

"This is his child," Maureen replied in English, pointing to the pram.

The girl gave Nils a sharp look. Maureen didn't move away, continuing to watch Nils' discomfort. How dare he have a girlfriend! Had he been seeing girls while she had struggled to survive? He was unconscionable. She felt betrayed. A look of recognition filled the girl's eyes.

"Yes, I am the hitchhiker girl." For once she was thankful that her picture and story was in the paper. Herr Classon had stuffed it up for his son; she hadn't. Maureen turned away, pushing the pram towards the wharf. Behind her she heard the roar of the car engine and a screech of tyres. For a while they walked in silence, Maureen a sea of emotions.

"You should have expected it," Sarah said.

"Well I didn't." What had she expected?

Sarah laughed. "Did you see her face? God you sure killed that romance!"

Inside the pram a little fist shot up and Maureen suddenly laughed. It was like a signal to tell her to forget about Nils. She had Henry Bernard now. "I think he's getting hungry. We'll have to go to the wharf café so I can warm up his bottle." After that she would go home, the spring had gone out of her day.

Her encounter with Nils had left Maureen despondent. Opening the door to her flat she saw two letters on the floor. One was from Paavo, the other from her aunt Audrey. She opened the one from Paavo first. Herr Classon had agreed to pay her a lump sum of two hundred pounds. If she accepted the lump sum, then she couldn't demand future maintenance payments from Nils or his family. She was to make an appointment with Paavo to collect the cheque and sign an agreement to that effect. Maureen put the letter back in the envelope and sighed. Nils could be rid of her so easily.

Seeing Nils with another girl had made Maureen's mind up. There was no reason for her to stay in Sweden. She had deluded herself long enough. She looked around the sparse room. It was more like a campsite than a flat. Around the wall were characters from a Peanuts comic strip which she had drawn to fill in time while she waited for the baby to wake up. On the white-tiled chimney, a painted face. Those images expressed her loneliness.

Henry Bernard began to cry. Maureen picked him up and

carried him to the couch to change him. Then she opened her aunt's letter and her spirits lifted.

Her aunt would be arriving in England next week! She was coming early to settle her two children in school while her uncle finished up his job commitments in Melbourne. Maureen could move in with them whenever she was ready. They had a flat organised. It was a gift from heaven.

How wonderful her aunt had always been to her, never turning her back or pointing the finger. Maureen would always remind herself of how much she had done for her. If she hadn't gone to live with her aunt Audrey in Melbourne, she wouldn't have experienced the world. Even with all the bad stuff that had happened she had come out on top. What would her life be like if she had married Nils? His mother would have taken control and made her life a misery. She'd had a lucky escape. Netta had been right about him.

The following day there was another letter waiting for her in Bernard's office, this one from her mother sent by express mail. She laughed at the description of her father's testicle operation and was amazed that she had gotten the farm back for him. She sounded so proud, explaining how they had stolen the horse and used it as ransom. It wasn't that different to holding a fake gun to a rapist's head, Maureen thought.

At the end of the letter she put it down, realising that the outcome in Eden had all been because her mother had wanted to find the fare to bring her home. The fare was waiting for her. All she had to do was open a post office account so her mother could wire the money. Maureen put the letters away and tucked a blanket around her sleeping baby. She looked across at Bernard engrossed in his accounts. She had a lot of people to be grateful to.

"Bernard, I'll be leaving Sweden soon but before I leave, I want to have the baby christened and I'd like you to be the godfather.

I'm asking Sarah to be the godmother. I have to organise it with the Reverend at the church. I'm hoping he can do it on Sunday. Would you be the godfather?"

Bernard's chair fell against the wall in his rush to get up. "Ma chérie. I would love that." He hugged her, kissed her cheeks. "I love the baby. I will be the best godfather. He can have my restaurant." Bernard was overcome with enthusiasm.

Maureen laughed. "He only needs you to keep in touch with us, Bernard."

"Ma petite, always."

"Could I use your telephone to call the Reverend to make arrangements?"

Everything was soon decided. The christening would follow the Sunday service in two weeks' time.

Dressed in a christening gown that had passed down Paavo's family line, Henry Bernard gazed up at the Reverend. Maureen looked at all the people gathered in the church. Paavo looked so happy for her. She felt sorry that she hadn't asked Paavo to be a godfather as well, but she would keep in touch with him and when Henry Bernard was at school and could write, she would make sure he wrote Paavo letters.

Bernard and Sarah stood side by side accepting their roles as godparents to a full church of smiling well-wishers. Henry Bernard didn't cry when the holy water splashed him. Maureen was full of pride.

At the afternoon tea that followed, Maureen said her final goodbyes to the people who had been kind and helped her. It was a tearful farewell.

Maureen wasn't a good sailor and the ship's captain had appointed a stewardess to help her with the baby while she lay on her bunk dry retching into a vomit bucket. The stewardess helped her off the ship and onto the train. She still had four hours of travelling ahead, but fortunately she didn't mind trains and the journey helped to pull her back together.

The trip hadn't bothered Henry Bernard. He had been a model baby, eating and sleeping as though he'd been born at sea. Maureen put it down to his Viking blood. When the train pulled into the station, Maureen got off and went to the luggage room where she collected the pram wheels. Once she had all her luggage, she carted it back to the platform to wait. How long would it be until her family arrived? And how would she be received?

"Maureen!" Her Aunt Audrey yelled and waved from the back of the crowd. Maureen pushed her way through the throng and fell on her aunt. They hugged and cried then Audrey peered in the pram.

"He's beautiful, I can't wait to get my hands on him. And by the way, your mother is coming to visit us. She's using your fare. Apparently, it was some money she got from looking after a horse!"

Maureen beamed at the unexpected good news and was thrilled that her mother could return to her homeland. Not only would Lillian meet Henry Bernard but she would get to see her brothers after a 40-year absence. And she could meet Netta too. What was it her Aunt Maggie used to say? 'Every cloud has a silver lining'. She pushed the pram forward and followed her aunt out of the train station.

Acknowledgements

Thank you, Spinifex Press, for welcoming my sequel to *Lillian's Eden*.

Housebound by COVID, I see why prisoners write on walls! However, my confinement was responsible for the completion of this book. It was also responsible for another housebound woman, June Close, having the time to read my first draft. June gave me an in-depth written review. I am grateful for her close eye to detail and positive criticism. Thank you, June, you were so generous and helpful.

Thanks also to reader Diane Kilderry who knew where a full stop should go and when I needed an ego boost. Thank you Joyce Spiller, for your encouragement. And thanks to my son Garth, whom I nearly gave up on because it took him so long to read! He did like it.

I want to thank Spinifex Press editors, Renate Klein and Pauline Hopkins. You are so easy to talk to and always available and caring. Love you all.

Other books available from Spinifex Press

Lillian's Eden
Cheryl Adam

With their farm destroyed by fire, Lillian agrees to the demands of her philandering, violent husband to move to the coastal town of Eden to help look after his elderly aunt, despite his ulterior motives. Juggling the demands of caring for her children and managing two households, Lillian finds an unlikely ally and friend in the feisty, eccentric Aunt Maggie who lives next door. In this humorous yet rich and raw novel, Cheryl Adam shows us the stark realities of life in 1950s Australia, and pays homage to friendship and to the rural women whose remarkable resilience enabled them to find happiness in the most unlikely of places.

A sparkling debut novel, reminiscent of Ruth Park and Kylie Tennant.

Lillian's Eden is a garden full of stolen roses, family secrets and ambivalence. It's also home to one very attractive snake. I couldn't stop reading till I found who got cast out.

—Kristin Henry

ISBN 9781925581676

Locust Girl, a Lovesong
Merlinda Bobis

Winner, Christina Stead Prize for Fiction,
NSW Premier's Literary Awards

Juan C. Laya Philippine National Book Award
for the Best Novel in English

Shortlisted, ACT Book of the Year Award

Most everything has dried up: water, the womb, even the love among lovers. Hunger is rife, except across the border. One night, a village is bombed after its men attempt to cross the border. Nine-year-old Amadea is buried underground and sleeps to survive. Ten years later, she wakes with a locust embedded in her brow.

This political fable is a girl's magical journey through the border. The border has cut the human heart. Can she repair it with the story of a small life? This is the Locust Girl's dream, her lovesong.

Don't be lulled by the lusciousness or lured by the love but make sure you are warned by the politics. Typically inscrutable, relentlessly seductive, Bobis uses a different quill ... and Australia can use the sweep of a different wing.

—Bruce Pascoe, author of *Dark Emu*

ISBN 9781742199627

Murmurations
Carol Lefevre

Shortlisted, Christina Stead Prize for Fiction,
NSW Premier's Literary Awards

Lives merge and diverge; they soar and plunge, or come to rest in impenetrable silence. Erris Cleary's absence haunts the pages of this exquisite novella, a woman who complicates other lives yet confers unexpected blessings. *Fly far, be free*, urges Erris. Who can know why she smashes mirrors? Who can say why she does not heed her own advice?

Among the sudden shifts and swings something hidden must be uncovered, something dark and rotten, even evil, which has masqueraded as normality. In the end it will be a writer's task to reclaim Erris, to bear witness, to sound in fiction the one true note that will crack the silence.

There is something of Elizabeth Strout's Olive Kitteridge in Erris Cleary, as there is of Stroud in Lefevre's exquisite calm prose, but there are depths to Erris that are foreign to Olive and that give *Murmurations* some of the suspense and speculation of a thriller.
—Katherine England, *Adelaide Advertiser*

ISBN 9781925950083

Symphony for the Man
Sarah Brill

1999. Winter. Bondi. Harry's been on the streets so long he could easily forget what time is. So Harry keeps an eye on it. Every morning. Then he heads to the beach to chat with the gulls and wanders through the streets in search of food, clothes, Jules. When the girl on the bus sees him, she thinks about how she can help. She decides to write a symphony for him.

So begins a poignant and gritty tale of homelessness and hunger, centred around two outcasts – one a young woman struggling to find her place in an alien world, one an older man seeking refuge and solace from a life in tatters.

An uplifting and heartbreaking story that demands empathy. Amid the struggles to belong and fit in, we are reminded that small acts of kindness matter. And big dreams are possible.

A tale of two people from the margins of society united for a moment by music, by kindness, this short novel ripples along with gentle insistence towards a surreal but ultimately hopeful climax.

—*The Sydney Morning Herald*

ISBN 9781925950069

*If you would like to know more about
Spinifex Press, write to us for a free catalogue, visit our
website or email us for further information
on how to subscribe to our monthly newsletter.*

Spinifex Press
PO Box 105
Mission Beach QLD 4852
Australia

www.spinifexpress.com.au
women@spinifexpress.com.au